LAUGHING DOLPHINS

A NOVEL OF COINCIDENCE

Amber Polo

Wordshaping Press

Amber Polo/Wordshaping Press
Camp Verde, Arizona
amber@amberpolo.com
http://amberpolo.com/

This is a work of fiction. Names, characters, places, and incidents are a product of the author's imagination. Locales and public names are sometimes used for atmospheric purposes. Any resemblance to actual people, living or dead, or to businesses, companies, events, institutions, or locales is completely coincidental.

Cover design by Connie Fisher
http://www.connieleemarie.com
Book Layout ©2013 BookDesignTemplates.com
ISBN: 978-1-7346622-5-2

Dedication

For Sharon Massey,
Laughing Dolphins' godmother,
with gratitude

Contents

"There is an odd synchronicity in the way
parallel lives veer to touch one another,
change direction, and then come close again
and again until they connect and hold
for whatever it was that fate intended to happen."
Ann Rule

Mount Desert Island, Maine, 1980

Sandy

Sandy's head pressed against the window of Jeff's borrowed Subaru hatchback. Jeff opened the door at a Dunkin Donuts and cold air rolled in. She wished the heater worked. Back on the road a Welcome to Maine billboard flashed by and, half awake, she snuggled Jeff's New England Patriots parka over her denim jacket. A Harvard Square café double shift had made her too tired to wonder why he refused to reveal their destination. An all-night road trip was the kind of weird fun stuff Jeff thought up.

Two hundred and fifty miles north of Boston, Jeff turned off Highway 95. A half hour later, the Subie's headlights illuminated a white wooden fence. He parked and helped Sandy out of the car and whispered, "My mom brought me here when I was a kid. She said if I made a promise as the sun rose on Mount Desert Island, it would come true. That morning I promised I'd be an artist."

In the frigid pre-dawn air, Sandy saw their breath but not much else. She snapped her denim jacket and zipped the parka closed. Jeff took off his Red Sox cap and scrunched it onto her head. Waves crashed on distant rocks and an offshore sea breeze tickled her icy cold nose. She hoped this would be worth it.

Jeff inhaled. "Smells salty and clean. Not like washed up dead things or diesel boats."

Sandy's teeth chattered. "Smells like hundreds of miles of open sea."

Jeff sniffed. "Molecules from countries we've never seen." He pulled two blankets out of the car and led Sandy along an uphill path.

Sandy heard people around them but couldn't see a thing. "What's this? A make-out spot?"

Hissing whispers shushed her.

As her eyes adjusted to the dark, Jeff led her close to the top and spread out one blanket and helped her settle next to a large rock. He sat and tugged the second blanket around them, leaving only their faces exposed. Hugging her shivering body close, Jeff whispered, "It'll be worth it."

She leaned into the familiar warmth of his body. She loved Jeff's quirky sense of adventure and wished she possessed that whimsical spark.

Jeff pulled her close and kissed her. "Our love is like a sunrise. Like a desert sun shining on ocean waves."

She giggled. "We've never even seen a desert."

"We'll go everywhere. Together. I feel in my heart we'll always be together. Now, promise you'll love me forever."

"I promise." She tried to sound as sober as Jeff.

"If I lose you, I swear I'll find you."

She laughed. "I'll never leave you." Sometimes he was so dramatic.

A glow lined the horizon. A speck of dark gold fuzz appeared, then broadened along the distant ocean. "There," Jeff sighed. "Now, don't blink."

Slowly, then faster, the sun rose above the water, its orange-red glow spreading up against layered purple clouds. The panorama was divided by a white seam holding water and air together as the sky lit the ocean in hues painters jealously craved to replicate.

Watchers released their breaths and uttered a spontaneous, "Ahhh." No artist could ever capture this sunrise or the feeling in her heart. Jeff insisted artists needed to experience everything, even if they didn't have the skill to translate their feelings into art. She felt hesitant to even try. Her life felt like a still life oil compared to Jeff's animated talent.

As the sun rose higher, a frisson of excitement traveled through her body. "That was really amazing. We were the first people on the whole continent to see the sun rise."

The sun globe now hung over the horizon. Through morning haze, the entire sky glowed luminous and soft. Jeff made her see the wonder in the world. When she was with him dreams seemed real. "I'll remember this for the rest of my life."

They tumbled back on the blanket and rolled together while the other watchers hurried down hill. Pulling apart only far enough to unbutton and unzip, their bodies wiggled, squirmed, and adjusted. Sandy and Jeff moved under the blanket and joined with the easy intensity of two people meant to be one.

***

Despite napping all the way back from Maine, Sandy was so tired. As soon as they merged into morning rush hour traffic, the honking kept her awake.

Jeff parked the Subaru and pulled her to the stairs to their second floor apartment. She hoped to sleep for a few hours before her Renaissance History Art class and the late afternoon shift at Sam's coffeehouse. Jeff bounded up the steps, then ran back down and pushed her up before him. "Come on. I've got this idea. It'll be great."

Inside the apartment Sandy put on a pot of coffee. When Jeff got in one of these moods there was no stopping him. He laid her largest blank canvas on the floor and began throwing tubes of paint down next to it. He took a knife from the kitchen counter, bent it until it looked like a trowel and began spreading layers of paint on the canvas. Sandy slumped onto the futon to watch. As her eyes fluttered and began to close, Jeff looked up. "You got to help. I see it. But I can't make it real alone."

"I can't see what's in your head. You have to do it yourself." Jeff was such a nut sometimes.

He teasingly pulled her off the futon onto the floor. "No way." He grabbed a slab of mouse-gray clay and pushed it into her hand. He started layering ochre, sienna, and crimson over the white-streaked ultramarine background. "Look, see the sunrise reflected in the ocean! You must see it. Now the ocean has to reach up to greet the dawn."

As Jeff talked and waved his arms Sandy began to knead the clay between her palms. As her fingers poked and massaged the cool mass, the heat from her hands softened it and she felt it grow more pliable under her touch. "I see a water sprite rising out of the cold dark ocean to welcome the love of the sun."

"Wicked cool! I knew you'd get it." Jeff reached out to hug her and they both fell on top of the canvas. Getting up, clothes spotted with globs of paint, they stared down at the canvas.

The sunrise scene was perfect.

Boston Art Institute, 1980

Sandy

The next morning Sandy stomped up the well-worn wood steps of the old art school humming 'Love in a Void.' Her head buzzed, fuzzy and foggy. She'd wanted Jeff to come with her, but she left him sleeping. Last night had been great. The best.

But now a nagging voice inside reminded her graduation was only two weeks away. She pushed thoughts of change aside as her boots echoed the beat of her favorite Siouxsie and the Banshees tape.

A girl in skinny jeans running down the stairs, saw Sandy, and stopped dead. "Cool. Where'd you find that wicked black lipstick and nail polish?"

Used to being stared at, Sandy considered herself a fashion pioneer around the school. "Check out the costume shop on Broadway. Ask for Nubian Nails and Stygian Nights lipstick."

"Thanks. And your hair—"

"Temporary black dye." She sneered at the girl's blond hair. "You'll need double strength." Soon too many Cambridge students would take on the Goth look. The record shop near their apartment now carried imported tapes by the Sex Pistols and Joy Division, but she'd been the very first local fan.

During spring break of her junior year she'd gone to London with her dad. Mostly, she'd visited art galleries while he gave poetry readings. One night when he was at some literary thing, she took a cab to a funky club and saw Siouxsie. Blown away by the sound and the sheer guts of the music, she copied her look the day she got back to Boston.

Her gaze raked the short blonde. "Are you an art student?"

The girl's head bobbed. "Starting this summer."

"Don't copy anyone." Sandy pushed her haystack of hair out of her eyes and continued up the stairs. On the top floor the large banner 'Senior Art Show' drooped a little to the left. A poster listed the names of the Institute's graduating seniors: Alexandria (Sandy) Shellborn, Jeffery Sanders, Sandi Sue Maddox, Jack Brandt, Sandie Foster-Smith, Brenda Whatley, Kevin McCracken, and Sandra Cox.

A thin man in jeans and a black turtleneck lounged against the department office door. McCorry, that pretentious visiting prof, was talking to the department secretary who wore mini-skirts like it was 1970. "Art students are so predictable. The ones with the least talent speak of their art as though it had a capital letter." He too-casually pushed back a shock of longish blond-gray hair. "My god, Brenda, they act as if they'd die if they didn't pursue their art. No. As if the world would cease to exist if that paintbrush was pried from their grubby fingers."

The secretary tittered.

"It's true! Art majors choose Art for because they think art is sooo cool. They think it will help them get laid."

"Does it?" Her coquettish tone made Sandy want to gag. She imagined Brenda fluttering her false eyelashes. She'd heard rumors the department secretary had once been a promising art student, but that just had to be silly gossip.

McCorry continued, "They haven't lived. They're not good at anything. And aren't ready to go to work."

As Sandy walked away, she heard him say, "It's fine for kids to have dreams. It gives art professors a job."

She stepped into the deserted studio gallery. Jeff's show hung on the far wall. He'd merely picked five of the manic giant abstracts he'd done during a Red Sox winning streak. Sandy crossed the paint-stained wood floor where she'd spent so many hours the last four years. She'd had her own key and a part-time job inventorying supplies. She knew every room in this building by smell.

Her instructors loved her versatility. She'd tried every media from papier-mâché to marble. Weeks ago she'd selected pieces for her senior show. Then, she'd read the rules. Every work had to be executed 'one hundred percent by the student artist.' Her best works were collaborations with Jeff. Her black lacquered woman had been boring until Jeff carved a piece of oak into a snake that fit against the figure's back. Her raku torso was adequate for art student ceramics until Jeff carved a seashell necklace that enhanced its texture. And the painting they'd done last night was great, maybe their best.

Jeff dared to be original and rebellious and he pushed her to experiment with new techniques. She admired and envied his gift and wondered if, compared to his talent, she was merely a mediocre technician. She had solid knowledge of art history, composition, and technique and was good at incorporating symbols into landscapes and still-lifes. She followed rules. But left alone she retreated to the safety of flat conventional subjects. Was she any different from ladies who dabbled in macramé or cross-stitch?

She'd finally chosen a watercolor, a charcoal and pastel drawing, one oil, an abstract, a landscape, enlargements from last semester's photography lab, and her portrait of Jeff for the show. The pieces made an eclectic but predictable display.

She walked into the office to check for mail. Her hand shook as she reached into a wooden cubbie marked Sandy S and pulled out an envelope addressed Alexandria (Sandy) Shellborn, Senior. Since her grades had been top in her class, this senior show critique was just a formality, but she was still nervous. Jeff's review had praised his creativity and innovation, criticized his erratic technique, and strongly suggested patience, discernment, and lots of discipline. What would her letter say?

She ripped it open. Ignoring a paper cut, she closed her eyes and unfolded the culmination of four years of art school. She was proud of her work and the praise her professors gave her. In the entire class only Jeff was recognized as a better artist, but he seldom followed directions or completed projects on time.

J.J. McCorry, last week's guest lecturer, had told her class, "Lighten up and lose yourself. Learn to celebrate life in the full range of nature. Find your mountaintop of ecstasy." She could imagine Jeff doing just that. But what did that kind of advice mean for her? McCorry talked about the transformational power of art and the need for a spiritual guide. She'd taken notes, but he'd made no sense. "Art is life and life is love." At twenty, what did she know about life? And what did she know of love?

And finally, that guy's most stupid statement, "Open to the coincidences and unpredictability of life." Platitudes. Just words. All fine when you were a student. But she was graduating.

Opening her eyes, she skimmed her critique. And rocked back on her Doc Martens. "Very nice show … good technique … not gallery quality. You're a competent artist. I am sure your art degree will be useful in whatever you choose to do. You might consider graphic rendering or another commercial field."

She was second rate. All that work and she didn't have the talent to be an artist. Her mother was right. All the art school wanted was her tuition.

She rushed to her professor's office, remembering too late he'd already left on sabbatical. She sat on the steps and sucked blood from her paper cut. She'd fooled herself for four years. Her future as an artist would be just more disappointments, like this. For the rest of her life. When at last she brushed away a tear and stood up, her mascara was smeared but her eyes were clear. Time to put away her crayons and grow up. She pulled her jacket around her and walked out of the art school.

Commencement, June, 1980

Jeff

Jennie Sanders leaned towards her son, a conspiratorial glint dancing in her blue eyes. "Do we have time for a drink? Not every day my genius son graduates from Harvard."

Jeff's blue eyes smiled back. "Mom, Harvard accepted me but I went to the Art Institute. Graduation's at two. After we're eating at the Parker House." He pushed back his hair, removed his ball cap, and again placed the mortarboard on his head. The stiff head thing refused to stay on since yesterday, his first haircut since his sophomore year.

"That stuffy roll place? Doesn't Boston have any fun spots?"

"Sandy's mother arranged the dinner. She's paying." Why had it seemed like a good idea for their parents to meet? Sandy said college graduation was a big deal for parents and since both sets were divorced, dealing with four parents would be easier. Easier than what?

"Sandy's a nice girl. But her mother…" Jennie rolled her eyes.

Jeff looked over at Sandy standing with her mother. He needed her to get him through today. Without Sandy he doubted he would have shown up for graduation. Or finished school. She reminded him to turn in projects and gave him ideas when he got stuck. And when they did art together he felt completely alive. Even here, a few feet away from her, he felt tingly all over.

***

Sandy

Sheila Shellborn picked lint from her daughter's graduation robe. "I'm so proud of you, sweetie. And so happy you washed all that nasty eye makeup off your beautiful face." Sheila placed her palms on either side of Sandy's head, forcing eye contact with her only child.

"Right, Mom."

"Have you decided what you'll do next?" Sheila pursed her lips. "You could work for a gallery in New York or Paris and later go to business school."

Sandy sighed. She might as well tell her mother now without Jeff listening. She'd struggled since reading her critique. Big Sam, her coffeehouse boss, complained she served all her orders cold. Finally the decision became clear. Now, saying it aloud would make it real. "I've enrolled in Simmons' Library Science program. The summer session starts Monday. And I don't want to talk about it."

With an exaggerated exhale of relief, Sandy's mom kissed her daughter's cheek. "Thank you. Thank you so much. You have made me so happy."

Sandy's dad emerged from the Green Line station, waved, and crossed Beacon Street. "Hey, baby." He hugged his daughter. "Big day!"

"Good to see you, Aiken." Sheila pointed at the patched elbows of her ex-husband's lumpy tweed jacket. "You could have worn—"

He grinned at his ex-wife. "Everyone calls me Jim."

"There's Jeff's father." Sandy pointed to Jeff greeting a tall man in a dark suit who peeled bills into a taxi driver's palm. Jeff's shoulders rounded in his dad's presence. He looked ready to escape. Wait 'til Mr. Sanders saw the Sex Pistols t-shirt under his son's robes.

Sheila strode over to introduce herself to Jeff's well-dressed father.

Jim smiled. "She can't stand being around me when I'm dressed inappropriately." He put air quotes around inappropriately.

Sandy shrugged. "Mom's tough on both of us."

"Ignore her. What about you? Your senior show was fabulous. The Chairman of Northeastern's Art Department told me my daughter was very talented."

"Right." Sandy rolled her eyes. "That makes one person who thinks so."

"What's wrong, honey?"

"I've decided to go to grad school. Mom will pay for any program that doesn't contain the word art." She put air quotes around the word art.

Jim nodded. "In her mind, the only thing worse than being an artist is being a poet."

"You're a great poet. And wonderful teacher." Sandy gave her dad a quick hug.

"Your mother doesn't measure success by literary reviews or student evaluations."

Sheila returned, wrote a check, and slipped it into an envelope and handed it to Sandy. "I knew I could trust you to come to your senses. Here's the dermatologist's name. I made an appointment for you tomorrow morning at ten. He'll take care of," she added with an obvious wink, "it. The check covers his fee and your summer semester expenses. You're such a smart girl. Now I need to call the Parker House to confirm our reservation. Too bad Jeff's mother has to come." She wrinkled her nose as she walked off to find a phone.

Jim shook his head. "Sheila believes only well-dressed people deserve to be in family photos. Grad school? Tell me more."

"Library Science." Sandy looked down her black robe to her inappropriate oil paint-spattered combat boots. At least they were mostly black.

"You're giving up art?" Her father squinted at her. "I thought you loved art. But, if that's what you truly want. All I care about is that you're happy. What does Jeff think?"

She didn't meet her dad's gaze. "I haven't had a chance to talk to him."

"I thought you and Jeff were serious."

"Jeff isn't serious. About anything." She looked at Jeff, stiff in his wrinkled black robe in uncomfortable conversation with his father. Jeff was serious about her. He'd believed her when she promised never to leave him. And she had meant it. It was just that she didn't think she was that art student who'd made that promise. Not anymore.

Jeff grinned at her over his dad's shoulder and for a second Sandy felt that happy all-over buzz. But she had to break it off. The magic of making art—and love—was all they had. And neither fit her plans. She was young and sure she would meet lots of men more grown up than Jeff. Now, all she had to do was tell him.

***

Jeff

All Jeff wanted was for this day to be finished. Over. Done. His father unconsciously mimicked the gesture, smoothing his own perfectly styled cut. "Well son, what next?

Have you reconsidered going for an MBA? You couldn't get into the Harvard B school with your," he scowled, "art degree. But there are several strong programs in the Chicago area. You could live near me and Jennifer."

"Dad, I'm an artist." He really wished he'd skipped graduation and avoided listening to his father's lectures on career choices. His head hurt. He wanted to escape to the pub for a beer.

"I won't pay for you to paint and drink beer with your friends forever. Why do you think I divorced your mother?"

"I thought you divorced Mom because she was a lousy corporate wife."

"She surely wasn't presentable." He looked at his ex-wife talking with Sandy. "Probably dying for a drink right now. Jennifer wanted to be here, but she's closing another deal in London. You know, son, if you really want to be an artist, you could work for her. Corporate interior design is a fine career and you could get that MBA later."

"Your son, the interior decorator?" Jeff hated the tone of voice his father used whenever he said the word artist, like Jeff's talent was a personal affront to his identity and artist was a synonym for bum. His father was good at making money. Jeff didn't care about that. When he was creating art he felt alive. His mind was on another plane. His heart thrummed with joy. No one was going to tell him how to live. If Standford Sanders thought he could convince his son to sell out, he was wrong. Dead wrong.

"Jennifer does very well with her hotel clients."

"I don't want to work for Trophy Wife Number Two."

"Watch your mouth. You don't want to wind up like your mother."

"Mom's happy." Jeff saw his plump rumpled mother hug Sandy. That too-tight red dress made her look like an aging hippie. But he never doubted his mother loved him and was proud of him, no matter what he did. As a graduation gift she'd sent in his test scores and paid his Mensa membership. All his high IQ had ever done for him was to raise other people's expectations. He wanted to create art and have a good time. Why couldn't anyone understand. He couldn't be creative if art was a job.

Sandy waved and walked toward him. The closer she got, the better he felt. He believed Sandy's talent was greater than his. Sometimes he had to push her to try new things, but she was a great artist. Like their art teachers, he admitted her still lifes were only competent. But when she sculpted the human body, each piece came to life. One day in the studio he'd watched her place her hands on a block of red clay. Her face transformed into this amazing portrait of peace. And when her fingers dug into the moist mass, her whole body seemed to glow. She shaped the torso with strong gentle fingers, as if she were making love. As he watched, he'd felt a bit jealous, but then she turned to him and he saw the love in her eyes. She'd flung herself into his arms and wiped red slurry all over his best Red Sox t-shirt.

Sandy loved him for who he was. She encouraged him. She supported him. He couldn't imagine not being with her.

***

Sandy

Excusing herself from the most excruciating graduation dinner ever, Sandy ducked into the ladies' room at the Parker House and removed her robe. She pulled down the neckline of her dress and examined the dog turd shaped birthmark incorporated into a cool dolphin tattoo.

16

When she was five, she'd lift her shirt and show everyone the crescent birthmark right over her heart. Her mother always treated the brownish-black growth like the devil's mark, while her father wrote a whimsical poem called 'My Piscean Daughter's Happy Fish Tail.' When Sandy wanted to wear a sundress to her ninth birthday party, her mother smeared theatrical concealer on her chest until the fish tail looked like a mashed potato smothered in pinky-tan gravy.

Last spring, Jeff got the great idea to tattoo dolphins around her birthmark. They worked out the design together and went to a guy in Charlestown who tattooed sailors. Jeff made her drink a couple of shots of flavored vodkas and she didn't feel a thing. When her mother saw the tattoo, she moaned and swore that her daughter had ruined both their lives. Jeff had promised to get one just like it, but he never got around to it.

Tomorrow morning after work she'd take the T to an office building near Brigham and Women's Hospital where the dermatologist her mother selected would remove both the mark and the tattoo. A little flesh was the price of her summer tuition and board in a grad students' dorm.

***

The next afternoon Sandy poured a cup of coffee without moving her shoulder. Getting both sets of parents together for a graduation dinner had been a stupid idea. Her mother actually flirted with Jeff's dad. Jeff's mom drank too much and literally fell off her chair. Her dad read a sentimental poem. Jeff's father thought it was a joke, then announced only wimps wrote poems.

She gently touched the bandage above her heart and flinched. That fancy doctor who removed both her tattoo and

birthmark this morning promised there would be no scar. He'd
also said it wouldn't hurt.

Her cotton blouse didn't cover the bandage, but Jeff
hadn't noticed or asked where she'd been all morning. At one
o'clock when she'd come home he was just getting up. He
asked her to make him coffee while he took a shower. She
wanted to talk and hoped getting caffeine into him might help.
She'd put it off long enough. She had to tell him how her senior show had been a total bomb and that she'd decided to give
up art. And tell him she'd be starting grad school next week.
And she was moving out.

she slipped her new Joy Division tape into Jeff's boombox with a click. "Love will tear us apart, 'Love Will Tear Us
Apart' started playing, but she heard the words she punched it
off. Taking different roads? Oh yes.

Jeff wandered out of the bathroom, pulling on the jeans
she'd washed.

"Can we talk?" She had to tell him now. This was it. No
more excuses. She knew he'd be pissed off. She'd promised
never to leave him. But that was before.

"Sure." He poured a cup of coffee and turned on the TV.

"What do you want to do next?" She spit out the words.

"Like tonight?"

"The future? Grad school? A job?" Her sore spot
throbbed. Gripping her cup with both hands, she stifled the
urge to scratch.

"I'll figure out something."

"But we've graduated. My mother won't pay the rent if
I'm not in school. What can we do?"

"I don't know. Ask Big Sam if he'll give you more hours
at the café." He stood, pulled on a shirt and grabbed his Red
Sox cap. "Yesterday was awful. I'm going to O'Brien's to

watch the game and have a few beers. Renko's pitching. I need some fun."

She wanted to yell, Do you think serving greasy burgers to rowdy college kids is fun? But all she said was, "I wanted to talk."

He opened the door. "Maybe I'll start tending bar to help you pay the rent. That would be cool."

Part I

"But really, there are no coincidences. Coincidences are just other people's choices, plans you don't know about."
Elise Broach

I.1. Boston, Massachusetts, 1980-81

Sandy

Sandy sat on the apartment's ratty futon examining the paint-spattered boots she'd worn all through art school. The temperature was almost eighty, warm for June and the apartment smelled like stale pizza. Opening the window, KC and the Sunshine Band's 'Please Don't Go' burst in from the third floor guy's radio. She slammed the window closed.

The girl in skinny jeans she met at the art school dove into a pile of pigments and pencils like a puppy searching for a toy. Sandy had once been that excited about art. The girl surfaced with a box of 468 color pastels in one hand and a sable brush in the other. "Excellent. Art supplies are wicked expensive."

"New art students need everything." Sandy's voice cracked as she stuffed sketchbooks into a black garbage bag.

"Why do you want to get rid of this good stuff?" The girl indicated a wooden easel and a stack of canvases. "Your paintings are so beautiful. You should put them in a gallery."

Sandy stood. "Paint over the canvases. Just pay me and I'll help you load your car."

The girl picked up a small bronze. "Dolphins! Wow. You're a great sculptor, too."

Sandy didn't feel great. She didn't even feel like an artist. Her scalp still itched from the harsh shampoo that removed most of the black dye from her hair. Just her paint-smeared jeans, boots, and black t-shirt still labeled her as an artist.

"You'll experiment with all mediums." Sandy reached for the dolphins. The sculpture slipped out of her hand, fell to the vinyl tile floor and cracked in two. She inhaled. The twin dolphins piece was the last she and Jeff had done together. Like her tattoo, they were symbols of their shared art and love. "It's okay." She set the pieces on the Formica table next to a box containing the last leathery slice of Santarpio's pepperoni pizza.

She began to take off the denim jacket she'd worn constantly through school. It wasn't much good. The sleeves were worn and the designs she'd painted faded. Only the dolphins on the back and Jeff's name over her heart were still clear. "I'm keeping this." She walked to the bathroom and tossed black nail polish, heavy duty mascara, eyeliner, and lipstick into a Coop bag and threw it on top of the art supplies.

"Cool." The girl looked around the studio. "What about the furniture?"

"The furniture belongs to Jeff, my... boyfriend. He'll be staying until he figures out what to do next. He's really talented and smart. Maybe he'll go to Paris. Or Italy." She pushed down her guilt at not telling him she was leaving. Roommates moved out without notice all the time. She'd not think about Jeff. Besides, since graduation he'd practically lived at O'Brien's and Fenway Park.

"You two splitting?"

Sandy swallowed. "We graduated." She turned away from the girl and checked the bricks and boards bookshelves. Her copy of *Make Way for Ducklings* had been jammed between the art books she was leaving for Jeff. She pulled it out, then decided to leave it, too.

"Art school has been my dream." The girl sighed. "I want to be a famous artist."

"I hope you make it." Sandy just wanted this girl to leave before Jeff came home from helping Jerry O'Brien unload a liquor shipment. He'd work all day in exchange for double header tickets and free beer. "I faced reality." Her voice sounded determined. She'd convinced herself her mother's pressure had nothing to do with her decision. "Since I'm not good enough to make art a career, I'll become a librarian and find a real job."

She took the girl's money and dragged the bag to the door. The girl followed, carrying an armload of canvases and the easel down three flights of stairs. Sandy helped her pack it all into a pea green Datsun and watched her drive away.

Back upstairs, Sandy fell onto the futon. She'd taken everything important to her grad dorm by cab this morning. Orientation was tonight. Her portfolio case, thick with her senior show work, leaned against the door. She'd never think about art again. Tossing her apartment key with a clink on the table, she grabbed her backpack and maneuvered the portfolio down the stairs and out the rear door. Without looking inside, she stomped and smashed the cardboard case until it fit into the stinking metal trashcan with the other garbage.

***

Jeff

Jeff inhaled the familiar smell of stale pizza and oil paint, tossed his Red Sox cap on the futon, and called out, "Sorry I'm late. Met Picasso at O'Brien's." He knew he should have come home as soon the game was over but figured Sandy would understand. "We won 36–30." Somehow the room looked different. He muttered, "Who'd steal...?" He circled the studio twice, then realized only Sandy's stuff was gone. He opened the refrigerator and took out a beer.

Their bronze dolphins statue lay broken on the floor next to that kid's picture book Sandy loved. "Damn!" He finished the beer in one swallow. She wouldn't take her stuff and leave? Not without her copy of *Make Way for Ducklings*. And not without one clue that she was planning to move out. It made no sense. She'd promised never to leave him. Sandy loved him. Sure, she kept asking to talk about the future, but he hadn't seriously thought she was serious.

He stuffed *Ducklings* in his backpack and ran down to the coffeehouse on Prospect where she waited tables.

Big Sam, the manager, scratched his head. "Sandy quit after the breakfast shift. She's been depressed since that prof slammed her show."

"Impossible. Her professor promised to get her work into a New York gallery." Jeff couldn't remember if she'd mentioned her show critique. He hadn't even looked at his until Sandy had picked it up and read it to him. Other people's opinion of art didn't matter.

Big Sam raised both hands. "Hey, all's I know is, the day the show closed, she cried."

That professor was some jerk. If Jeff had any idea Sandy was unhappy, he'd have cheered her up. He had to find her. He tried to think where she might have gone. Maybe the Boston Garden. He'd been promising her a swan boat ride since April. That's where she'd go if she were sad. He stopped at a package store to buy a six pack of St. Pauli Girl. When the wimpy clerk asked for his ID, he spat, "I'm twenty-two, not a kid."

Jeff disappeared underground at the Harvard Square T Station, slouched into a vacant seat, and popped open a green can. By the time the Red Line stopped at Park Street, he'd finished two cans and stuffed the others in his backpack. With the ease of a Boston native, he switched to a Green Line train and rode standing to Arlington. He shot through the folding door out the train and up the steps, emerging in front of the Garden's wrought iron gates. Ignoring flowers and families, he followed the path to the swan boat dock.

Fishing quarters out of his paint-encrusted jeans, he stepped on board. Seated on a bench at the bow, he quickly finished another beer. His hand trailed into the water long enough to fill and submerge the can. The boat captain gave him a disgusted look and crawled behind the big swan.

A tall, blond couple with a dark-haired toddler took the seat next to him. The woman was telling her husband, "I hope our little Ginnie will go to MIT someday." Jeff pulled his Red Sox cap lower and leaned away from them. Why did Sandy love these stupid boats? He stared at the receding shore. Now he was stuck on a fifteen minute ride to nowhere. Then he spotted a girl in a denim jacket like Sandy always wore. He stood up. The captain yelled, "S' 'own!"

As the girl ducked around a tree and headed out of the Garden, Jeff yelled, "Sandy! Wait!" leaned over the gunnel and plunged head first into the water.

He hit mucky bottom, surfaced, spit out a mouthful of cold slimy water, and readjusted his beer-filled backpack. Crotch-deep in historic pond water, Jeff was still wiping mud from his face and hair when two lifeguards rowed close and dragged him into their boat by his backpack strap, scraping his belly on the splintery edge.

"Put me down. I'm fine," he sputtered when the big guy lifted him onto the dock. His soaking shoes, jeans, and that damn backpack made it hard to move. The other lifeguard handed him his dripping cap. The backpack gushed more murky water over his Celtics T-shirt. "I'm outta here."

"Son, you're not going anyplace," a gravelly voice boomed five feet above him.

Jeff looked up at a Park Ranger uniform atop a tall horse, then at the gathered crowd. In the first row was the girl in denim. Not Sandy. Not close.

"I'm going to have to book you for public drunkenness." The Ranger's horse nosed him forward.

"I'm not—"

"No swimming in the lagoon. Can't you read?" The Ranger cocked his head to the crowd. "These college boys think they're so smart, but can't read. Com'on. We're outta here."

***

Sandy

Sandy unpacked the last box into the dorm room closet and stuffed her old denim jacket into the bottom dresser drawer. The room was bland, but fine. Lisa, her new roommate, had great taste, if you liked Boston Marathon posters.

She looked in the mirror. Bare of makeup, her eyes seemed small. Tan slacks, white blouse. Her art school friends wouldn't recognize her. With a quick trip to Filene's Basement, she'd put together a wardrobe in boring New England neutrals. Pantyhose put the final seal on her conservative preppy image.

Telling herself she'd feel better when her stiff brown loafers were broken in and feeling strangely anonymous, she left the dorm room. Jeff's name was on the old apartment lease, even though she always paid the rent. Here, she didn't need her own phone and she'd filled out all her school forms with her real name, Alexandria Shellborn.

Now she lived only one mile from the Art Institute. But this place felt a million miles away. She wasn't worried about running into Jeff. He spent most of his time in Cambridge and at O'Brien's. Art students didn't hang around here. Besides, dressed like this, he wouldn't give her a second glance.

She'd miss Jeff. They'd been inseparable since the first day of art school. In their junior year, she'd found an apartment to share with two other art students. For a while others came and went, but she and Jeff stayed together. She'd believed they belonged together. She'd promised never to leave him. Maybe that was why she couldn't face him now.

Jeff had been the only boyfriend she'd ever had. Everything had been for the first time. But, like being an art student, he was part of her adolescence. He was a hugely talented artist and had a future in the art world. She couldn't be with someone who constantly reminded her of her own inadequacy. He couldn't expect her to stick around cleaning his brushes, attending his gallery openings, and waitressing. A clean break and new life was better. If she'd told him she was leaving, he would have argued that she was as talented and talked about how they were meant to be together and do their art together. Jeff never worried about the future. He didn't get it.

Finished with kids' stuff, like the grubby apartment with no real bed, she crossed the Fenway and walked down Arlington to The Classic Beauty Hair Shoppe. Across the street, a crowd surrounded a mounted officer. She hoped it wasn't a swan boat accident in the Public Garden. She loved those boats but hadn't ridden in one for a long time. Jeff promised to take her, but never did.

Inside The Classic, she told the plastic-faced receptionist, "I need a haircut."

"With?" The blonde tossed her small head as if showing off the salon's latest blond shade.

"With… anyone! Fast and cheap." She ran her fingers through her light brown hair, which reached to her shoulder blades. The ends were split and residue of black dye clung to strands.

The blonde touched Sandy's hair. "To get this color out, I'll have to cut a lot off. It's wicked damaged." She looked at Sandy's rough hands. "You need a manicure and some nice clear polish. Whatever did you do to your hands?"

"Art school."

Ninety minutes later, Sandy arrived at her graduate school orientation, neat hair swinging around her ears. Sliding into a front row chair desk, she took out her spiral notebook and wrote 'Day One.'

***

Jeff

The next morning Jeff sat in a dark pub, clothes still stinking of pond water, staring at his empty glass. He'd used all his cash to pay the fine to get out of jail. The pub's familiar beer and whiskey smell soothed his nerves, but the quiet was weird. At ten, the place had just opened and Jerry O'Brien hadn't turned on the TV. "Hey, O'Brien, get me another beer."

"No." The tall good-looking bartender turned away from his only customer.

"Corin, honey, you do it," Jeff appealed to the waitress.

"Stuff it," she said without moving her lips and turned back to wiping tables.

"You two are bartenders, so bartend." Jeff looked at the Black Irish O'Brien twins. Corin was thin and pale, with what the Irish called a brooding expression. Her handsome brother Jerry had an easy, charismatic smile. This morning they were feuding—again. Tired of being ignored, Jeff walked around the bar and drew himself a second draught of Guinness.

"On the house," Jerry called. "As usual."

"Doesn't anyone care that Sandy's left me? I don't know where she went. I can't find her father's phone number and her mother hung up."

Jerry stopped straightening the wall of bottles. "Forget her. Whenever she came in with you, she always had her head in some book in the back booth. Never once drank at the bar or watched the game." He clicked on the TV. "Don't even remember what she looked like. Just a lot of black lipstick and those weird eyes."

"Sandy's wonderful. Didn't like beer much or the Sox. Or Irish music."

"See, I told you. Lots of women out there care about the good life. Like your mother. When she was in town for your graduation, she was something else. Drank a couple of good men under the table. Even tried to pick me up. Claimed neon barlights made her look younger. I shouldn't talk about your mom, but that lady knows how to have a good time. And she said you weren't just a great artist, you were smart. A member of Mensa no less. What a woman!"

Jeff grimaced, not wanting to remember the night he brought his mother to his favorite pub.

Corin came out of the kitchen holding a tray of clean glasses. "Soon you two will forget what I look like. This barmaid's moving on."

"Where do you think you're goin'?" her brother asked.

Corin tilted the tray, stepped back, and watched a dozen glasses shatter across the wood floor. "I got my scholarship to

Harvard Business School. And a student loan. No more smellin' like a brewery and livin' over a bar."

"You can't leave me here with Dad." Jerry's mouth dropped open. "I'm… going to… to… Paris."

"You're crazy." Corin sneered at her brother. "Think you're going to be a famous *artiste*? You flunked out of art school."

"No." Jerry sounded sure. "I'm going to learn the art business."

"Do you even speak French?" Jeff should be the one going to Paris.

"I will." Jerry grinned. "*Mon ami.*"

Jeff slid off the stool onto a pile of glass shards. This was supposed to be the place where he could forget his troubles. Where everyone knew his name. Now these friends were acting crazy. Why couldn't everyone just stay put and have a good time?

***

Sandy

Sandy pouted as Lisa's Toyota turned off Route 2 onto a narrow country road under arched foliage. Her roommate maneuvered Boston traffic like a typical maniacal native.

"Alexandria, stop acting like I kidnapped you. We need a day off. Classes only started last week. You are not behind."

Sandy didn't like to admit it to Lisa, but she already loved everything about grad school. She loved the classes and all the subjects. Something about the orderliness of the discipline fit her. She actually liked reading lists so long no one could possibly read everything.

Her goal was to be first in her class. This was a field where success could be measured. And hard work would make her successful. The dream of running a perfectly organized library energized her. Libraries were systematic, harmonious, and methodical rather than haphazard, disorganized messes. In art, no matter how hard you worked, you were judged by fluctuating standards where chaos and jumble beat out order and skill.

"So, where are we going?" She didn't like being called Alexandria as much as she'd expected. "I saw a sign to Walden Pond."

"I know my way around here," Lisa told her. "My folks lived nearby before they moved to Colorado."

Maybe this wasn't such a bad idea. She needed to stop thinking about Jeff. Changing her hair color hadn't erased him from her mind. He'd be fine with his art, friends, and beer. He'd forget her. Maybe he'd already left for Paris.

When Lisa drove under a banner that proclaimed, The De Cordova Art Museum and Sculpture Park, Sandy grumbled, "I don't want to go to an art show."

"It's just fun. And we need exercise. I only ran three miles this morning."

Sandy returned to pouting, but soon found herself admiring the turreted red castle. So what if sculpture scattered the placid New England grounds. She wasn't an artist anymore.

Lisa giggled and pointed at the cartoon-style chicken. Sandy relaxed a little as Lisa flirted with a flute-playing mime. Lisa pulled Sandy to the food tent and bought her a Ben and Jerry's cone. A joyful boy about six, a dolphin painted on each cheek, skipped out of a tent filled with clowns. Sandy lost Lisa in the crowd and turned from the laughter, choosing a path to the pond, away from the crowds. Away from the art. A middle-aged couple strolled in front of her, hands drifting close but not touching.

"Please, J.J.," the woman's voice rasped. "I shouldn't have come to the reunion."

"Admit you expected to see me. You came from Kansas without your husband, Osmond."

"Oscar had business back on our farm."

"Martha, do you think I came to Boston to critique art school seniors as a favor to an old friend? I'm an artist, not an art teacher. I swear five students were named Sandy. I couldn't keep them straight." He looked into her eyes. "We haven't seen each other since we were art students."

Martha turned away. "You went to Paris, became famous, and married Rene."

"You'd already married Otto and become the Midwest soybean queen."

"Oscar! He's a wonderful man." She still faced away.

"Marti, Rene died five years ago. All I have is my son. I know you still have feelings for me." He playfully took her hand.

Sandy felt like an eavesdropper. If she met Jeff in twenty years, would they play out a scene like that? No. He'll have forgotten her. She followed a path into a grove of trees. Two huge dull black bronze hearts loomed in front of her. The artist had molded coffeepots, hammers, and bric-a-brac all over the casts. Every view of the hearts revealed more fascinating details. "If I could create work like this..." she whispered.

A half hour later, Lisa, a daisy painted on one cheek, found Sandy sitting in the car reading a cataloging textbook. "Come on. Today is for fun. The face-painting clowns are wicked cute art students. Way cooler than the guys in our classes."

"We should be getting back to Boston."

"You must really hate art."

"Art is for children."

34

***

Jeff

Jeff squatted on the sidewalk rearranging paintings on a thin blanket. Standing, he stepped back. His display looked more flea market than fine art, though his stuff was better than most at Central Square's Fall Arts Sale. He shrugged and sat on a crate.

Picasso had helped him unload, then drove off. Sandy, always the perfect image of a cute eccentric art student, was good at sidewalk sales. She'd smile and chat and people would hand her money and leave with a painting or drawing. Even her goth makeup didn't scare people. She loved Central Square because she believed people from one hundred countries lived in the ten blocks surrounding Mass Ave and Prospect. He smelled jerk chicken from the Caribbean street vendor's cart. Sandy had gotten him to try the spicy dish, but now, even if he had the money, he wasn't hungry.

Damn, but he needed a few sales. Sandy had been gone three months and he was way behind on rent. The cash from his face painting gig at the DeCordova was long gone. Everything was a mess, and he still hadn't decided what to do next. Keeping his options open. Waiting for her to return.

A woman in a black business suit stopped and examined a painting of Sandy sprawled in the grass on the quad. "How much is that?"

"Oh, about a hundred." He needed money, yet still didn't like to part with his work.

"What about that one?" She pointed to a sketch of a pair of dolphins.

"Not for sale," he snapped. The woman moved quickly on to the next space and bought a small oil painting and a handful of greeting cards from a wild-haired woman in a purple peasant dress.

When the buyer left, Jeff called over, "Nice sale."

"Cha-ching!" The purple gypsy laughed, bent down, and pushed aside the fringed scarf that covered a folding table. After she replenished her stock, she stood back up, fluffed her russet electric hair, and reached between beaded necklaces to push her bosom back into her purple bodice. She appraised Jeff's work. "Nice. But not displayed well."

"Don't I know it. Suggestions?" She stepped closer and he noticed gray hairs mixed in her wild red curls.

She smiled. "I'm Sammie. Samantha Swampscott." She checked the signature on the closest painting. "You're Jeff Sanders. And you're very good."

"Thanks. But I haven't sold anything."

"I figured." Her gaze held his. "Want my honest opinion?"

"Yeah. I mean, I could use some help."

"First, lose the beer." She raised her hand to stop his protest. "Yeah, I saw the six pack behind the big canvas. Customers can smell it on your breath. Then, set firm prices or decide if you're willing to haggle. Want me to tweak your display?"

"Tweak away." Jeff watched her hang his blanket on the backdrop, move a low table to the front of the space, and then add some of her extra crates to prop up his canvases. Pleased, Jeff asked her to help him set prices.

When Sammie finished pricing the last one, a woman with a tapestry briefcase asked about a small canvas of the Charles River. Jeff told her it cost $59. She said it reminded her of a friend who crewed. Jeff offered it to her for $50 and she handed him five tens.

Sammie suggested he make up small items, like greeting cards that could be sold cheaply. "They'll pay for your space rental. Cha-ching!"

"Sammie, I owe you. Let me buy you a beer. There's this pub—"

"No thanks. But I'll buy you a cup of coffee."

After the sale closed, Sammie sat opposite him in the molded white plastic booth, its table and two seats bolted to slick pink and orange walls, rehashed the art sale. Jeff leaned back, inhaling the burnt roast smell of brewed Dunkin Donuts coffee and yeasty donuts.

He sipped from a large styrofoam cup and by the time he finished the last bite of his second gazed donut, he realized he was laughing for the first time since Sandy left. "Sammie, thanks again for all your help."

"Usually, I sense an artist's state of mind from his work." Sammie brushed bits of sugar glaze from the bosom of her purple dress. "None of your pieces reflect a troubled soul. What have you painted lately?"

"I haven't painted for... since... well—"

"Woman trouble?" Jeff nodded and she continued. "The work you were selling today was not painted by an unhappy man."

"That stuff is all from last fall and winter. Sandy... well... she left right after we graduated."

Sammie focused her attention on a chocolate frosted. "Did you two have plans?"

"Sure. I talked about grad school. And maybe going to Paris. Or Italy."

"And this Sandy?" She nibbled thick frosting.

"The same. I guess?" His sadness flooded back. "Then she was gone. I've looked for her. She might come back."

"What do you want to do, now?" Sammie watched Jeff struggle with the question. Her face softened. "It's not a test. I'm trying to help. I like you."

This older woman looked like a wild gypsy, but talked like a friend. "Right now," Jeff hung his head, "I need to pay my rent."

Sammie leaned forward. "I have a loft in Medford. Not fancy, but there's a bed and you can share my studio."

"You're kidding? You don't even know me."

"I know people. I know art. And I like you."

Jeff grinned. "Thanks, really. You're such a *serious* artist."

She laughed. "I'm competent and have a knack for marketing. Cha-ching! But my dream's always been to own a diner back in Nebraska." She winked. "Now. I have three house rules. Paint every day. Help me with shows. And no booze."

"No problem."

"That includes beer."

"You're kidding?"

"You can't be addicted to both alcohol and art. You have to choose."

A mother and a little girl walked past. The dark-haired child stopped and pointed at Jeff. "Mommy, that man's mommy let him go swimming with the swans," the child whined as her red-faced mother scooped her away.

Overhearing the girl, an elderly couple looked over at Jeff. The woman said loudly, "I saw him on the news."

Sammie grinned. "You're the guy in that *Globe* photo. The one who fell off the swan boat."

Jeff looked down at the dregs in the bottom of his cup. "Maybe I do need help?"

"I am old enough to be your mommy," Sammie whispered.

"What?" Jeff looked up.

"What that kid said. I'm over forty and you're about… twenty?"

"Twenty-two." He looked at her, really seeing her for the first time. "It doesn't matter. Maybe you're my fairy godmother."

***

Sandy

Sandy dropped her textbook in the grass, closed her eyes, and flopped back onto the blanket. This fall New England postcard day was perfect for watching rowers along the Charles and doing nothing. "Makes me want to barf," she hissed, angry at herself for unconsciously sketching a tree in the margin of her notes.

"What's wrong?" Lisa looked up from her book and leaned against the maple tree. "Oh, you're sketching, like that art student." She pointed to a shaggy-haired guy with a Red Sox cap walking near the river, sketchpad in one hand and a beer bottle in the other.

Sandy kept her eyes closed. "This drivel is making my neck feel wicked weird."

"Take a break. You can study tonight."

"I'm sort of busy." Lisa's eyebrows lifted. "I'm going to a lecture at MIT."

"With?"

"A math post doc named John. I met him in the library. John said some guy from IBM is talking about a PC. A personal computer. And after John offered to show me his TRS-80. Whatever that is?"

"Sounds like super fun." Lisa pruned her lips.

Meeting John had been an accident. They'd both been sitting at the same table when one of her bound journals knocked his math text off the edge. They'd talked a little and went for coffee to her old coffeehouse, though John drank tea. They talked for almost an hour and Big Sam's other waitresses didn't even recognize her. John was focused and nice and talked about computers, huge and powerful machines, organizers of information. She liked that idea. And she liked John. Lisa would think he was boring, but that didn't bother her. He seemed to be a good match for her. Just like Lisa was her perfect roommate. Happy and easy going. Not demanding and no competition.

Sandy changed the subject. "I've got to read four more chapters and write a paper."

"Grad school's hard." Lisa patted Sandy's hand. "I only have time to run five miles a day."

"Hard is not the problem. No one expects us to think."

"Cataloging class is intense. I hardly have time to go to the gym."

Sandy shrugged. "It's more like grade school than grad school. Memorize. Fill in the blanks. Painful."

"You have to do the work to—"

"To get the degree. I understand they don't want creativity, but when do I get to use my brain? Fall Orientation was a bunch of old ladies sounding like… like… old ladies. I was waiting for the one in the gray pantsuit to say Shushing 101 was a required course. At least in Collection Development we'll read porn."

"We won't read porn! It's about censorship! Anyway, give it a chance. With your Bachelors in Art, you'll be all set. You can be an art librarian in a museum like the Met or maybe work for Disney World."

Sandy shook her head. "I have no intention of being an art librarian."

"Too bad. With only my English lit major, I don't have a chance at the good jobs. Science and business degrees bring the big bucks. I should have listened to my Dad, gone to law school, and joined his firm in Denver. I'll end up sitting at a reference desk in some podunk public library."

"Ladies, may I join your conversation?" asked a deep voice behind the tree.

Sandy's eyes flew open and she pushed herself up.

A red-haired man in his late thirties appeared. The beard that covered his lower face drew attention to his piercing blue eyes. He knelt on their blanket and stuck out his hand. "I'm Barry Kohl. I was resting on the other side of the tree and couldn't ignore your conversation."

"Lisa Fitzpatrick. And this rebel is Alexandria Shellborn."

Sandy moved her backpack and hid the copy of Anaïs Nin's *Delta of Venus: Erotica* she was reading—not reading about.

Barry grinned. "I can tell. Sorry that orientation was so dreary." He settled on the blanket and stretched out his short legs, avoiding any chance of grass stains on his chinos.

"You teach?" Lisa checked out the well-dressed man.

He nodded. "I just got back from a conference in California. Gladys and Margaret can be deathly dull. I'll liven things up."

"You're Professor Kohl who teaches Computer Services." Lisa poked Sandy. "Oh my god! The one they call Professor Cool."

He chuckled. "You'll be my students, that is, if you choose my class as an elective." He raised an eyebrow. "So, which one of you is the artist?"

"I was," Sandy admitted.

"Interesting." He looked into her eyes. "I'm designing a prototype computer system for a mega art library in New

York. If you don't have a practicum lined up, you could work for me. I need a student with artistic flair to jazz up training materials. And for data entry."

Lisa asked, "Any work for a non-artistic girl?"

He grinned. "You're both hired." And looking only at Sandy added, "Come see me in my office."

***

Sandy and Lisa settled down to study for final exams, kept awake by cups of Dunkin Donuts caffeine and surrounded by shiny pink and orange walls. Lisa put down her book and sipped from a large styrofoam cup. "Did you know that Pope Pius XI, Mao Tse-Tung, J. Edgar Hoover, and Casanova were librarians?"

"I bet they didn't have to read this crap," Sandy mumbled. "I can't wait to graduate next week."

"Speaking of Casanova, it sure has been wicked dull since Professor Kohl took that job in Columbus. He liked you," Lisa teased, still flushed from her morning run along the Charles.

"You're crazy. He's married and has a bunch of kids." Sandy tried to control the blush that crept up her neck. Barry did flirt outrageously and was sort of touchy-feely—but he treated all his students that way.

"And he's old."

"Not so old," Sandy snapped, then continued more slowly, "but working for him was lots of fun. I'd like to do something with computers."

"I didn't like the computer stuff that much. I want a job in a law library where I could meet successful guys. Everyone in my dad's law office wears wicked nice clothes." Lisa indicated the front counter. "Not like her."

Sandy turned to see where Lisa pointed.

An overweight woman with wild red hair picked up two coffees and a bag of donuts. When she bent to pull cash out of her sack, her floppy purple blouse drooped low exposing the tops of large breasts.

"Oh my god, an arty type," Lisa said. "Probably doesn't shave her legs… or underarms."

They heard the other counter guy ask, "Hey, Sammie, you and your cute young man going to another art show?"

The woman nodded and pulled a shawl around her shoulders.

"Guess, it's better than working," the guy said with a gravelly laugh. "I should try my hand at artsy stuff."

Lisa sniffed. "She's probably a street person."

"Stop talking like a stereotypical blonde." Sandy looked back to her notes.

"I'd rather be a blonde than some old maid librarian type. It's different for you. You're engaged to John, that dorky math post doc who takes you to Neil Sedaka concerts." Lisa began snapping her fingers. "Love will keep us…"

"Stop it. John's serious. We get along just fine. We've discussed our future. I'll find a job wherever he gets a job. I hope he finds something around Boston or D.C. where there's tons of great choices for me. My mother's not happy he's an academic like dad, but his MIT degree does impress her."

"Even so, you have boring John. You never talk about that artist boyfriend from your undergrad days. I bet he was way cool."

Sandy ignored Lisa, regretting she ever told her roommate about Jeff. She tried not to think about him, but from time to time she wondered if he was still looking for her as he promised.

"I'll go back to Denver. Get a cat. Never earn enough money to buy really good running shoes."

Lisa was a good friend, but she wouldn't miss her six a.m. aerobics routines. "All year you kept telling me libraries are more than dull discussions of bibliographic control theory and collection management. You said that after graduation, we'll do important things. Bring order to chaos and help people."

"Right." Lisa sighed. "We're going to challenge that old image. But before we graduate, let's have some fun. Some of us are going to this funky Irish pub called O'Brien's. Want to come? You could bring John."

"No. Absolutely not"

I. 2. Ohio, 1982-1983

Jeff

Jeff, sweating through a muggy Lake Erie haze, carried a four-foot square box from Sammie's van to the downtown Cleveland art gallery.

"Twenty-two!" Sammie stood on the loading dock, flapping her low-cut purple tunic away from sticky damp flesh. "Six more. And don't you dare chip one piece. My show, my whole tour, my whole entire career would be ruined. I didn't lose twenty pounds for nothing. Cleveland might be a joke to you, but it's an important art town."

"If you say so," Jeff grumbled and set down the box. A radio played 'Born to Run' and he hummed along with the Boss. Since leaving Boston he'd become driver and porter to this suddenly self-centered artist.

After Jeff brought in the last box, Sammie inspected the circle of tables in the main gallery. She jiggled each of the twenty-eight white-clothed tables, then called, "They're stable. Start unpacking. We're late. Who'd think traffic could be bad so far from Boston?"

"The big Boston artist should have gallery staff to handle setup," Jeff groused, wondering how Sammie could have changed from free spirit to temperamental artist in the few weeks since this tour was booked.

"I want the effect perfect before anyone sees it, even gallery staff. The press will be at this evening's reception." She ran her fingers through her hair, creating an even wilder effect, then pulled her tunic neckline lower. "Do you think I've lost weight in my breasts?"

Jeff ignored the question, but had noticed her red hair was redder and no longer shot with gray. He opened the box marked 'One' and lifted out a three-foot diameter bubble-wrapped ball and began unwinding. Wrap removed, he handed Sammie a cotton-covered ball. She peeled off the cotton and reverently placed a twelve-inch-tall coffee mug on the first table.

"What the big deal? I liked your New England landscapes better. And your raku teapots always sold."

"Get over it. The media loves political eroticism. Cha-ching!" Sammie turned the giant cup's white chicken feather-covered handle precisely perpendicular to the table's edge. She stroked the lumpy scalloped lip where baby pink deepened to rose.

"Perfect. From this angle you can't even tell it's a vagina."

She ignored him, making sure each one of the twenty-eight ceiling lights would shine directly into a cup. "Twenty-seven more to go. And Jeff, wear something nice tonight. And don't talk to media people."

***

Sandy

Sandy leaned forward and pleaded, "Please hurry." The cabby slid open his window and a cloud of cigar smoke hit her face.

"Lady, give me a break." He hit his horn. "It's Cleveland rush hour."

"I'm meeting someone at the bar in the Sheraton." She heard the nervousness in her voice, anticipation at seeing Barry Kohl, her grad school professor again. "I can't be late."

"Good luck! A buddy of mine says some big convention's in town. 20,000 librarians, if you can believe that. A bunch of old maids who don't tip. So, the bars laid off half the bartenders."

Sandy unpinned her library conference badge from her navy suit lapel and stuffed it in her pocket. The red Joyce pumps and new briefcase must have made him take her for a business woman, not a librarian.

"There's a hot art exhibit opening tonight." The motor-mouth cabby pointed down St. Clair Avenue. "Look at that. Already a line around the block. Show's about women's privates." He pulled to the curb. "Close as I can get ya."

Sandy checked the meter, counted bills, tipped more than she'd planned, and pulled her briefcase out the door after her. Two Nike-clad women with bulging plastic bags scurried toward her as the cab pulled away. Their conference badge lanyards swung as she clicked past them into the hotel bar. She heard the taller one in the baggy brown pants suit say, "Cleveland cabbies are rude. Every one's been nasty when I asked for a receipt."

Inside Sandy paused, blinded by the hotel barroom's dark interior. As her vision returned, Barry in the farthest booth raised a hand and she hurried past the men seated at the bar.

"Alexandria!" Barry stood to hug her. His cashmere jacket enveloped her as he held the embrace a heartbeat too long. She stood in the aura of expensive aftershave. His auburn hair was longer and he seemed taller than she remembered. She settled in the booth across from him. His sparkling eyes and cock-eyed half grin were as intoxicating as ever.

"You're starting your first job." He chuckled. "In Zinzin-nati."

"Well, my husband, John—you remember I'm married now—got this great appointment in the Math Department." Barry drummed his fingers on the lacquered table, but she continued, "I start next week in the Main Library Special Services Department."

"Sounds dreary." He let out an exaggerated sigh. "I teach two super boring classes in Columbus, but most of my time is spent planning for a library computer system company. I've got top-gun programmers lined up and a mega investor in Texas. All I lack is a beta test site."

Two hours later Sandy left the bar. Exactly like when she'd been his student, Barry made her brain spin. She wished she could work on his exciting project. When she told him Lisa had returned to Colorado to head her father's law firm library, he didn't remember her former roommate who'd also worked for him.

Back in her hotel room, Sandy flipped through American Library Association group and committee acronym flashcards: LITA, LAMA, LRRT, LALA, certain dropping these into conversations would make her sound super-professional. By the time she finished, it was too late to call John. Her husband would arrive on the last day of the conference and they'd drive to their new apartment in Cincinnati. After one frustrating year shelving books at Boston Public while John finished his post doc, she was now back on her plan and their joint careers were off to an excellent beginning.

***

Jeff

Swerving around picketers at the front entrance, Jeff drove the van close to the Cincinnati art gallery loading dock. "I'm worried, Sammie. Cleveland was one thing, but this town has a bad reputation for controversial art. And you are way controversial."

"Get over it. If my show gets closed down in my tour's second city, I'll make national news. Then other cities will give me more press. My cut of entrance fees will skyrocket. Catalogs, prints, and postcards will sell like ET dolls and orders for limited edition reproductions—Cha-ching!"

Jeff faked a newscaster voice. "Collect Sammie's vagina cups now! A better investment than Barbie dolls or baseball cards!"

"Don't call them vagina cups! I've trademarked the Yoni Chalice name. I'm thinking mass market. Boutiques. Crystal shops."

"Coffee shops!" Sammie had gotten him to stop drinking, but on this trip he sure wished he could retreat back into that friendly fog.

"What's your problem? Can't you be happy for me?" Struggling in the van's cramped quarters, she poked Jeff as she took off her jacket and shimmied into a purple silk tunic imprinted with her Sammie signature logo.

"I'm tired of being treated like shit. Those libber women who booked your show refuse to even make eye contact with a guy. One referred to me as your hod carrier. We've been together three years. If we'd gotten married before the tour, at least then I'd be the *artiste's* husband." Jeff wasn't even sure he meant that. Life with Sammie had been fine up until this show, but marriage was another deal altogether. Not that he loved

Sammie. Or didn't love her. That part of him was a closed book, but he'd trusted her not to abandon him.

"The feminist community is my main support. If we get shut down here, I'm calling Marge Polanski. She can drive and list more than you. And does not complain." Sammie grinned out the window at the milling crowd.

Jeff turned off the engine. "So then, what would I do?"

"Go back to Boston and produce art. That Irish guy offered you your own tour. You wouldn't even return his call. After my tour is a big success, you could create a counter counterculture spinoff. Every great art movement needs a backlash."

"That spoof of your cups project was a joke! I was just being goofy."

"You never took my vaginas seriously. You think I'm just a hack who didn't go to some fancy schmancy art school. I may make money, but I'm not a real artist. Try paying the rent with your authentic art." A siren screeched in the distance. "Get out of the van! I'm driving around to the front. There'll be photographers." She ran her fingers through her wild red hair. "Does my hair look all right?"

Jeff got out of the van. Sammie slid to the driver's side and pulled away without a backward glance.

***

On the third day in Cincinnati, censors officially closed the Yoni Chalice Exhibition. Sammie, jubilantly manic at press interviews, was intolerable in private. Desperate to get away from her, Jeff escaped from the hotel.

He entered a downtown bar and let the distinctive smell of alcohol tickle his nostrils and travel through his brain. Cheap beer or expensive scotch, all bars smelled the same. Living with Sammie had taught him alcohol and art didn't mix.

Not for him. Sammie was strict. It had been hard at first and, he was pretty steady. She kept him busy preparing for shows and working producing stuff that sold. He didn't like all the results, but was starting to feel like he was making a contribution. Some people could drink and work. But after a couple of relapses he was sure he wasn't one of them. He hadn't been back to the old pub. Or tried to find Jerry or Corin. He still thought about Sandy, but accepted she was out of his life. Gone back to their old apartment and asked if she'd come back, but the new manager just laughed.

He ordered a ginger ale, then with an indifferent jerk of his head toward the people at a long table, asked the bartender, "Who're they?"

"Come in once a month. Tip fifteen percent. To the penny. To the penny." The bartender leaned across the bar, lowering his voice. "The woman in red is a total babe so I asked one of the guys how I could join. He says you need a certain IQ to get in. So's I figure they're a little slow, not retards exactly. Well maybe the Tweedle Dum look-alike with the red *Beam Me Up* t-shirt."

Jeff, desperate for social contact outside the phony baloney art world, picked up his glass and walked to the table. He stood awkwardly until the group stopped talking and looked at him. "I'm Jeff." He swallowed. "Is this the Mensa table?"

"Welcome, Jeff," said the guy in the *Beam Me Up* shirt.

Jeff fumbled in his pocket. "I have my card here somewhere. I'm just passing through town."

The woman in the red sweater moved her chair so he could squeeze one in from another table. The round Beam Me Up man said, "Don't need no stink-een card. I'll give you the official Cincinnati Mensa test." He looked around to see if everyone was paying attention. "How many of the following have interested you sometime in your life: One: Science fiction. Two: Puzzles and games. Three: Bad jokes."

Jeff had only wanted to sit and listen. He'd worn his good jeans.

"And," the red-sweatered-breasts leaned close to him, "sex."

Jeff blushed. His mother had kept paying his dues because she was so proud of his brain. He bet his mom didn't know certifiable geniuses behaved like this.

"I'm Ralph," the suited Mensan introduced himself. "We talk about most anything at our get-togethers but those topics are always of interest to upper two-percent types."

"Especially sex," Red Breast breathed.

"Especially bad, sexy jokes," Beam Me Up added.

Ralph ignored them. "Many Mensans were socially mal-adjusted gifted children. Some are still under-educated under-achievers working through adolescent fantasies."

"Wait just a minute, Ralphy." The Beam Me Up guy turned to Jeff. "Ralph has a year of med school, a year of law school, and six months at the Cordon Bleu. Hasn't a clue what he wants to be when he grows up."

Jeff nodded. As if he had a clue what he wanted to do. Where were the brainy confident eggheads he's imagined? Four people on one end of the table began a joke-off and three on the other end talked about the last Mensa Gathering, which sounded like an orgy with junk food.

The woman in the red sweater asked, "What are you interested in—this week?"

Jeff swallowed. "I'm an artist." He half-hoped someone would begin a serious discussion of art, the kind he always despised as pretentious and faux intellectual.

"Wow. Then you should see that amazing Yoni Chalice exhibit."

Another woman leaned over the table. "I heard it got closed down before I could see it. Too bad. It's the feminist art event of the century."

The red-sweatered woman noticed Jeff tense and laid her hand on his arm. "Relax. I'm Sharon, Librarian at the UC Math Library. If you want more serious conversation, you can take me out for a 5-way and talk about nuclear physics, Aristotle, or whatever you think the smartest people in the world talk about."

Jeff pushed his chair back and excused himself. He didn't fit in here any more than in Sammie's radical art community.

***

When Jeff returned to their hotel room, Marge, the muscular feminist, had arrived to pack up Sammie's successfully censored show. No one paid attention when he grabbed his backpack and walked away—with nowhere to go.

Now heavy rain pelted Jeff's back as he hurried down Clifton Avenue past university buildings. He and Sammie had been just fine. For three years they'd gone to street fairs and sold their work in galleries in Lexington and Hingham. He'd developed a small following of collectors who liked his dark acrylic collages, heavy on black paint and body-part prints from medical textbooks. Sammie told him that he'd sell more if he lightened up and produced stuff like her commercially spiritual street fair angels, dolphins, and frogs. He told her he'd never sell out, but he'd done more pieces that appealed to the college kids.

Then on a lark she'd made the first of those damn cups. Gallery owners insisted Boston was not ready for vaginas, but somehow a snotty New York agent found her, booked a tour, and arranged major publicity. Overnight Sammie turned from his fairy godmother providing food, paints, and sex to hellish bitch goddess. From then on it was all about her.

"Damn. Damn. Damn," he mumbled. The two block walk from the gallery had left him cold and wet, but still hot under the collar. He couldn't drive back to Boston because the van belonged to Sammie and he had no cash for a bus ticket. And there everything was hers.

"Excuse me," a voice behind him interrupted his thoughts. "Jeff? Jeff Sanders?"

Jeff turned to a man shadowed under an enormous black umbrella.

"Remember me? Jerry O'Brien. O'Brien's pub. Boston." The man stepped closer, offering to share his umbrella.

Jeff recognized Jerry's Irish crooner looks. "What're you doing in Cincinnati?"

"I read the article in the *Globe* about you. Well, actually about Sammie and her tour. I drove straight here. Some butch woman at the gallery told me you were walking in the rain."

Jeff looked away and muttered, "Leave me alone." He didn't need one of Sammie's stalkers using him to get to her.

"Just listen. I'm setting myself up as an art promoter. Sort of an agent. And I thought of you, my old friend, *mon ami*."

Jeff shook his head. Water dripped from the brim of his ball cap. "This vagina cup thing isn't my gig. I'm splitting from Sammie and heading back to Boston."

"Here. Here's a library. It's warm and dry and they can't throw us out." Jerry led Jeff up marble steps, past a man wrapped in aluminum foil, and downstairs into a deserted reading room. They passed the librarian's desk. Two women deep in conversation ignored them.

Jeff stared at the librarian with the rainbow legwarmers and whispered, "Don't you think she looks like my old girl-friend?"

"No way. That freaky chick would never become a librarian. Librarians don't wear black lipstick. How could you even kiss those lips?" He looked back to the desk. "Besides, the sign reads Mrs. Olson. You're hallucinating." Jerry shook off his umbrella and they settled on worn lounge chairs near a hot air vent.

Jerry turned his charismatic smile on Jeff. "Now that you're on your own, old buddy, we can work a deal. The Hingham gallery owner that exhibited your work last year said you only used black paint, but told me you had a quirky streak. Showed me one of your forks."

"What!" Jeff burst out. One of the women who'd been talking at the desk, the one with the bun and the lumpy brown dress, walked by with an armload of books and glared. Jeff whispered, "He kept that joke?"

"How about we drive back to Beantown? I give you a place to work and you make more forks. I'll set up a one-man tour for you. Same deal as Sammie's. Lots of publicity, interviews. The works."

Jeff gritted his teeth, knowing without the price of a bus ticket he had no other choice.

∗∗∗

Sandy

After only six months working in the library, Sandy hated everything about her job. Rainy Friday evenings were the worst when the university library overflowed with nerds working on papers. And perverts.

A man, head and shoulders covered with crumpled aluminum foil, crinkled up to her desk and asked to borrow a pencil, the most challenging question of the night not involving restroom locations. Compared to Boston, this place was a wasteland. Betting which local art exhibit would close first was the popular cultural pastime.

A woman in a shapeless brown dress clomped out of the staff elevator.

"What's with the outfit?" Sandy asked Nora. "You look like a 1940s librarian."

The Head of Circulation smoothed the bun at the nape of her neck and poked wire-rimmed glasses higher up her nose. "Please, hon, it's a costume. I'm going to a party. After college my family expected me to get a job at P&G. My Hamilton friends tease me about being the library lady. This is still the expected image. Besides, look at you." She pointed to Sandy's legs. "Rainbow legwarmers aren't standard librarian gear."

"It's cold down here." Sandy's hand knitted legwarmers were her one non-conservative expression of individuality. John hated them and told her it was the sort of thing only art students wore. She had six pairs and was kitting another. "You aren't exactly a librarian. Yet."

"Don't I know it." Nora sighed. "But they think anyone who checks out books is one. Someday I'll be able to afford to get my Masters."

"That's great." Sandy paused, realizing how much she hated her boring job and working three nights a week in this drafty basement. She scanned the deserted reading room and noticed two men in the lounge area near the door. "Look at those guys. The one on the right reminds me of someone I used to know in Boston."

"Ripped jeans and wet ball cap? Probably some undergrad who spends his scholarship money on beer instead of books and baloney. A million like him on campus. Now the guy with the black umbrella has potential. I wouldn't mind taking a walk in the rain with him."

"You're right. The ball cap guy's just a kid. I can't imagine why I even thought... Besides, I'm a happily married woman." Her marriage was perfect. She and John made a good team. If only she could get a more fulfilling job, her life would be great. John was happy and if she didn't have to work so many nights and weekends they'd be able to spend time together. When he wasn't working.

Nora looked up. "Looks like you got a customer."

A neatly dressed man in a dark overcoat stepped up to the desk. "Please excuse me." He stared at Sandy's shoes and asked, "Are you the young lady who has the expertise to add paper to the copy machine?"

Sandy smiled and led him back into the Copy Room.

When she returned Nora told her, "I've got to get back upstairs," then added, "look out for that polite guy. He copies messages from religious aliens and exposes himself in the stacks."

"He seemed so normal."

"If you call Security, they'll come in like Rambo and create tons of paperwork. Just tell the guy to put it away."

"What about the creepy foil guy?"

Over her shoulder, Nora whispered, "Chair of the Philosophy Department."

Nora's insights into how this place worked really helped Sandy get to know the university and the library system. The phone rang and Sandy listened to her husband recount the latest Math Department gossip and the enthusiastic reviews of his latest paper. John taught four freshman classes and wrote papers nights and weekends, hoping his publications would earn him early tenure. He was excited about his work, but never noticed her disappointment in hers.

When John finished, she put down the phone, pulled up her legwarmers, and went back to reading an article by Barry

Kohl in a library computer journal. Barry was doing the exciting work she dreamed about.

***

The next morning Sandy entered Marion Stillman's office. She knew the Associate Library Director had hired her because of her faculty wife status and would happily replace her as soon as she became pregnant.

"Mrs. Olson," the older woman greeted Sandy.

"Ms. Shellborn," Sandy corrected, standing taller.

"But you're Professor Olson's wife." She looked at Sandy's waistline, then at her red slingbacks. "Sit down."

Sandy nodded and sat.

"So, you are unhappy with your schedule."

"Working three nights and supervising Xerox machines and sorting mail isn't professionally challenging."

"You're gaining invaluable management experience. Whatever did you think you'd be doing without specialized reference or cataloging skills?" She pretended to refer to Sandy's personnel folder. "Oh yes, you have an undergraduate degree in Art. Art History? No, just Art. Be patient. A position may open in the Art Library in a year or two."

"I don't want to be an art librarian." Sandy crossed her legs and kicked one red toe at the modesty panel bolted onto Ms. Stillman's gunmetal gray desk.

"Too bad. At least you don't have a visible tattoo. I understand many artists favor body art. My advice is to acquire a second Master's degree as soon as possible. That always looks good to faculty committees."

"A Master's in what?"

"It doesn't matter. Most of us have Masters in English or Education. Even Art History would be fine." She paused. "Or you could apply for the Tobacco Leaf Experiment Library

58

when an opening comes up. Of course, the TobEx position requires management experience."

Sandy bit her tongue.

"So, about your schedule."

"Never mind, I've registered for a class that meets on Monday, Wednesday, and Friday mornings. Working those nights will be fine, for now."

"What class?" Ms. Stillman's eyebrows pushed up.

"Computer Science." Sandy smiled as her supervisor's nose wrinkled in distaste.

Dismissed, Sandy met Nora in the staff lounge. "Marion Stillman's a bitch, but I have a plan. You're going to teach me about circulation. And I'm going to take a computer course. We're getting out of the basement."

"How will we do that?"

"I heard a rumor that next year the Director will hire a computer services librarian to write an RFP to select a computerized circulation system. By that time, I'll be the most qualified." Sandy smiled, knowing Barry was still searching for a beta site.

That evening, Sandy told John about her decision to take a computer science course.

"Hum." John stared into the current issue of the *Journal of Esoteric Mathematical Models* and mumbled. "You could become an electrical engineer. Funny thing happened to me today. Sharon in the Math Library suggested I join Mensa."

"The high IQ group?" Sandy put away her knitting and pulled a packet of forms out of her briefcase.

"Whyever would a scholar with a PhD want intellectual stimulation outside of their department?" John turned on his lecturing voice, first listing the credentials of each of his colleagues, then the benefits of solitary contemplation.

By the time he finished, Sandy's application was complete.

***

Jeff

Four months later after he'd worked frantically in Jerry's Boston garage to create thirty pieces, Jeff's first show opened in Cincinnati.

Jerry locked the gallery, patted Jeff's shoulder, and led him across the street. "Let's grab some chili and pound down a few beers. After all the publicity I got you, I can't believe only four people came the first day. The show's great."

Jeff's body tensed at the word beer. Not meeting Jerry's eyes, he looked back across the street into the gallery window. "Not for me." He still knew that in order to create art, even art that he considered crude and opportunistic, he needed to stay away from alcohol.

Jerry's display mimicked Sammie's record-breaking traveling vagina cup show, though the gallery was smaller and in a less artsy neighborhood. Like hers, spotlights shone directly on tables. Thirty-one lights on thirty-one penis barbeque forks. Over the door a neon sign flashed 'The Prick-nic.'

"I just don't get it." Jerry shook his head. "Your work is brilliant. I expected national coverage. Penis art to compete with vagina art!" He smiled. "This weekend's *September Oktober-fest*. A lot of beer flows at these local street fairs. I'll hand out flyers. Attendance will be better. Guaranteed." He led Jeff into a brightly lit restaurant, found an empty booth, and ordered. "You'll feel better after a bowl of chili."

Jeff, tired of Jerry's promises and excuses, ignored his agent's talk until the waitress slid heaping plates in front of them. He stared at his mound of cheese-covered spaghetti. "Where's my chili?"

"Please." The waitress rolled her eyes. "Hon, in Cincinnati, this is chili. You got a classic 3-way. Spaghetti. Secret recipe chili. Shredded cheese."

Jeff stuck his plastic fork into the stack, twirled spaghetti, watery sauce, and cheese, and took a bite. "Tastes like bland pasta sauce with meat. With cinnamon?"

"Greek recipe. Also comes as a 4-way with onions or beans or a 5-way with both," Jerry explained, apparently familiar with local cuisine.

Jeff remembered the Mensa woman. "Oh, that's a 5-way."

"Eat up," Jerry ordered. "This show is going to be huge. Just a slow start. It'll get coverage in a couple of prestigious men's publications. Don't think sleaze. Think money, *mon ami*."

Jeff cringed. He'd wanted to be a serious artist, but he'd lowered himself to take a chance on a bad joke. After Sammie's successful vagina show, he couldn't stomach the pseudosophisticated jargon she and her entourage tossed around. Now he'd sold out to Jerry's hype and marketing gimmicks.

Jerry pulled a handful of envelopes out of his pocket. "If your show did well, I was going to turn these down. But, well, businesses are offering lucrative commissions for your work. I'll take a cut, of course."

Jeff laughed. "What for? Personalized BBQ forks?"

"Not exactly. One guy has a chain of bars in Pittsburgh. He needs an artist with real creativity to design the men's rooms. Give them an upscale theme. Professional sports murals. That sort of thing."

Jeff stopped eating and stood up.

"Where're you going?"

"Back to Boston. Keep the forks."

"Jeff, there's nothing back in Boston. For either of us. We have to go forward."

***

Sandy

Nora closed the door of Sandy's new fourth floor office. "Sandy, hon, you are one hotshot librarian."

"Told you I'd get us out of the basement." Sandy flopped into her chair, hiked up the skirt of her navy suit and pointed one red Etienne Aigner toe at her desk plaque, Associate Director for Automation Services.

Nora mimicked a scream. "And as your assistant I have my own assistant! Still can't believe you made it happen."

"I documented that all University Library Directors in the state had high level computer people on staff. To represent our library, I needed a respectable title and perks. I snowed the Director with techie jargon. No one here knows a byte from a CPU."

"Or how to dress," Nora added. "Lots of work to do, but, on my new salary, now I can afford grad school. And a suit with shoulder pads like yours."

"Enough celebrating." Sandy stood. "Let's go to the Information Retrieval Committee meeting and get this show on the road."

Sandy and Nora hurried to the conference room and watched four people file in. Sandy whispered, "They're all catalogers."

"Of course," Nora whispered back. "Phase One is creating machine readable records and tossing out the card catalog. Only catalogers care. Remember, whatever you do, don't say anything bad about cats."

Four catalogers sat, two on each side of the conference table. Sandy called the meeting to order. Marc, in a dashiki, and Tammy wearing a long ethnic skirt covered in cat hair, were the younger staff members. Irene and Elaine in matching sensible shoes, who'd cataloged half the library's collection during the past twenty years, crossed arms over cat-appliquéd sweaters.

"Why are you wasting our time?" Irene whined. "I don't have time to catalog books and make those preposterous electronic records."

"Right," Elaine added. "And I heard, if you put records into a computer, hackers can steal your books."

Marc, the young Serials Cataloger, snickered. "But what about patrons who rip cards out of the catalog to remember the call number."

Tammy said, "Automation is great. I won't have to be so careful assigning subjects. Computers find anything, even if it's misspelled."

Irene sniffed. "That would be oh-so-helpful in the evenings when there isn't a real librarian in the building who knows a main entry from a uniform title."

Marc replied, "You mean who knows a 240$b from a 245$b? Or a double dagger from a dollar sign?"

They sniped and argued until Sandy adjourned the bibliographic ping pong match.

Back in their office Sandy flopped into her chair. Nora told her, "Hon, catalogers are crazy. My first week working here, Irene tried to run me over with her booktruck. And Marc belongs to CatNipNet, that subversive ALA roundtable for catalogers fighting to take their cats to work."

The phone rang. Nora answered, listened, then trying not to giggle announced, "It's Mr. Barry Kohl, President of Megga-Tech Systems Ltd. Bet he's still looking for a test site for his new computer system."

Sandy grinned as she took the phone. "Barry, meet me in front of Skyline Chili. I'm on my way." She hung up. "Nora, call John's office and leave a message that I'll miss the Math faculty dinner."

I. 3. Texas, 1983

Jeff

Jeff held his head in his hands, elbows on the glossy mahogany bar, and listened to Willie Nelson croon 'Always On My Mind.' The mirrored backbar reflected liquor bottles, steer horns, and his old friend Jerry O'Brien. Jerry thrust his snakeskin boots deeper in the stirrups of the saddle barstool and winked at the cowgirl bartender.

"I hate painting men's rooms," Jeff moaned over the grind and roar of the mechanical bull. "No more bar jobs, Jerry or Jerome or whatever you call yourself today."

"Come on, buddy. Only one more," Jerry pleaded, putting his arm across Jeff's shoulders.

Jeff shrugged Jerry off. "Are you crazy? The Klondike Pub?"

"They need the lounge finished for the Iditarod." Jerry flashed his charismatic smile. "Do it for me."

"Do it yourself!" Jeff glared at Jerry's new pressed jeans. His own were worn, ripped, and paint-spattered. He stood in his stirrups, threw a leg over the saddle, and crunched down on the peanut shell covered floor.

"I'm through with bars, too." Jerry followed Jeff down a dark hall. "I'm opening an art gallery. I made great contacts on my Paris trip. People here in Houston actually believe I'm French."

Jeff rubbed his saddle-sore crotch. All the anger of the last six months rose up. He spun around and snapped, "Lost your South End accent?"

"Pretty much, *s'il vous plait, mon ami.*"

"You are so full of it, Jerry O'Brien." Jeff stepped around the sandwich board that blocked the men's room door.

Jerry followed. "Jerome Oberon."

"What does your sister think of that? Corrie always said you were full of bull."

"Calls herself Corin now. With her fancy MBA, she's working for a big time brokerage firm. Got more money than Guinness has beer."

"Corrie was okay. You were always too tough on her."

A man in a gigantic hat, so white it glowed, loomed behind them. "Hey partners, when can my gents use the Stallions' Room?"

"Bull's dry," Jeff told him, "But the urinal wall bronco needs another hour to dry." He lowered his voice, "before you pee on it." He began packing paint cans into boxes. "Jerry." Damn it, he was not going to call him Jerome Oberon. "Help me load this stuff in the van, *monsieur.*"

Jerome bent to help, gingerly avoiding getting paint on his jeans. "Who's the beautiful cowgirl you painted in the Filly's Room?"

Jeff concentrated on folding tarps. Jerry sounded sincerely interested, but he'd never tell him the cowgirl was his old girlfriend from Boston, the one Jerry had called weird. "None of your business." Why had he painted Sandy in that red cowgirl outfit? He kept thinking about her. And his promise to find her. He wondered if she was doing art. Wondered what his life would be like now if she hadn't left. He sure wouldn't be painting stalls in Houston.

Maybe the alcohol fumes were making him nostalgic for the girl who disappeared from his life. Now he just wanted Jerry to disappear. "I quit. Finished. I can't take it anymore. You made a ton of money on my work. The lobster shack in Maine. The crab house in Baltimore. The Big Ten taverns." Jeff shook his head. "The porn movie houses were the sleaziest." When he thought of Sandy seeing him like this, he knew he had to quit being Jerry's lackey.

"You accepted those jobs." Jerry looked confused. "If you quit, what will you do?"

"I've got a job faux-painting a house west of the Galleria. *Faux* is a French word. *Trompe l'oeil* means to fool the eye, like you pretending to be a Frenchman."

Jeff left Jerry and drove out to meet his potential client. Though he'd told Jerry he had the job, he was only answering a newspaper ad for a muralist.

Inside the Houston mansion's foyer the flower arrangement looked as big as his old Boston studio. "Mrs. Kohl," he began shyly, trying to make a good impression. He needed this job.

"Call me Mona Sue." The tall, big-boned blonde's smile lit up her face. "I'm so excited having a real artist paint my walls. Come see my little ol' living room."

Jeff followed her bouncing bouffant hair. He pulled his gaze away from her tight pink jeans and looked up at the two-story cathedral ceiling. "Everything in Texas is so big."

"I have five children," Mona Sue said, as if that explained it all.

"I need to go back to my van for my sketchbook and tape measure."

She followed Jeff to the door and waited for him to retrieve supplies from his battered van. "Do you live close by? With family?"

"I rent a room near Gilley's." He didn't tell her he'd spent the last two nights sleeping in the van. "I'm new to Texas," he added in explanation.

"You can stay in my little ol' pool house. It's comfy and will be close to your work."

Jeff jotted notes as he followed her through the house. Oh yes, he needed this job.

"The family room stays rustic, just like Daddy's ranch house in Nacogdoches. Each of my children will choose a theme for their bedroom. The rest of the house is all yours to decorate. But I do favor that old Roman stuff for the master bedroom and bath."

She led him to the kitchen. "We just moved in a few months ago. Some oilman went bust before this place was finished." She waved an arm at the white walls and meager furniture. "We lived in Ohio when my husband was on the faculty at State. Now he's started his own high tech company and I'm pleased as a Lone Star on ice to be back in Texas. The North is nice, no offense, but kinda cramped. Barry thought a bigger house would be nice for the kids. Daddy helped. He wanted his grandbabies close to the home spread."

Jeff only half listened as his head clicked with ideas how to make this bland rambling house his canvas. It might not be real art, but he knew he could do a good job. When they reached the den, he asked, "What kind of a man is your husband? I mean, for the theme. Outdoorsy? Sporty?"

"My husband golfs... for business. Entertains... for business. He became a librarian because he got a grad school scholarship." Mona Sue thought for a moment. "Basically Barry's a salesman. He swept this flight attendant off her little ol' feet."

***

Sandy

The white-jacketed waiter ceremoniously placed a truffle-studded goat cheese burrito in front of Sandy. She whispered to Barry, "Real French truffles!"

"*Bon* appetite." Barry raised his wine glass. "The most expensive restaurant in Houston is the perfect mega beginning to launch your Megga-Tech career." He smiled his enticing half grin and reached for Sandy's hand.

He often touched employees, customers, and even competitors, yet tonight Sandy sensed his gesture meant more. This afternoon when he'd picked her up at the Houston Airport, he complimented her new suit and said her big curly perm was the perfect look for a Texas company. Then he explained he'd booked a hotel room near the Galleria until her company condo was furnished and mentioned twice that his wife Mona Sue and their children were visiting her family.

"You deserve the best." He handed a gilt-wrapped package across the table. "You're going to help me take Megga-Tech to mega heights."

She unwrapped a monogramed leather day planner. "Thank you. This gift is perfect. Now I'll have to get used to working for you. Not being your customer." She lifted a forkful of sculptured appetizer to her lips. Beautiful but no flavor.

"How'd your old boss take your resignation?"

"He wasn't surprised. Nora can do my job while she finishes her degree. He made a nasty crack that since I was already working for you, I might as well get all the perks."

"How much money will it take to get Nora on board?"

69

Sandy shook her head. "Nora wants stability."

He shrugged. "Most people settle for lives of dreary desperation."

The waiter pushed a cart to their table and served Barry a massive cut of Texas beef and Sandy an entire duck à l'orange with perfectly browned skin and sculpted Mandarin orange garnish. A side plate held a cornucopia of potatoes filled with miniature vegetables and swirled with balsamic vinegar spirals. She sliced off a piece of her entrée.

When her mouth was full, Barry asked, "And your husband, what's his name, has he decided to stay in Zinzinnati?"

She nodded. Sandy had only hinted to Barry that John would remain in Cincinnati. When she'd received Barry's offer, she'd told John that moving into Barry's company as a vice president was the chance of a lifetime. Computers were the most exciting part of the library world and Barry was positioned to make it big. When John asked if their marriage meant nothing to her, she'd told him she was unwilling to be limited to jobs where he wanted to work, explaining that perhaps they'd married too young, before their careers were settled.

John had been stoic and she'd pretended sadness as she packed her clothes and a few books for her move to Houston. But inside she'd felt elated, freed after a few years of putting someone else's interests first. Only a small voice blamed her for rushing into marriage with a man the complete opposite of Jeff. Neither relationship had worked out any better than her wasted four years in art school. Now it was time to throw herself into a life of her own choosing. She sat taller. "John's no longer part of my life."

Barry smiled and switched the conversation to plans for the library tech show in San Antonio. "You'll love this one. Not as large or boring as ALA or as provincial as state conferences. I've booked the largest hospitality suite and we'll host a mega open bar. I want everyone to know Megga-Tech is the future in this business."

Sandy's duck was raw in the middle and dry and tough everywhere else. Too excited to eat, she gave up and poked at the concrete cornucopia.

"I got you on both the LARUIT and HAGYT committees. Of course, you'll be chairing the Megga-Tech Users' Group."

"But I work for Megga now. I'm no longer a user."

"Who better to tell customers our new release can do anything?"

The waiter interrupted to serve coffee, brought two silver bowls, one filled with packets of sugar and sweetener and another with plastic containers of half and half. "I may not eat in many five star restaurants," Sandy admitted, "but I expected a cream pitcher and sugar bowl."

"It's all show. Tell everyone your new boss took you to the most expensive place in town."

They left the restaurant and Barry drove to her hotel. Sandy felt his hand on her waist as he guided her up the metal stairs. She'd expected one of those glitzy high-rise hotels like she'd stayed in when she came to Houston as a Megga-Tech customer. This two-story motel was just one step up from seedy. Not the usual business class she was used to even on the library's minuscule budget.

She slowed as they reached the top of the stairs. His fingers seemed to drum a nervous beat on her back, but his words came fast in his usual enthusiastic patter. "Sorry this so far from the office. When your condo's finished on Monday, you'll be just next door to Megga-Tech and be able to be in your office in no time." His hand shook as he fumbled the key into the lock. She'd never seen Barry nervous. From the day she met him, she'd been drawn to his confidence and sparkling blue eyes and the way he made her feel as if she were the most important person in the world.

Now, Barry's charisma was legendary in the library automation business. That's why she'd joined Megga-Tech. Right? Because the chance to work with him was the most exciting opportunity in her field. She'd left everything. Her job. Her marriage. Her home. To be here. With him.

He opened the door and set her carry-on inside. Closing the door behind them, he didn't reach for the light switch and for a moment in the streetlight's glow coming in the window she saw the silhouette of a short, slightly overweight, prematurely balding man. Stale cigarette smoke lingered under the odor of cheap bleach.

He took a step closer. "So, here we are."

***

On Monday morning, the first day of her new job, Barry greeted Sandy in the marble and brass Megga-Tech lobby with a firm handshake and a wink. She'd been hesitant when he'd left the hotel this morning. How was she supposed to pretend they were just business associates after the last two days? Wouldn't everyone know just by looking at her?

But Barry acted just the same. He escorted her down a plush carpeted hall and introduced her to the office staff. Abilene, Odessa, and Yellow Rose, all with big Texas smiles and hair, towered over their short boss.

"Everything is wonderful." Sandy noticed empty offices as she walked down the hall next to Barry. "But where's the staff?"

"Now contract programmers write programs off-site. Greg Bertram in Georgia working on the circ system. Bright guy. Wrote a super hardware store inventory package. Todd, our database guy, is back in Columbus. All the top library programmers are based in Columbus. Herb Vernon's in Utah. He's working on patron lists, bar codes, and the book reserve system."

Surprised at the changes, Sandy asked, "Will it all fit together?"

"You must see our computer room." Barry laid his hand on her shoulder and led her into a closet-sized room filled with metal shelves heaped with electronic gear. A scruffy teenager with flaming red hair and a five o'clock shadow crawled out from under a table and greeted Barry with a "Hiya, boss."

"Sandy, Meet Danny Picasso, our hardware guru. Picasso, this is Sandy Shellborn, my Sales and Marketing V.P."

Sandy, certain the kid stayed on the floor to look up her short skirt, backed out of the room. "He's so young," she whispered as they moved down the empty hall.

"Don't worry. His MIT credentials are mega good. Customers will never see him. Leave the tech side to me. Now, Ms. V.P., here's your office." He opened a door with a flourish. A space as big as her old apartment held a massive desk, two couches, and a conference table for twelve.

Sandy walked to the phone-covered desk and looked across the room and out the window at the Houston skyline. "How did you furnish these offices so quickly?"

Barry came up and stood close behind her. "An oil company went bust and I picked up the lease cheap, right down to the paper clips. I even bought the owner's house. This classy setup will show people who we really are."

***

Jeff

Three months later, Jeff sponged the last dab of ochre paint onto Barry and Mona Sue's bedroom wall. Mona Sue touched the ancient marble patina behind the headboard. "This is so real. And my kids just love what you've done to their rooms."

Jeff grinned, proud of his work. "Barry Jr. said he wanted to be an oceanographer, so I made an aquarium wall. Belinda never stopped talking about her horse, so I painted the back of her door as a half-open stable showing Buttercup's head."

"The baby adores the Seven Dwarfs."

"I'm happy you're satisfied. But I should finish up and let you have your pool house back." She'd given him a lot of freedom to design creative murals. She treated him like an artist and helped him gain back his self-respect. This may not be avant-garde art, but looking at the results made him feel good. The generous pay included room and board and use of one of their five cars. He'd gotten used to this comfortable life, days painting walls and evenings watching episodes of *Dallas* with Mona Sue and her kids.

"Don't worry your head. After our big open house shindig, you can start on the guest wing. But today we're going shopping."

As usual, Mona Sue had her way and Jeff followed her through a dozen antique shops before she led him up the stairs of a one-story house on Westheimer Street. The Victorian was shadowed by the adjacent twenty-story atrium office building which housed Mona Sue's husband's company.

Jeff read the sign 'Ariel's Fortune Telling' on the porch and hesitated.

"Come on," Mona Sue coaxed. "I want you to meet Ariel. She's my oldest friend and helps me with my little ol' problems. Then we'll go get you fitted for a pair of real Tony Lama Texas boots."

Jeff vowed not to buy into this psychic crap just to please Mona Sue, nor accept expensive gifts.

"Sometimes you seem so sad." Mona Sue lifted the brass knocker. "Maybe Ariel can help."

A voice called, "Y'all come in," and Mona Sue led Jeff through the foyer and into a front room. They passed a table holding a computer and three telephones. She pulled aside a curtain divider and they passed through to what had been the dining room. Oak woodwork, Chinese red walls, and oriental rugs created a feeling of old-fashioned elegance.

A woman in a white silk robe sat at a round table. Her long hair shone silver in the candlelight, but Jeff estimated she was only in her late thirties.

"Blessings." Ariel nodded to Jeff then stood and hugged Mona Sue. "You pure, sweet spirit."

The woman indicated two chairs and they sat.

Mona Sue blushed and turned to Jeff. "Ariel was the one who told me I needed to find someone to paint my house. And I found you. She also told me that when my house is finished, my time of change will begin."

"Don't be afraid," Ariel told her. "You're stronger than you think."

"Do you have another job besides telling fortunes?" Jeff asked.

"Ah, you saw the computer I use for telephone readings."

"Ariel's a big-time consultant to oil companies. She has clients all over the world. Although Barry doesn't believe in psychic stuff at all, she called me in Ohio to tell him about the office space next door. And it's worked out perfectly for him."

"The oil company that went bankrupt was not one of my clients." Ariel grinned. "I'm grateful Barry taught me to use computers, but the time's not right for a spiritual internet." Her voice was casual, but her gaze never left Jeff.

"Internet?" Jeff asked.

"It's a word Ariel made up," Mona Sue explained. "Barry wants to copyright the name."

Jeff, so uncomfortable he could not meet the woman's eyes, focused on the crescent moon birthmark on her left cheekbone. The longer she stared at him, the more he focused, until he saw the mark was not a moon at all but an arching dolphin.

At that instant she spoke. "Your journey is just beginning."

Jeff, despite his intention not to buy into this psychic stuff, asked the one question that haunted him. "Will I stay an artist?"

"Everything is art," Ariel told him. "Coincidences await." She placed a cool hand over his. "Pay attention and keep following the laughing dolphins."

***

Sandy

After Nora finished her Masters, Barry offered her more and more money until she agreed to work for Megga. On her first day she trotted to keep up with Sandy as they crossed the cobblestone bridge over San Antonio's River Walk. A boat with a three-piece band playing Lionel Ritchie's "Can't Slow Down" floated under them.

"Are you okay?" Nora asked for the third time since they'd met at Sandy's hotel.

"I'm fine. Just busy," Sandy said over her shoulder. "Have to get back to the Convention Center for a presentation in an hour."

Sandy knew Nora would never understand. She loved being part of something big, building Barry's dream. Her dream. Some called her obsessed. Some said she was addicted to be being in control, but Sandy wasn't stressed. She loved the never-ending deadlines. Those few times she was caught up, she'd started a new project, made new appointments, or researched foreign markets.

Nora pulled Sandy to a stop. "Slow down, hon. Take a break. Walk over to the Alamo with me. You've lost weight and those dark circles under your eyes didn't come from too much sleep. You haven't even asked about your ex. Did I tell you John's seeing Sharon from the Math Library?"

"Good. They're both so boring." Sandy tapped her foot on the stones. "My job'll be easier now that you're here to help. I spend a lot of time traveling. Investors want updates. Prospects with RFPs have thousands of questions. I demo the prototype system at shows. And clients need so much hand-holding. Barry's found a new programmer in Maine I have to brief. And—"

"Wait a minute. Sounds like you're doing it all."

"It's a start-up company."

"But Barry told me all was on schedule. Before I left Ohio, the prototype was supposed to be installed in two campus libraries. I used the operator's manual you sent me to train staff who, by the way, still think computers are filled with snakes. All except Marc. He's so happy to be taking over my job, he's stopped asking to bring his cat to work."

Sandy didn't smile. "That manual's a great promotion tool. Barry and I wrote it in one weekend."

"But, it's the way the system actually works. Right?"

"Sure." Sandy looked at her Rolex. "I have to get back to the booth. Go on to the Alamo if you want." She walked away before Nora could answer.

Back in the exhibit area, Sandy pushed through to the Megga-Tech aisle, ignoring the pain radiating from her aching feet up her legs to her back after four days of standing in three-inch heels.

The Megga-Tech booth was packed with middle-aged men wearing dark suits. They circled Barry, who shook hands, patted shoulders, and handed out invitations to the party in their hospitality suite. Behind the booth young bearded men in rumpled jeans watched Picasso reconnect cable.

Barry waved. "There she is now, the best little V.P. in the State of Texas."

His energy buoyed her and Sandy forced a big smile and plunged into the booth shaking hands and passing out technical literature and business cards.

As soon as the exhibits closed, she hurried to her hospitality suite bedroom to change for the party. No time for a shower, she stripped off the navy suit and pulled her red one from the closet. She looked in the mirror at the skin above her heart where her birthmark had once been. The wrinkled skin looked like an alien had bored through that weak spot into her heart and now a good poke could make a hole. That Boston doctor had promised the scar would heal, but pale tissue, like a skin graft from some albino fish, didn't feel like part of her. Barry asked her about the spot, but she refused to talk about it. She had no weak spots. Her life was perfect. She was successful, and though she didn't make a lot of money yet, the Megga-Tech perks gave her a jet set façade. Even her mother was impressed when they met at Logan during a brief layover.

Sandy slid the narrow red skirt down over silky pantyhose, buttoned the matching suit jacket, and re-checked her image in the mirror—business suit in a party color, no blouse, just the expensive gold pin and earrings Barry had given her.

Barry walked out of the shower, towel around his soft waist. Barry was excellent at what he did. But as men went, he certainly wasn't the most handsome or the smartest. He was short and thick and only expensive suits prevented him from looking like a dumpy kid. Ten years older than Sandy, he possessed the energy of a much younger man and his vigor kept her motivated. He was driven. And he had charisma. One wink from his flashing blue eyes made her feel like the most important woman in the world. She was always with him, working on the same projects, traveling, entertaining. It was like a marriage. She certainly spent more time with him and had more in common with him than his Texas-born wife. Since Sandy had no time for a social life or to meet men who weren't her clients, she'd fallen into an affair with her boss. A post-divorce affair cliché. But right now her life was exactly what she wanted and in a way she still had her freedom— didn't she?

As Barry straightened his tie he asked, "Did you request two bartenders? We're spending mega bucks. We need two."

Sandy nodded as she toed into strappy red sandals. They'd looked fabulous in Neiman Marcus, but by the time she walked into the hospitality room, she knew they'd torture her for the next four hours.

Early birds helped themselves to bottles of Lone Star from a tub of ice while waiters unloaded braziers of Texas BBQ. She phoned the catering supervisor and complained waiters had delivered the wrong ice sculpture. She'd ordered a computer, damn it, not dolphins. Finding Picasso stuffing his mouth with tacos from the Mexican buffet, she whispered, "I can't believe you're eating food that's never seen the inside of a vending machine. Go back to your room. I don't want our guests seeing you."

She walked to Barry's side as he touted Megga-Release 8.62 to the Saskatoon Library Commission. "Megga's software will do anything you want it to do. Absolutely bulletproof." He slipped his hand around her waist. He'd become bolder when he thought no one noticed. It made her uncomfortable in business meetings, but he'd told her everyone knew he was a toucher and at parties clients were too drunk to remember.

Sandy felt a chill run up her back. A tingling spread through her body. As Barry's hand slid lower, she sensed someone watching her. She turned her head. Mona Sue stood behind the departing ice sculpture. And for a second, their eyes met.

Mona Sue turned and pulled a man in jeans out the door.

***

Jeff

Jeff's fingers clutched the door as Mona Sue drove her pink Cadillac back to Houston without regard for Texas law or Jeff's comfort. Right before Mona Sue pulled him out of that hotel room as if he were a wheeled toy, Jeff remembered a powerful blast. He'd wanted to go in and find out what could make him both feel so good and so helpless.

That morning he'd put the finishing touch on the last dolphin's fluke, completing the pool house's coral reef wall, when Mona Sue bounced in and announced that a dealer in San Antonio had acres of really old Etruscan stuff she wanted to see. He enjoyed her company but frequent shopping excursions and lunch dates definitely slowed his progress.

Nestling a pink Stetson on her mountain of blond hair, she explained that Barry was doing a trade show in San Antonia and she wanted to surprise him.

They'd driven to San Antonio and spent most of the day shopping and reached the Megga-Tech suite just as guests arrived for the evening party.

"I'm Mrs. Kohl," Mona Sue had told the security guard.

A big, tall man rushed over and with a rude glance at Jeff's worn jeans, took Mona Sue's arm and rotated her back out the door.

"Floyd, leave me be. I want to see Barry. There he—" She'd pointed to her husband's unmistakably short frame, in tailored suit and elevator shoes, talking to a group at the bar. One arm waved dramatically, the other hung casually around the waist of a woman in a red suit.

As Mona Sue froze, Jeff felt hit by a powerful surge of energy from inside the room. A waiter pushed a cart with a dolphin ice sculpture past them, obscuring his view. He felt dizzy.

Mona Sue had pulled herself up to her full six-one in boots and announced, "We all don't have time to stay after all."

Jeff felt sorry for Mona Sue. She was an amazing woman and deserved so much better than that ass of a husband. It was bad enough he spent no time with her or their children, but to flaunt an affair in public was disgusting. One glimpse of the backside of the woman in the red suit gave him the strangest feeling. He instantly hated her for hurting his friend, but at the same time he was drawn towards her. If Mona Sue hadn't pulled him out of that hotel room, he didn't know what he'd have done. One thing was sure, he wanted to knock that short guy's hand off the woman.

***

Sandy

One hundred eyes stared at Sandy—one pair from every state. The new software refused to boot for her demo to the State Library Directors' Coalition. Worse, Sandy's old boss Marion Stillman was now Coalition Chairperson. The Library Director had retired after Megga missed two deadlines, too embarrassed to face his board after authorizing expenditures for a system he no long believed would ever work.

Holding a tiny screwdriver between her teeth, Sandy adjusted cables at the back of the computer and again tried to log in. She twitched phone lines, then called the Houston office. Everyone but Picasso had gone home early to get ready for Barry's open house.

"I'm trying to dial-in to demo the system," she told Picasso. "What's wrong?"

"Reloading the main system. Can you wait till midnight?"

Sandy slammed down the receiver. A man in a rumpled suit asked, "How does your system handle the hyphen versus em dash controversy?"

Sandy said through clenched teeth, "Later."

Marion stood. "Ms. Shellborn, this Committee has better things to do than watch you attempt to make that useless box work."

"I can fix this little glitch." Then, before Marion could say more, Sandy faced the group. "Please step out in the hall and enjoy a refreshment from Megga's complementary bar." Everyone except Marion quickly rose and filed out. Soon Sandy heard the familiar clink and buzz of contented conference attendees.

Marion glared and hissed, "If you cannot get that thing to work at my library by the next payment date, I will break the

Megga contract and sue for fraud. You'll never sell so much as a mousepad to a library anywhere in the country."

She heard a fizzle and saw a puff of black smoke spiral from the back of the computer. Sandy took a long, slow breath, walked into the hall, and asked everyone to bring their drinks and came back in. She proceeded, more lecture than demo, using an overhead projector to show a series of mock screens from the operator's manual.

That night in her hotel room, Sandy kicked off her sensible black Easy Spirits. She was still upset Barry had sent her to do this demo the night he'd invited the entire company to his home. There'd been gossip about the lavish decorating Mona Sue had done. Yellow Rose said some artist had painted palm trees and dolphins on a wall behind the pool and that they looked more real than the real thing.

Barry had been a little cool for a while after the San Antonio conference, but now everything seemed to be back to normal.

When Sandy called her office phone for messages, she heard Barry's familiar recorded voice. "Good news. I'm driving in right after this shindig is over." Then he said the code words she knew meant he loved her. "You're always there for me."

She whispered her usual response, "Always," to the silent phone.

***

Jeff

The evening of the gala open house Jeff just hoped Mona Sue would stay calm. He'd overheard her arguing with Barry last night on the patio. She'd accused him of having an affair with one of his employees. That woman in the red suit. Barry had insisted she was mistaken and told her to trust him.

When the first of the two hundred guests arrived, Mona Sue's eyes were still puffy, but she looked damn good in a low-cut pink cocktail dress and diamonds that would have made a smaller woman look cheap. In her foyer, transformed by Jeff into an Italian garden, she greeted every guest with a hug and a big Texas smile.

Barry held court in his den before shelves lined with faux books, while liveried caterers scurried trays heavy with colossal hors d'oeuvres. Jeff overheard him say, "Just like the Sistine Chapel and cost as much."

An hour after the party started, Mona Sue discovered Jeff had returned to the pool house and led him back to the main house to help her give tours.

"Meet my artist-in-residence." She touched Jeff's arm possessively. "You must see what he has done in my bed-room," and led them to the master suite.

One woman admired the dramatic detailing of the nude faux Roman statues scattered around the steam room, sauna, and six-person Jacuzzi, and raised an eyebrow at Mona Sue and the cute young artist on her arm. Several women asked Jeff for estimates and he imagined he could spend the rest of his life in Houston painting nouveau mansions.

At midnight Barry excused himself to drive to Austin, saying he had a mega important breakfast meeting with some government types. An hour later, Mona Sue said goodbye to the last guests and asked Jeff to follow her upstairs. In the bedroom she removed her jewelry and the pink gown.

"I'll leave so you can rest," Jeff told her, his gaze avoiding her pink slip.

"Please, stay. I need you." She choked back tears.

Jeff eyed the four massive posts supporting the California king-size bed and tried to imagine her short husband in such a big bed.

"Jeff," she said softly, "one more thing. In the bed-room…"

He began composing a polite refusal.

She took a photo from her dressing table. "Here's a picture of Barry. Paint me a faux-husband next to the bed. That's all little ol' me has left."

I. 4. Colorado, 1984

Sandy

Sandy jumped back into Megga-Tech's trade show space in the Denver Convention Center yelling, "Damn you," at the fork-lift driver's lifted finger as he careened past an inch from one red Jimmy Choo.

The new booth was near-ugly but at least Mile-Hi, that local graphics company, had delivered it on time. She'd erected the modular felt walls and hung the graphics without help—again. After two years and thirty shows, she could setup in her sleep. Sandy loved the buzz. But she missed the graphic design. After the first year, Barry insisted she hire an outside firm to design advertising literature and company logos. Nothing they produced was up to her standards and this booth was just another mistake.

Red eye flights, caffeine and sleeping pills. She'd take a vacation next year after the next release. Or after Megga had fifty contracts. For now the company was her life. Sleep deprived, she was always short tempered with those working a mere forty-hour week. Barry couldn't run Megga without her. And she liked being indispensable. Megga was exciting. Decisions to be made. Problems to solve. No time to think how others lived. This was a startup. Later, she could sit back and enjoy her accomplishments.

Satisfied all was secure, she plugged the booth phone into the cable.

A librarian in a baggy cat-print dress stepped up to the skirted table and held out an empty Demko bag. "Do you have anything free?" She looked at Sandy's tight jeans with raised eyebrows.

"Exhibits open tomorrow." Sandy ran fingers through her sweaty hair.

"I don't want to miss out on the goodies, especially buttons for my collection." She pointed to her jacket covered with advertising and library association buttons.

"We'll have mousepads. Tomorrow."

The woman eyed the boxes marked 'Mousepads.'

Sandy shook her head. "Tomorrow." The phone rang. Sandy mouthed, "Go away!" to the gatecrasher, snatched up the receiver, and switched to her business voice. "Shellborn, Megga-Tech." She heard Barry's familiar voice whisper, "It's me."

Her heart quickened. After all this time his voice could still do that to her. Over the past years they'd fallen into a routine. In Houston they only saw each other at the office or with other staff. Barry had convinced her no one suspected their long term affair and pointed to Mona Sue's polite manner as proof. She hoped he was right. On the road was a different story. Clients and other vendors treated them like a couple, inviting them to parties, ignoring handholding, and pretending they slept in separate rooms. Sandy suspected their limited time together sustained an excitement that wouldn't hold up in an ordinary marriage. Plus, the clandestine habits they'd developed to maintain their furtive relationship preserved a level of excitement. Barry had time to spend with his family and Sandy was free to work long hours without the interruptions of a normal social life. He told her he'd convinced Mona Sue there was nothing between him and Sandy and hinted his wife had been pretty cozy with her live-in painter. Barry reassured Sandy all was copacetic. At times she felt cheap, but chose believe him.

"My god, Barry, you're late. Everything except for the computers is set up." He didn't reply. She raised her voice over the noise. "Where are you?" Then she said softly, "I hoped we could have time... you know a quiet dinner and... time. My room has a view of the mountains." One of the perks of traveling was that she had his complete attention, except for clients and phone calls. "This connection is bad. So much noise here." She couldn't hear him. Barry was never at a loss for words. She kept talking. "InterTech, our big competitor at this show, has the entire sales staff dressed as cowboys and saloon girls."

"That's the first laugh I've had all day." Barry paused. "Sandy, listen. I have to miss the show. You'll manage just fine. Floyd's flying up from Houston."

"But I need you." Barry couldn't be serious. Floyd Landers, the company's financial guy, was an ass-kissing asshole who hated her. "Where are you?"

"A hospital. Here. In Denver. Just a little problem at the airport. But they won't let me out. Make excuses and handle everything. You're mega great. Always there for me. Got to go, this nurse—"

Sandy's fingers grew cold around the phone. The word "hospital" numbed her. Barry never got sick.

She sat on one of the plastic chairs to catch her breath, but before her head stopped spinning, Floyd, Barry's Finance V.P., strode up the aisle carrying a garment bag and a snake-skin briefcase that matched his boots. Behind him a porter pushed a dolly stacked with the missing computer equipment.

Floyd's gaze raked Sandy. "My god, you look awful. Go change. We're having dinner with prospects. And, Sandy, make it conservative. Not as sexy as usual."

Sandy bit her tongue. "Tell me what's going on?" she said in the tone that always intimidated this seven-foot Texas number-crunching wimp.

This time he didn't cave. "Barry had a stroke. He's in no shape to be seen here. I'm in charge."

"This is my show. I'm V.P. of Sales," she said, automatically tipping the porter who still waited behind Floyd.

"I'm Acting President." Now Floyd actually leered. "Mona Sue, the major stockholder, appointed me. You remember Barry's wife?"

Suppressing shock, hate, and fear, Sandy forced her face into a neutral expression. "Sure, Floyd, I understand. Meet you in the lobby." She focused on the sound of her shoes clicking down the aisle. She needed to do her job and hold on to her power in the company. Neither would be impossible—if only Barry was just her boss and not the only important person in her life.

***

Jeff

Jeff gasped for air as he jogged on Treadmill #29 next to Lisa on #30 at her favorite downtown Denver gym. Her blond ponytail bounced. How could she run and talk at the same time?

"How's your job at Mile-Hi Graphics going?" she asked over the hum of bikes and grunting gym rats.

He slowed his pace to answer. "Today I sketched kittens and angels... for the guy... working on the new 'My cat is heavenly' cat food ad... campaign. Then I delivered a truly ugly booth to the Technical Library show… Convention Center… Texas company… Megga… something."

"Your job is so creative. I have no time for fun. I wanted to go to that show, but my law school classes on top of managing Daddy's law library make me frantic." Lisa slowed and jumped off.

Jeff gratefully stopped his treadmill and picked up his towel, ready to head for the shower.

"Let's go to the weight room and catch a salad on the way home. I've got a mountain of work."

"How do you do it?" Jeff followed her, wiping his brow.

"Just keeping in shape for the rat race."

A few minutes later, Jeff saw Lisa curling fifteen pounds. "Hey, slow down. I lift pencils and tiny brushes for a living. You heft law books."

"Ha!" She softened and kissed his cheek. "We're so lucky we found each other. What a coincidence we were in college in Boston at the same time. We may have known some of the same people."

Jeff shrugged. "Boston's a big city."

"I wouldn't have met you if you hadn't come to Daddy's law firm for help. A bright, talented guy so down on his luck."

"Not my fault I was robbed at the bus station. Or that the trucking company lost my commodes for the Loveland sculpture show. It could happen to anyone." They were a strange match, but he enjoyed being around a happy woman who treated him like a regular guy. And Lisa thought he was smart because he belonged to Mensa.

"Colorado has mountains. Who needs sculpture?" She moved on to the bench press station. "Wonder what happened to all those decorated toilets?"

Jeff looked away. Life in Denver with Lisa was great, but she sure didn't share his love of art, nor did he share her exercise compulsion. He was disappointed the graphic design job her father arranged for him didn't leave free time for painting. But Lisa always had weekends planned and he had no free time. Still she was so upbeat and she'd started to talk about getting married. Maybe if he could just convince her they needed more space with room for a studio and a yard for their Golden Retriever, they'd get along better. "Say Lisa, how about we start looking for a bigger condo?"

"Great idea! We could use the extra space for our own workout room."

The next morning, Dick Hill, Jeff's boss, caught Jeff before he got to his cubicle. "Hey Jefferino! Sit in on this meeting."

Dick hung his arm over Jeff's shoulders, steered him to the meeting room, and with a conspiratory wink, whispered, "You got to meet Tonto." Jeff cringed. Old Dick Slickerino was an asshole. Jeff was enjoying graphic design more than he'd expected. He'd always put it down as selling out. Too commercial. But after learning a few techniques, he liked the flexibility of moving images around on his lightboard. He also liked the challenge of working with different clients' products. He might start the day designing a sign for a florist's truck and move to working up ideas for a restaurant menu. He loved laying out newspaper and magazine ads. He'd gotten good at imagining what a client already imagined and then gently introducing a better idea. What he didn't like was working for idiots and Dick was first class. No imagination and not one iota of artistic ability or sensitivity.

A handsome Native American about Jeff's age sat at the fake mahogany conference table, long hair pulled back into a silver ponytail. Jeans, a white shirt, and a tweedy jacket with elbow patches showed off an angular athletic build.

"Jeffer, meet Steve Whitehawk. He's here looking for advice from the best admen in the business. Okay, guy, make your pitch." Dick spread his fingers. "Five minutes."

The man ignored Dick and turned to address Jeff. "I want to open a healing center."

"Whoa!" Dick scratched his head like an idiot. "What the hell is healing?"

"I had a healing school in Virginia Beach."

"So, what happened?" Jeff asked before Dick could interrupt.

"I gave it to my partners. Their dream was a massage school. I just want to teach people to heal."

Dick leaned forward close to the prospective client's face. "So, how much do you charge for this here healing?"

"Enough to cover expenses," Steve replied.

Dick nodded. "Cool. Non-profits can really bring in the bucks. You could make a fat salary and our advertising work becomes a write-off."

"No," the man stated quietly.

"Whoa! What do you mean? You wanted expert advice." Dick feigned mock surprise. "I'm giving it to you."

"I just need a logo and an ad."

"You're crazy, but if that's all you want... That would cost..." Dick scribbled numbers on a yellow legal pad and pushed the pad across the conference table.

Steve shook his head. "You're the crazy one."

Dick stormed out and Jeff walked Steve to the lobby and slipped him his card. Before he left the office Steve had called and told more about his dream of setting up the healing center. Jeff wanted to help. He needed something to believe in. He wanted to be excited about a project again.

That night Jeff told Lisa about the meeting and how Steve called him.

"You have a private client!" she cheered. "Soon you'll open your own agency."

"Well, this client is sort of pro bono."

"Jeff, you sure don't know much about business. Pro bono is only for companies already making tons of money off other rich companies."

***

Sandy

On the final day of the trade show, everything closed down at noon. As Sandy placed the last CRT in its box, Barry phoned. "Take a taxi to the hospital's south entrance, elevator to 4th floor. Room 421. Tell them you're my sister from Cleveland," he told her with familiar firmness.

Since the news of Barry's hospitalization three days ago she'd moved in a trance. Finger food at obligatory parties passed her lips, but she'd not felt hungry. No one noticed she didn't eat or drink. She talked with clients until late into the night, wrote proposals, faxed them to Houston, then prepped for the next day's meetings.

Stepping out of the hospital elevator, Sandy checked the Fourth Floor signs and followed Barry's instructions to Denver General's Intensive Care Unit. He'd sounded so sure, so in control—like his old self.

She walked past the nurses' station with the confidence of a hospital administrator and looked into room 421. A pale bearded man lay against white sheets, tubes and monitoring equipment filling half the room. This must be the wrong room.

The man turned his head to her and life flooded into his face. In two strides she'd crossed to his bed. Afraid a kiss would dislodge the plastic, she bent her lips to his right hand.

94

A smile spread over her face while tears cascaded down both cheeks.

"Hey, no crying." His voice sounded thick and raspy as he brushed away tubes to take her hand.

"So happy to see you. To see you are all right."

"I'm mega great. This is dreary. Wish I was in that classy hotel room with you instead of flying back to Houston. Can't miss the SLC meeting."

Even in her state of shock, she knew he was confused. That meeting had taken place last month. "Sure, it's all set up," she lied.

He squeezed her fingers and looked up into her eyes. "Thanks for coming. You're always there when I need you." He pulled himself up from the pillow and she thought he was going to try to kiss her, but his eyes jerked from her face to the door. "You're back?"

Sandy turned. She felt her face freeze and her body go numb. She couldn't breathe. All her relief at being with Barry turned to fear. Barry's wife stood in the doorway. It was one of those weird moments when all Sandy could think of was how much taller Mona Sue was compared to Barry.

"Your phone call, dear. You kept asking when I'd be coming back to the hospital. You asked again and again. I thought you needed me. So I came right away." Her normally tanned skin was as pale as her pink dress. She raised her chin. "I see you don't need little ol' me. You look tired. I'll send a nurse." Focusing on a spot above Sandy's head, she added, "Ms. Shellborn and I will chat in the lounge." She turned on her heel, leaving Sandy staring at the empty doorway.

Sandy closed her eyes and took a deep breath. Her face tightened into a mask of dried tears and makeup. She saw Barry, weak, old, and not at all in control. Her cold wet fingers touched his hand. "Remember I love you," she whispered and wondered if he understood she was saying goodbye. As the nurse began rearranging tubes, Sandy walked away, out the door to meet Mona Sue.

***

Jeff

Jeff entered the brightly lit Chinese restaurant and walked to the green and yellow booth where Steve Whitehawk waited.

Steve stood. "Jeff, thanks so much for meeting me."

Jeff grinned and gestured Steve to sit. "Hey, I hear there's something to this New Age healing stuff."

"I want to help people. I'm a good healer." Steve turned to the waiter and said a few words in Chinese, then to Jeff, "I ordered tea for us."

"No tea for me. Coffee," Jeff told the confused waiter. He settled into the booth and, too excited to wait, flipped open a sketchpad to show Steve a half dozen thumbnail logo sketches.

Steve examined each one. First his eyes, then his lips, and finally his entire face burst into a smile. "Yes." He pointed. "I like this one. Mountains and sun."

"I prefer this one with your profile shadowed against the mountain. People need to remember you." Jeff hesitated. The quiet man's penetrating gaze made him uneasy. "I'd also suggest a better name. Something short and catchy. And unusual."

Steve nodded. "My Lakota teacher called me Seva."

"Perfect. Then you are Seva." Jeff sketched the name into the design.

Their drinks arrived and Jeff took a sip of the tan liquid. Tea would have been a better choice. He continued to sketch. "So Seva, tell me about yourself."

96

"When I was twelve, my adopted parents told me my mother was Lakota and my dad a Swedish physician."

Jeff smiled. "So, you *are* a blond Indian."

"My hair turned gray when I was twenty at the same time my Lakota grandfather sent me to begin my studies with healers of many traditions." He pointed to the sketch Jeff had drawn. "You're very talented."

Jeff tore out the drawing and handed it to him. "There'll be a charge."

Seva's face turned blank. "I can't afford much."

"I think I need healing."

Seva smiled and nodded.

That evening at the gym, Lisa slowed to her cooldown rate after an hour on the step climbing equipment. "I have a big surprise for you. My midterms were so spectacular Daddy insists I take the whole weekend off."

"That's good." Jeff slowed. "I worry that you're overdoing—"

"I've signed us up for a rappelling intensive with one of the best—and toughest—instructors in the Rockies. We go to orientation Friday night."

"Can't. I'm going to Pagosa Springs with Seva."

"That Indian guru hasn't paid you."

"He's taking me on a retreat instead. He says it's time for me to make soul choices. It's just one weekend. I'll learn a lot."

"Not about rappelling." Her lip curled into a pout. "How can you be my climbing buddy if you don't take the training?"

Jeff lowered his head and said softly, "Maybe, Lisa, I don't want to be your climbing buddy." But she'd already put on earphones and picked up her pace.

That weekend Jeff was the last to arrive at the camp. He didn't know what to expect at Seva's retreat. He'd always stayed away from the kind of people who chanted and twisted into pretzel poses. There were a lot of Subarus and Jeeps and a few Volvos, no psychedelic VW buses with flower power designs. The people walking around actually looked a lot like Lisa's hiking friends and her law school buddies in boots and the latest LL Bean gear.

He saw Seva and walked into the clearing behind the tents. As he got closer it looked like Seva and two couples were arranging roundish rocks in a circle. No, not quite a circle, more like a spiral. He caught Seva as he left the circle to find more stones. "Can I help?"

"Sure, Jeff. We need more stones to complete the labyrinth for our walking meditation."

Jeff fell into step and began to tell Seva about the drive to the camp.

"Jeff, here we try to keep conversation to necessary communication. It helps quiet the mind. There'll be some mandatory silent times, but mostly we practice mindful speech."

Jeff slowed, taking in Seva's words and tried not to feel rebuked. After Lisa's nonstop patter, a weekend of quiet would be a welcome change. For the next hour he carried rocks the size of small deep dish pizzas to the circle and began to notice the cries of birds and chatter of squirrels.

When he heard a gong, he followed the others to the largest tent. Each camper stopped to take off boots before entering and Jeff did the same, wondering about the smelly foot odor of twenty people in a confined space. Inside there were no chairs. Not one. Everyone was sitting on mats on the ground. A guy at the door handed Jeff a thick pillow and Jeff found a spot in the back and managed to bend his stiff denim covered knees into a sort of sitting position.

Nothing happened. Seva sat in front facing the others, eyes closed. Jeff looked around. The others seems bored, too, but not fidgeting. He tried to find a more comfortable position. And failed. He watched an ant crawl across the ground in front of him. This was definitely not what he expected. He didn't know what he expected. Maybe Seva giving lectures. Advice on how to become like him. Maybe a chance to walk in the woods. Or swim in the pond. Nature stuff. Native American stuff. But not just silence.

Then Seva opened his eyes and looked at Jeff. Right at Jeff. He hit the gong and Jeff felt every molecule in his body hum, and hum, and hum.

It felt good. Very good.

***

Sandy

It was morning, but Sandy couldn't remember if she'd slept. She sat on the king-size bed in the art deco Brown Palace suite she'd booked for the trade show. Though Mona Sue had warned her not to visit Barry again, she'd stayed on in Denver.

She used the room phone to call her office number in Houston for messages. The ring cut off and the call transferred to an operator who informed her Nora was unavailable and all Sandy Shellborn's calls were being transferred to Acting President Floyd Landers.

Next Sandy called Nora's home, a number she knew well, since most mornings for the last year she'd call her at least once before Nora left for the office. Often she'd also call late at night. And at odd hours on weekends, sometimes when Nora was at a local stables taking riding lessons. There were always so many emergencies. Nora was an invaluable assistant and her best friend. When Nora answered, Sandy pleaded, "Please, tell me what's going on."

"Please?" Nora's familiar voice could be sarcastic, but the venom had never before been directed at Sandy—her boss, her mentor—not until now. "I'm taking a week off. Remember. I'm getting married."

How could Sandy have forgotten? Nora was her closest friend. "Right. You and Charles."

"Christopher. His name is Christopher." Nora let the silence hang on the line for a while, then said, "This must be rough for you. Floyd announced you resigned. I was assigned the task of clearing out your office and making arrangements to have the contents of your company condo put into storage."

"You're kidding. They're packing my house? Where do I live?"

"For now, hon, nowhere. After the rented furniture got picked up, there's not much left. It's not as if you had a life." Nora must have heard Sandy crying, for her voice softened. "Sorry, you've got to get yourself together. We all saw it coming. You didn't think your balloon could burst. I'm sorry the end happened this way. You're through at Megga-Tech. And I'm a little busy with my own life right now. Plus, I may not have a job when I get back from my honeymoon. Being your assistant is no longer the fast track to success here."

Sandy sobbed, unable to say anything. Nora sighed. "Okay, okay, hon. I'll do you one last favor. I'll find you a place to stay until you decide what comes next. It'll be outside Denver and definitely not in Texas. Don't go anywhere 'til you hear from me."

"I won't," Sandy said softly to the dial tone. She reached for her briefcase and mechanically took out the proposal she'd been working on. She was indispensable. Barry couldn't run Megga without her. Then tossed it in the trash. It was over. All over.

***

Jeff

Jeff pedaled harder. Uphill was torture at 7,000 feet elevation. Why did he ever think this mountain biking trip would make up for missing last weekend's rappelling?

Perky, tireless Lisa stopped twenty feet ahead. Straddling her bike, she looked back and called, "Race you to the top of the hill!"

"Hill? This is a mountain. I'm whipped," he gasped. "You go on. I'm going back... to the campground."

"Why?" Lisa sounded displeased.

"I want real food and coffee. Veggies aren't helping my stamina."

"Keep pushing. Remember you pooped out of rock climbing to sit and meditate."

Ignoring her, he lifted the bike around, stiffly swung up, and coasted down the trail. Behind him Lisa called, "Be that way. But take Dolf." At the mention of his name, their Golden Retriever stopped peeing on a tree and shot after Jeff.

Back at the campground, Jeff considered showering, but remembered that the showerhead shot icicles. He ducked inside the tent and, crouching, struggled into clean jeans and a Denver Rockies sweatshirt. He found keys to Lisa's Volvo in her hiking boot and signaled Dolf to jump in.

***

Sandy

Sandy's rubber-soled shoes flip-flopped across the parking lot from her hotel room. She'd pulled her robe tight over her bathing suit and entered The Springs Bathhouse. Thanks to Nora's arrangements and a rental car, she'd managed to drive from Denver to southern Colorado and check into this Pagosa hotel adjacent to the famous hot springs.

The bathhouse's athletic girl attendant was telling a guy, "These are not like swimming pools. They're hot. Like 120 degrees. Hot enough to cook fish!"

Sandy waved her room key, picked up a still-warm towel, and flipped through the women's locker room to the springs. Even at midday, steam rose fifty feet over soaking pools terraced above the cool river. One two-person pool had a sign which read '115 degrees—The Lobster Pot.' Sandy touched her toe to the water surface. "Too hot." Slightly above 'The Family Bath' temperature sign read 96 degrees. "Too cool." She dunked her foot in to the ankle at the 'Bubble Machine' and found its 102 degrees just right.

Slipping out of her robe, she tossed it and her tote bag on a chair, and walked down the steps. Inch by inch, immersion in the heated mineral water soothed her body. She closed her eyes and settled her head on the edge until her hair floated. Inhaling, the sulphury steam tickled her nose. She positioned her lower back precisely in front of a bubbly outlet.

Letting the water envelop her, she realized how cold she'd been. Not the outward cold of frigid temperatures and chilly winds, but the unyielding frost of an inner core that would not bend to the feelings of others. She remembered that cold Maine sunrise when Jeff had warmed her with the heat of his body and the intensity of his love. With him she'd felt more human. And then she'd left him. Turned cold and walked away. She doubted that Jeff still looked for her, regardless of his impetuous vow. She wasn't worth being found.

A half hour later, wrinkly and soft, she emerged, showered, and wrapped in her robe. Muscles warm, she looked forward to a massage.

An hour later, inside one of the Springs Spa massage rooms, enveloped by the smells of flowery spicy oils, her body gave up another layer of tension and long held stress. She struggled to remember when she last been this relaxed. And failed. Not since her college days had she felt a true minute of peace.

***

Jeff

As Jeff drove out of the campground, he thought about Seva's retreat. Last weekend had changed his life. He'd never imagined two days of sitting with his own thoughts would have made such a huge difference. He was convinced Seva's calm energy entered his mind, offering just the right words when Jeff's thoughts began to drift. For the first time Jeff looked at his life from the outside. A few intuitive exercises helped, but it was mainly Seva who seemed to know how Jeff struggled and drew him aside from time to time for a consult or what Seva called satsang. Seva helped him see he'd been blaming others.

He'd blamed Sandy for leaving, Sammie for changing, and Jerry for taking advantage. He needed to take responsibility. Even now he was letting Lisa pull him into her life. He understood all that, but when Seva suggested he also needed to forgive, he told him he had forgiven. Yet the look in Seva's eyes made him realize that had not happened. He left the retreat wiser and more aware of how little he understood himself. He already felt he'd known the gentle spiritual teacher forever.

Seva had told Jeff he'd be performing a hot air balloon wedding at the Pagosa Balloon Festival and balloonists always needed extra crew. Jeff wanted to help but explained floating in a flimsy basket was not his style.

Seva shrugged. "Look for the yellow and red one called Coincidence."

Seeing no fast food on the outskirts of Pagosa, he kept driving. An old-fashioned sign with an arrow pointed him to The Springs. Curious, he pulled into the parking lot in front of a pseudo-Greek revival building. Leaving Dolf in the Volvo, he walked inside.

***

Sandy

Sandy left the Springs Spa relaxed and contented, her oiled body again wrapped in warm terrycloth, carrying her still-wet bathing suit. Halfway back across the parking lot to her room, a large Golden Retriever mouthing a tennis ball blocked her way.

"Not now, baby," she said with a laugh. Big mistake. The goofy dog interpreted her laugh as an invitation to play. He dropped the ball, grabbed one end of the sash that held her robe together, and tugged. A vision of the dog disrobing her in the middle of the public parking lot flashed in her mind. Holding the robe closed, she heard the belt begin to rip.

Just in time, a tall man with wheat-blond hair stepped up and grabbed the dog's collar and smiled down at her. "I'll take care of your playful friend. I saw him jump out of that green Volvo. The driver's inside the bathhouse. I'll find him," he said, adjusting two camera bags to secure his hold on the dog's collar.

"Thanks," she said, self-conscious under his friendly stare.

The blond man grabbed the ID tag that dangled from the squirmy dog's collar. As Sandy walked away back to her room, she heard him say, "Dolphin. What kind of a dog's name is Dolphin?"

***

Jeff

Jeff read the brochure, 'Natural Springs—Temperatures from 97-120 degrees,' and grinned at the young woman who smelled of freshly laundered towels.

"Want to soak?" she asked from behind a tower of towels.

"Do I need a... soak?"

"Our mineral waters, like, heal anything." She stacked the towels and grinned.

"You believe that?" he asked, half flirting.

"Yeah, but you have to, like, come more than once," she flirted back.

She was cute. Her taut, tan muscles reminded him of Lisa. "Didn't bring my suit."

She looked him up and down and shrugged. "If you were younger, I'd ask you to come back after hours."

Jeff left the bathhouse, retrieved his dog from a stranger in the parking lot, continued his search for caffeine and greasy red meat before heading back to camp.

The next morning as the first light of dawn appeared behind the San Juan Mountains, John Denver's voice singing 'Rocky Mountain High' echoed inside the Volvo. Lisa braked to let Jeff out, then without a word drove off. Jeff waved goodbye to Dolf's head lolling from the window and the yellow diamond 'Runner on Board' sign in the back.

Jeff turned toward the field where lights illuminated a dozen huge hot air balloons in various stages of inflation. In the early morning glow, he watched a red and yellow checkered puffball grow bigger and bigger. He took out his camera. When Lisa saw these pictures, she'd be sorry she'd left. They'd argued all night and finally he told her to return to Denver without him. It had irked her that he'd said he'd get a ride back with Seva and she'd frosted him with silence as they broke camp at three a.m.

He sat on the cold ground and attached a wide-angle lens to his Nikon. As he finished, he heard Seva call, "Jeff, over here." Standing he snapped a couple of shots of the field, ethereal light behind the mountains, mist wrapping the balloons.

Seva hugged Jeff. "You have been sent to save me."

Jeff grinned. "Me?"

"The Nebraska photographer I hired to shoot this wedding got an assignment from some aviation magazine. It wouldn't be right to hold him to this little job. But here you are, my talented artist friend with a camera."

"Sure. I can get a couple shots as you lift off."

"Oh no, you'll go up with us. You, me, the pilot, and the blissful bridal couple."

Jeff, unsure of his new role as skyborne wedding photographer, but not wanting to disappoint Seva, pocketed a spare roll of film from his camera bag.

The couple arrived and Seva introduced the bride, shivering in a gauzy white Mexican wedding dress, as Nora and the tall, skinny bearded groom in a white dashiki as Christopher. Equally nervous, they eyed the basket warily.

"I thought this would be romantic." Nora clutched a veiled circlet and apologized to her bridegroom, ghostly pale in the dim light.

Jeff attempted to take cute candids of the couple in front of the inflating balloon, but they refused to look at each other. He did get a few shots as they were boosted, stiff, cold, and scared into the basket.

The ground crew checked ropes as the pilot helped Seva and Jeff climb into the basket. The whole rig bumped around as the balloon strained at its ropes. The pilot gave a rehearsed talk about what to expect. At last the crew chief released the crown line and with a gentle burp the basket floated off the ground.

Camera swinging from his neck, Jeff gripped the edge and watched solid earth move away. The balloon continued to lift as the sky lightened. The mountains began to glow and Jeff forgot his fears as he photographed balloons backlit by the sunrise.

A noisy blast from the burners returned his attention to the bridal couple. Seva stood in front of Nora and Christopher. Jeff realized he'd used up too much film on the sunrise and had just taken the final picture on the first roll. He reached into his pocket for his spare roll to replace the exposed film, switched rolls, and—the basket lurched. The bride's veil blew off, hit the groom, and rebounded into Jeff's face. Trying to protect his open camera, he let the canister of exposed film fly into the air and arc out of the basket like a Fenway pop fly.

The burners stopped. The groom yelled. The bride cried, "Land this blasted thing. This balloon idea was as dumb as the two of us getting married."

The pilot pointed down and Jeff looked over the rim at the town below. Steaming hot springs water flowed out of the pools and down to the icy river. There'd be no wedding but

Jeff still had film. He leaned over and started photographing The Springs.

***

Sandy

That night, unable to sleep, Sandy rubbed her tingling neck and decided to watch the sun rise from the hot springs. She entered the pool area through the hotel's connecting gate before the attendants arrived and left her robe and bag on the edge of her favorite pool. Body submerged, mineral water steam swirled around her head as first light rose up behind the San Juan Mountains.

Before she left Denver, she'd signed the Megga-Tech resignation papers. Mona Sue had been more generous than necessary and offered a severance package with enough benefits and cash for a new start anyplace. Any place but Texas. Sandy had no choice. Fighting would have made Barry's life worse. She loved him, but she couldn't help him. He needed Mona Sue, his kids, and hopefully a chance to salvage some self-respect. Mona Sue told her everyone knew about the affair, but people would forget—if Sandy disappeared. Walking away hurt. Her life felt empty. Empty of love, purpose, and hope.

Her body had been numb. She cried more than she'd ever cried in her life. Emotions she'd buried for years, rose up and she cried more. Driving from Denver south to Pagosa, she pulled over every few miles to weep and clear tears from her eyes. She cried for Barry, for Mona Sue, for John, and for Jeff. And for herself, for being unfeeling and cruel. She'd thought she was successful but she had been a complete failure at all that was important.

Tears flowed into the hot springs. Days of soaking and massage began to soothe her body enough for her mind to begin to clear. Now for the first time in years she had nothing to do and nowhere to go. She realized how stressed and unhealthy her life had been. Soon she might know where she'd go and what she'd do. Even if Mona Sue's tightly written non-compete agreement didn't forbid any connection to her old life as a librarian, industry gossip would prevent her being hired even by the smallest library. Fear had replaced her mega confidence. Plunging on to her next goal was no longer an option. She didn't know where or what she'd do to start over—alone.

Sinking deeper into the pool, she tilted her head back to keep the water level below her lips. She enjoyed the mystical quality of the dawn and remembered that sunrise in Maine. Breathing in the steam, she couldn't smell the sulfur anymore, just the water's salty mineral scent. She drifted asleep. When her chin tipped forward and touched the water, she jerked awake. Her eyes opened. Spiraling red, yellow, and blue circles spun above her. To her right, a dark green and white one twirled like a child's top. In the dawn's light, rainbow striped globs poured over the hill. Dots and spirals spun around her like a Miro kaleidoscope.

She heard a whoosh. Something hit her forehead. A splash of water. A white tunnel of brilliant light appeared and instinctively she wanted to dive in and escape having to choose a new life.

***

Sandy became conscious of an insistent voice calling, "Miss. Miss." Her eyes flashed open. Surrounded by white, pure white, she remembered the tunnel. Was she still inside that magical white light? No.

"Miss?" the voice began again. "Can you talk?"

A hoarse croak came from her sore throat "Of... course. But where am I?"

"Room 421, Denver General," the woman in white told her.

"How long?"

"You've been in a coma for two weeks."

Sandy shook her head in denial. A tube stretched and pulled at her nose.

"Do you remember," the nurse coached, "sitting in the hot springs during the Balloon Festival?"

"Balloons?"

"A roll of film hit you. I developed the pictures hoping they'd help us find your family."

The nurse flipped through the photos. A Golden Retriever. A red and yellow hot air balloon. Aerial shots. Three people in the basket of a hot air balloon. A woman in a white veil looked like Nora. A tall skinny man just looked scared. A second man, dark-skinned with light shoulder-length hair in a loose white outfit seemed to be performing a wedding ceremony. His peaceful demeanor held her attention. Just holding the photos made her feel better.

PART II

"There are no coincidences in the universe, only convergences of Will, Intent, and Experience."
Neale Donald Walsch

II. 1. Virginia Beach, 1990

Jeff

Jeff stood under the lobby chandelier in the Virginia Beach Boardwalk Casino Hotel, noticing how his best suit, the only one without paint spatters, turned mouse gray in the glitter and glaring lights. How he'd come so far from the Colorado mountains?

After he and Lisa broke up, Jeff followed Seva from Denver to the East Coast helping with workshops and presentations. At psychic fairs Jeff met penniless spiritual musicians needing album cover design and developed a following. At one fair, he ran into Ariel, the Houston psychic Mona Sue consulted. When Seva went back to the West, Ariel asked Jeff if he wanted to move to New Hampshire and share a house with a group of artists.

Once settled, Jeff reconnected with an old college friend who told him Picasso was trying to get in touch with him. After a couple of intriguing phone calls, Jeff agreed to drive to Virginia Beach to meet with friends of Picasso who'd started a company called Yippee and were looking for a freelance artist. Ariel, who'd promised a friend in Virginia Beach she'd fill in at her tattoo booth, volunteered to share the driving. So, for six hundred miles Jeff had listened to Ariel's soothing voice explain chakras, auras, and energy healing.

At last Picasso, in what looked like pink scrubs, hurried through the lobby. "You're just in time."

"I don't even know why I'm here," Jeff told him. "I'm not a computer guy."

"Cuz you're smart and this could be a great gig for you. These two kids I knew at MIT wanted me to work for them, but after Megga-Tech I lost interest in computers."

"How's Megga doing?" Jeff asked, remembering his faux painting job for the owner.

"The boss was in lala land 'til he died. His wife stepped in and took over the boss's babe's job. Mona Sue's little ol' Texas gal routine worked miracles. She even made programmers talk to clients."

"So, why'd you leave?"

"I took a vacation and found some rocks. The next thing I know I'm enrolled in massage school here."

"Quite a change from M&Ms and Big Macs." Jeff noticed that his old drinking buddy snacked on trail mix and no longer looked like a fifteen-year old MIT student, pale from basement computer lab marathons.

Jeff followed Picasso into the hotel bar and squinted into a dark booth at two rumpled teenagers Picasso introduced as Chip and Mike.

Chip ordered four strawberry mango virgin daiquiris.

Jeff asked, "You guys look pretty young to have been in school with Picasso?"

Chip grinned. "You don't want to know our real ages."

Mike added, "I made these fabulous real-looking IDs, but Chip won't let us use them. Boring to have a best friend with ethics."

Jeff sipped his daiquiri. Excellent for a virgin. After Chip ordered four bags of Fritos, Jeff asked, "What kind of work does Yippee do?"

Mike giggled. "Work? Man, we play."

Picasso laughed. "You guys haven't changed."

Chip took a noisy slurp. "We have a whammo website with links to the best deals on the net. Mostly from kids with garages filled with the hottest electronics."

"Also the hottest," Mike giggled, "jokes."

"Fill me in," Jeff asked. "I've heard about the internet, but I don't really understand what it is."

"Okay. The web is graphics, but that's just the beginning, like," Mike waved one arm in a big circle, then the other, "the difference between *The Birth of a Nation* and *Jurassic Park*, that's the internet now and what the web will be in a few years. Big companies are too scared or too dumb to jump in. Not us."

"I know nothing about computers." Jeff leaned back. He'd probably come all this way for nothing.

"Picasso says you're really smart and an artist," Chip said. "We'll teach you to make web pages for our clients. We live in Boston, but you can work anywhere. A PC, modem, and a little software we designed and whammo—you're in business."

Jeff watched Mike wave to a desperately thin girl clunking through the lobby in Doc Martens and a black tube top. She didn't look more than twelve. Being with these kids made him feel old. He turned back to the boys. "So what's the deal? How much do you pay?"

"Pay?" Chip and Mike said together.

Picasso shook his head. "Guys, Jeff's a professional artist. He doesn't live with his mom."

Mike shrugged. "Geek-heads help us out for fun."

"Okay," Chip offered, "we'll pay by the number of pages you design. One hundred bucks for every website and twenty-five each additional page."

Picasso raised an eyebrow. "I don't know? Jeff's really smart."

Chip added, "And stock options."

Mike giggled. "Yeah, two thousand shares a month. And bonuses. If we like your pages."

Jeff needed money. The New Hampshire artist co-op gave him space to live and work and a schedule of chores to keep him on track. Weekends, the artists caravanned to flea markets and craft fairs. He was doing serious art again and, like Sammie, produced small fast-selling pieces. Some of the artists had jobs at a nearby New Agey summer resort called Alpha Camp. Since that did not appeal to him, the Yippee kids' offer had the potential to generate the steady income he needed without jeopardizing his serious art. Jeff nodded. "It's a deal."

***

Sandy

Sandy changed into shorts and sandals for an early morning walk on the beach. She grabbed her room key and put on her old denim jacket and walked out into the salty air. Even her comfy old jacket scratched the sensitive place on her neck that prickled with a weird frisson no matter how much many therapeutic modalities she tried.

Her massage school graduation was only a few days away and she was more than a little scared. From the first massage she'd given, she knew she'd chosen with her heart and spirit and not her head and mind. She'd be good at this work, but not famous and certainly not rich. Six months ago she'd moved from Pagosa into this shabby motel in the old section of Virginia Beach with fewer possessions than she'd packed for a four-day trade show in her old life. Other than her used Datsun, obtained by trading in the impractical Mercedes convertible, her folding massage table was the largest thing she owned.

A young man with flaming red hair and beard lifted a rock the size of a medium-sized dog from the bed of a Ford pickup truck and carried it into the motel unit next to hers.

"Need help?" Sandy assumed the man was a new massage school student as she watched him take out two smaller gray rocks. "They look like ordinary rocks to me."

"Haven't you heard of hot rocks massage?" the redhead told her.

She shook her head. His voice sounded familiar.

"Hot rocks is the absolute latest thing. I'm developing a method of using rocks for weight loss. Maybe I'll call it Ter-ra Firm-a? Or cuz you know, my stones are filled with Zen. Maybe I'll call it Zen-Zen Massage."

"But they're... ah... just rocks."

He unwrapped more rocks from a wooden crate. "This one is basalt from the Grand Canyon. And this is granite from an island in Lake Superior." He kept unwrapping. "Egypt. India. All the most sacred spots on earth."

"You went to all those places?"

He nodded. "Machu Picchu. Stonehenge. The Pyramids. My stones will bring energy from sacred places to ordinary people."

"Can you just really pick up stones in these places?" Sandy couldn't believe this guy was serious. Stones from Stonehenge? "And put them in your luggage?"

"Well... no. Cuz most places have nasty signs. And there's all those snarling border officials and rude customs bureaucrats. But when a stone's energy begins to peter out, I promise to take it back to the place I found it. I'm just sort of borrowing them." The man looked up from his rocks, pushed hair from his eyes. "Hey, weren't you Sandy Shellborn! Megga-Tech 1984." He stared. "You look years younger than that pushy bitch."

She stared back. "Picasso? Barry's hardware guru. You're starting massage school?"

"My second career."

She nodded. "My third."

"Meeting you. What a coincidence! Hey, did you know Barry Kohl died? Cuz you know, now Megga can stop those disability payments."

"Yes, what a coincidence." Sandy turned and walked away towards the beach. A gust of wind blew sand in her face and she wiped at the tears in her eyes. She'd thought she'd left the sad memories and shame from that materialistic and oh-so-selfish part of her life. From here she didn't know where she'd go, but she'd fallen off that obsessive track. Or been pushed. What had started as a job, after her divorce, had quickly become an obsession. Now from a distance, she could see that Barry had filled a need. More than a need, a hole in her soul. She'd loved him more than he was worth loving, because she desperately needed to love. She'd given him more than he deserved. She'd been there for him. And he'd never been there for her.

She ran the rest of the way to the beach and looked out to the horizon, hoping today would be the day she'd see a pod of bottlenose dolphins. Every morning since January she'd looked for them. Locals told her dolphins could only be spotted from June to September, when the waters off the Virginia coast were warm.

After Barry's stroke, losing her job, and that freak hot springs accident, she'd stayed in Pagosa Springs. When winter came to the quiet mountain town, she'd taken a job folding towels at the Springs Spa to be close to the healing waters. Accepted into the community of massage therapists, ski bums, and urban ex-patriots, along with the healing waters she'd absorbed a new slower way of living and viewing her life.

Pagosa was the first time in her life she felt free of pressure. As a kid her mother's expectations seemed to rule her life. Rebelling and entering art school hadn't really changed anything. She saw now she'd created her own expectations and always worried about deadlines and grades. She chose projects she thought would please her instructors. She was proud she finished first in her class. But now all that meant little.

Her values had been so screwed up. She never noticed. Thinking about her decision to leave Jeff and start grad school made her cringe. She'd panicked because of one professor's opinion. She gave up the art she loved. And gave up Jeff who she loved. She'd promised not to leave him and had not even had the courage to face him. She'd never thought of herself as a dishonest person, but she was. She lied to Jeff by not telling him she was going.

She married John because it suited her cock-eyed view of who she thought she was. He never deserved her lies.

Her entire relationship with Barry was built on lies because he fed her ego and she didn't think she was good enough for more than leftovers.

She'd hurt many people because she couldn't be honest with herself. She'd keep learning about herself and try not to hurt herself or anyone. And maybe, just maybe, learn to help some.

As she folded warm towels and soaked in pools steaming below snow-covered Colorado mountains, slowly she warmed and melted. Simple life in a small town. Simple satisfying work. Gratitude for the kindnesses of co-workers and neighbors. No one asked where she'd come from or why she stayed. To them she was Sandy who worked at the Springs. Sandy who hiked the trails. Sandy who cooked for potlucks and volunteered at the library. Sandy who always had time to help and care for newcomers. She was accepted and liked for who she was.

She wanted to help people heal. And she wanted a life with time to walk on the beach. She'd enrolled in massage school and moved to the ocean.

Months of training had flown by, every class convincing her she'd made the perfect choice. Her hands became strong and flexible, her mind steady and calm. She was proud to become a massage therapist, though her mother thought she'd become a prostitute, no matter how many times she explained therapeutic massage was not prurient.

Graduation was only a few days away, but she hadn't decided what she wanted to do—next. Most students were returning to their hometowns and starting massage practices or getting jobs at spas. All she'd done was buy a Rand McNally Road Atlas.

A movement in the water fifty feet from shore drew her attention. She stopped and stared. The first pod. She counted at least twelve dolphins. Then two broke from the rest and dove closer to shore, surfaced and seemed to look at her before submerging and rejoining their family. She closed her eyes, feeling blessed by her encounter with those gentle intelligent creatures.

She heard a call and turned to see Nora hurrying towards her. "Wait for me. I'll walk with you."

Sandy accepted the coincidence that her former assistant was now here with her. After Nora's disastrous hot air balloon wedding, Nora admitted she had no interest in men and Christopher had been just a good friend. Later both agreed they'd been lonely and the idea of getting married in a balloon seemed like a solution. Most surprising Sandy and Nora had switched roles. Now Nora often made decisions and gave Sandy advice. Sandy, feeling guilty for having been a heartless boss, became a loyal friend. It had taken a hit on the head to wake her up.

She waited for Nora and they walked along the still deserted boardwalk. Nora handed Sandy a flyer on ugly goldenrod-colored paper. "Look what I found on the floor near the job board." Cleaning the school's office was one of Nora's extra jobs along with shifts at the cotton candy concession, though she preferred helping with pony rides. "This job is perfect for you."

Sandy read the flyer: "Alpha Camp—Holistic Summer Camp—Where It Begins—Lots of Spiritual Teachers—Sunny, Bucolic Setting." The print was small and blurry and a few words were spelled wrong, but by the second reading Sandy understood this place wanted to hire a massage therapist. A five-month seasonal job would be the perfect opportunity to think about what she wanted to do next. "But what about you?" Sandy asked Nora. "Summer in sunny New Hampshire sounds lovely."

"Me?" Nora announced. "I'm going back to Texas. I've enrolled in Equine Massage Training. I like horses. Better than people."

"That's great." Sandy smiled, truly happy for her friend, as they listened to the peaceful sounds of the ocean. As different as they were, they shared the same joy every time their sesame-oiled fingers reached out to touch and offer healing energy to sore bodies and depleted spirits. And then, to replenish their own spirits, they were drawn to the beach.

Further down the sand Sandy noticed a skinny girl in black jeans, Doc Martens, and a tube top, looking into a trash container. Her straight Asian-black hair was matted and dirty. What was a kid so young doing on the Boardwalk?

Nora interrupted the comfortable silence. "After my morning class, I'm giving a room massage at the Casino Hotel. Some woman named Mona Sue in the President's Suite requested a strong masseuse. Never thought I'd meet another Mona Sue."

Sandy had seen a banner for the Compu-Fest convention and thought that it would be too much of a coincidence if it was the same Mona Sue. Meeting Picasso and Nora here was weird enough.

***

Jeff

Jeff stepped onto the boardwalk, hands in his suitcoat pockets. For two days, he'd been following the Yippee kids around the Compu-Fest conference, waiting for them to find time to train him. The flashing lights, electronic gadgets, and signs without one word found in a standard dictionary gave him a headache. He gotten very used to the quiet of his rural New Hampshire town.

A flyer taped to a post advertised cut-rate student massages. He thought about going for one of those 'soma soothing' treatments. But he couldn't imagine some strange woman, or worse yet, a guy, rubbing his naked body, so he stared out along the horizon where gray-blue water met blue-gray sky like a watercolor seascape. Families and couples began to swarm over the strip of sand separating boardwalk from ocean and splashed in the shallows. He shivered, remembering the bone-numbing ocean on the Cape, and felt isolated and unconnected here.

On a whim he bought a cone of cotton candy, but when he sat on the bottom step to one-handedly remove his shoes and socks, the pink fluff rolled away along the beach, gathering sand like a snowball on a dirty city street. He tied his shoelaces together, tossed one shoe over his shoulder, and ignored the sand trickling down the back of his suitcoat.

Distracted by clusters of people standing in front of a turreted hotel, he strode onto the beach, avoided shards of broken plastic beach toys, and let cool sand push up between his toes. Through the crowd, Jeff saw a sand sculpture of a mermaid in a clamshell. The artfully contrived sea creature was kitschy, but pretty. A girl dressed in black leaned close and reached out to touch the sculpture. The artist grabbed her skinny arm and shoved her back.

Jeff's hands itched to build his own sculpture. Further along the beach a tanned man in a red Speedo madly scooped sand into a mound. As Jeff approached he understood the man's frustration. "Looks like you got a late start."

"Right." The artist ran fingers through his sunlit gold hair. "I had to work all morning. No way can I finish in time for the judging."

"May I help?"

The artist looked up at Jeff's wrinkled mouse-gray business suit. "Sure, why not?"

Jeff peeled off his jacket and rolled up his sleeves. He paused, then unzipped and dropped his trousers. His red-striped boxers were not so different from many of the swimsuits on the beach. The artist showed him a sketch of a seated woman reaching for a dolphin.

Nice." Jeff nodded. "You do the figure. I'll do the dolphin."

The artist shrugged. "What do I have to lose? I hear the judge is French. I hoped this contest would get me a little cash."

Jeff dropped to his knees. His palms and fingers fell into a graceful rhythm scooping and patting as the warming sand seemed to breathe beneath his touch.

A half hour later the artist completed the woman's figure and turned to his volunteer. Instead of an amateurish attempt, he smiled at a reasonably accurate replica of his dolphin sketch. Except, instead of one, Jeff had built two dolphins arching toward each other. The blond artist nodded. "I get it. The woman is reaching out to the dolphins, longing for her own lover." Before he could say more, the black-suited judge strode up.

"I'm Jerome Oberon, from *La Parisienne François Gallery*. This is Entry Number 28, Monsieur Jake? Just Jake, *non*?"

Jeff took in the thick accent, European clothes, patent leather loafers sinking in sand, and the familiar dark wavy hair. He snickered at his old friend's new persona.

Jake began. "Yes, sir. I'm Jake and this is my associate—"

"Jeff Sanders." Jeff swallowed his urge to laugh.

Jerome did not meet Jeff's gaze. "It is good. *Très bon*."

"It's a joint work," Jake insisted.

Jeff put his arm around Jake's shoulders and faced Jerome. "I'm sure this artist's work is worthy of an award."

Jerome nodded. "*Mais oui*, of course. For an old friend."

Jeff's old anger at Jerome for the rotten treatment had cooled. Seva taught forgiveness and responsibility for one's own life. Jeff was trying. Seva also preached doing good to others. And Jeff was trying.

***

Sandy

After Nora left, Sandy walked farther down the beach. She stepped into the surf to wash away a glob of sticky pink cotton candy that had blown across the sand and stuck to her ankle. This water was cold, but not icy like the bone-numbing needles of the ocean off Cape Cod.

The banner fluttering on the Casino Hotel entrance caught her attention. *Bytes on the Boardwalk.* A computer trade show. Healing with her hands was so much more rewarding than selling computer stuff that failed to deliver on its promises.

In front of the hotel that same dark-haired girl in black begged for change and Sandy dropped coins into the girl's outstretched hand without making eye contact. Further up the beach, a crowd swarmed in front of a castle-like hotel. She detoured and took the stairs up to the boardwalk.

Today the red and yellow Tabby's Tattoos sign she'd ignored hundreds of times drew her in. Sandy looked down at the ghost-white spot on her tanned chest. The scar no longer appeared scary, but since everything inside her felt different, perhaps it was time to change her outside body, too.

She walked to the counter and browsed through photos of hearts spreading across bulging biceps, vicious knives on scrawny calves, and floral triangles pointing between women's buttocks.

A woman with flowing silver hair and a moon-shaped mark on her left cheek smiled. "What design do you want?"

Sandy shrugged.

"If you don't see one you like, I'll draw whatever you want."

"So Tabby, you're an artist."

"Just filling in. My name is Ariel. I'm a psychic and an artist." She looked into Sandy's eyes, then opened a binder to a page filled with drawings of angel fish, shells, and dolphins. "What about one of these?"

Sandy didn't hesitate. "That dolphin's perfect. But I want two."

Ariel pushed paper and pencil across the counter toward her and Sandy drew for the first time in ten years. The first strokes were awkward, but as the pencil warmed in her hand she made sure strokes.

"Nice," Ariel said when Sandy finished.

Sandy pointed at the scar above her heart, the location of her old tattoo and birthmark. "Put the dolphins right there." Her father's Piscean daughter had found her ocean at last— just like Dad's poem.

Ariel quickly prepped her for the tattoo and began before Sandy could reconsider. By noon Ariel covered Sandy's sore, stained skin with a light gauze pad and instructed her, "Take your mind off the tattoo. Walk down the beach and see the sand sculpture a guy named Jake from Nebraska is sculpting."

Sandy looked for her bag to pay. It was gone. Seeing that kid in black hurrying away, she raced after the girl, calling to Ariel, "I'll be back to pay."

By the time Sandy caught up, the skinny kid was stuffing a hot dog into her mouth. The ridges of her black tube top absorbed grease and mustard dribbling down her chest.

Sandy grabbed her bag and yelled, "Do you know the crap they put in those?"

"Yes," the girl glared back, "I do. But they're cheap."

Sandy seethed. "You bought that hot dog with my money. How old are you?"

"Sixteen!"

"No way."

"Like it's your business."

"You stole my money! Where do you live?"

"None of—"

She grabbed the girl's bony wrist. "Talk to me or I'll call the cops." She saw fear flicker into the girl's big dark eyes and felt her pulse quicken.

"I sleep under the boardwalk."

Sandy hadn't wanted to believe this kid was a runaway. "Why'd you leave home?"

"I'm adopted. My parents don't understand me. They're engineers. And blond."

"Parents don't understand their kids. It's the way it is." Sandy held tighter.

"I want to be an artist. They want me to go to MIT," the girl whined, "and take boring vacations with them."

"I went to college and majored in art," Sandy shot back in the same whiny tone.

The girl sniffed. "Like, what do you do?"

"I was a librarian." Seeing the kid's bored look, Sandy added, "I sold computers systems."

The girl sneered. "Like an engineer. Then what are you doing on the Beach?"

"Learning to be a massage therapist."

"You aren't an artist! Who are you to tell me anything? I'm going to be famous."

Sandy wanted to smack this lippy juvenile. But the kid was right. She'd never used her art training or talent—if she'd even had any talent. "Come with me." She dropped the girl's arm and waited. The girl didn't move. "You need a shower. Come back to my room." Still the girl stared defiantly. "You stink." Sandy turned and walked back to pay for her tattoo.

The girl picked up her backpack and followed.

***

Jeff

That night Jeff walked past the Casino Hotel's Lobby Bar, brushed away thoughts of strong drink, and considered spending his limited cash on another virgin strawberry mango daiquiri. After four hours with the Yippee kids, he was zonked. These kids talked computers the way other people discussed what they ate for breakfast. Out of school for twelve years, this work hurt his brain. In a few more days he could go home. Ariel's friend was due back from the Virgin Islands and Ariel, tired of tattooing, wanted to head home to New Hampshire.

"Jeffy, it is you!"

He immediately recognized that loud, buttery Texas drawl.

"Sweetie!" Mona Sue Kohl drew him into a big hug against her pink business-suited chest, then stepped back and looked him over. "You broke my heart when you left."

Jeff was pleased that she looked great. "Heard you found a taller guy," he quipped.

"My Floyd is a big man," she winked, "and a good accountant, but no one paints like you. *Houston's Huge Homes Magazine* did a spread on my spread when Floyd and I got hitched and now you and your fake paintings are famous. Can't move to something a bit bigger because I can't take those walls with me."

"Mona Sue, anything bigger than that house would require taxi service between the living room and dining room."

A man, close to seven feet tall in snakeskin boots, walked up. "Mona Sue honey, we're due at the Users' Group meeting."

"I'll be there in a minute, Floyd sweetie," she cooed.

The big man's eyes narrowed as he looked down at Jeff. "Don't ah know you?"

"Ah, no," Jeff gulped. He felt hot breath on the crown of his head.

"You look like that puny artist guy."

"Oh, no, this is the little ol' temp the agency sent to pass out goodies at our booth. Have you ever seen an artist in a suit?"

"Ah guess you're right."

Jeff and Mona Sue watched Floyd walk away, look over his shoulder once, then turn the corner to the bank of elevators.

"I can't pass out trade show promotions."

"Of course you can. And you will—for me. For four days, you will stand and smile because Floyd will be watching every minute." Mona Sue flashed one of her most charming smiles. "I love that he's crazy jealous. After my years with Barry, that's very important to me."

***

Sandy

Nora lugged the forty pound bag of clay up the steps into the massage school classroom. Sandy followed, carrying three large rolls of paper. "Tell me again why we're doing this."

"We get to attend a workshop for free with a famous feminist artist. It'll be fun. Why are you in such a hurry, anyway?"

"I left a runaway kid back in my room. She's probably stolen everything I own. Besides, you know artsy stuff doesn't interest me. And my new tattoo is starting to hurt."

"Stop whining. I need your help."

Following Nora's instructions, Sandy mixed clay with water, and eucalyptus and lavender oils in five-gallon buckets. At noon, ten women who'd paid for this expensive experience arrived. A school instructor introduced Sammie Swampscott, a large woman in a purple caftan and amethyst sequined sandals.

With a toss of her blowzy russet hair, Sammie announced, "Welcome to this deluxe detox and body art experience."

Assured that the space was totally private, five of the women and Nora stripped to their panties and lay down on plastic sheets. Sandy oiled Nora's body, covered her with the mud concoction, and wrapped her in brown paper like a large deli sub.

By the time Sandy removed the paper and loosened the dried mud, the ocean breeze had lulled Nora to sleep. The mud separated from Nora's torso in one piece with a smack. Nora's eyes snapped open. "Neat. Now your turn."

Nora oiled and packed Sandy with mud, careful to protect the area around her new tattoo with plastic wrap. After her torso dried and popped off, Sandy looked at the mold. It looked like a medieval breast plate, made to protect her vulnerable chest from spears and arrows. Once she'd lived her life as if she were protected from the people around her by the thickest shield. That defense was gone.

Sammie lectured, "The molding process produces a chest copy which we'll decorate with feathers, jewels, and personal mementos, turning your body into a glorious work of art. My famous yoni chalices are examples—"

Sandy got up and slipped out the back door. She refused to paste rhinestones to her clay chest. The sketch she'd made at the tattoo booth had left her longing to create art again, but not with showy sparkles, feathers, and doodads.

Back in her room, Sandy confronted the girl, trying to sound more like a friend than an adult. "So, where are you going?"

"Like, I don't know." The girl sprawled on Sandy's bed wearing Sandy's favorite 'Massage Therapists Rub You the Right Way' sweatshirt. "Famous artists need life experiences." She set a mug of hot chocolate on Sandy's completed *Anatomy Coloring Book*, and stuffed a handful of microwave popcorn into her mouth.

"You're only thirteen!" Sandy heard her mother's voice emerge from her own mouth. She snatched back the coloring book of bones and muscles, the closest thing to art she'd done in years.

"Seventeen!" the girl choked, spewing kernels onto the blanket. "Sixteen!"

"Your school ID says thirteen," Sandy said softly.

"You snooped in my bag while I was in the shower," the girl accused.

"When did you eat last?" Sandy's mom voice asked.

"I met some guys in the Casino Hotel lobby. They treated."

This kid was in trouble. "Never talk to strange men. Never."

"They're, like, rich geeks. From Boston."

Sandy stared her down. "Ginnie, I know you live in Boston, too."

"You know my name. I suppose you're going to call my parents."

"Not yet. Sleep here tonight. Eat some decent food. I'll figure out what to do with you tomorrow."

"Can I wear your clothes?" Ginnie asked.

"No."

"Like just the black stuff?"

"No." How had she become responsible for a smart-mouthed thirteen-year-old who was so sure she'd become a famous artist?

"Did you sneak a look at my sketchbook, too?" Ginnie asked, more curious than accusing.

"Yes, I did." Sandy smiled. "Ginnie girl, you are good. Really good." She watched the girl's eyes widen, then added indifferently, "You should go to art school."

Ginnie grinned. "I want to study art in Japan. I'd feel normal there. I look more Japanese than Swedish. My parents are unreasonable. If I refuse to apply to MIT, they want me to become a kindergarten teacher—because I like paints."

"If you say it's okay, I'll call your parents and see if I can convince them you should go to a good art school."

Hiding her pleasure, Ginnie scrinched her face. "Okay. But if they don't agree, I'm, like, hitching a ride to New Hampshire with this older guy, a friend of the geeks."

"Over my dead body."

***

Jeff

Jeff sat next to Jake on the boardwalk stairs below Tabby's Tattoos. His rolled-up pant cuffs dripped water. He'd hoped walking in the cold surf would numb the aches in his legs and feet from standing on the Convention Center's concrete floor. For four long days, he'd smiled and passed out Megga logo buttons, sticky notes, and mousepads. Convention-goers were greedy pigs. One guy circled ten times, faking surprise each time he came down Jeff's aisle to grab freebies.

Jake listened to Jeff's complaints. "I've got to leave this town. A big artist's judging the art show next weekend, instead of that fake French guy." Jake held his head in his hands. "J.J. McCorry."

"McCorry has a great reputation." He remembered McCorry from art school graduation.

"He's my father." Jake leaned back and looked up at a bi-plane flying fifty yards out over the ocean, pulling a sign advertising suntan lotion. "I've been traveling picking up odd jobs and meeting people. I really want to fly, not be an artist."

"If I could see the world from the air," Jeff sighed, "I could paint the world from a new perspective." He laughed. "A very new perspective."

"Paint? I just want to see it."

Jeff smiled. "When you do, send me pictures."

"Someday I'll do just that." Jake shrugged. "Now I want to go to New Hampshire with you."

"If you're sure, our co-op house has room for one more. We can leave as soon as Ariel is ready."

Still aching from the trade show, Jeff walked stiffly up the steps, while Jake clowned, pretending to hold him up, but pushing him over. By the time they got to the tattoo booth, both were laughing like kids.

Ariel, pleased Jake would be joining them, told them, "I'm ready to leave after just one final customer. Jake, help me."

Before Jeff knew what was happening, Jake tussled him into an old-fashioned dentist's chair while Ariel tied back her long white hair and prepared needles and inks.

"Not a tattoo," Jeff yelled when he saw her intent. "Not for me."

"Jake," Ariel cooed. "Please remove this ingrate's shirt. I'm offering him free body art. I'll even use my psychic powers to choose a tattoo that reflects his soul journey."

Jake held Jeff while Ariel closed her eyes for psychic vision. Her hand searched the counter among loose sketches until it settled on Sandy's sketch. "This one is perfect. You'll get the dolphins my earlier customer drew."

Jeff relaxed. There was no arguing with Ariel when she began talking about soul journeys. A long time ago he'd promised someone he'd get a dolphin tattoo and he often regretted not doing it. Now he'd get one—whatever design that woman drew. He still didn't know where his journey would take him, but he was beginning to enjoy the trip.

***

Sandy

Sandy arrived an hour late to her massage school graduation. Traffic to the Norfolk Airport and back to Virginia Beach had been awful, but she'd gotten Ginnie safely on a plane to Boston. The kid actually cried when Sandy bought her a plush dolphin to remind her of her Virginia Beach friend.

She buttoned her denim jacket against the ocean breeze and ran down the beach towards two blazing bonfires. Reaching Nora's side, he stumbled to a stop. The most beautiful man she'd ever seen stepped across the sand in front of her. Sandy couldn't take her eyes off the lithe man with long silver hair silhouetted in bonfire flames. A feeling of peace filled her. "Nora," she whispered, "who's that?"

"Steve Whitehawk, one of the school's founders. They call him Seva. Isn't he cool?"

As the man walked closer to the fire, he appeared to float. His white clothing shimmered in the firelight and his dark face appeared luminous as flames accentuated his angular features. He raised his left hand and threw an object into the fire.

Sandy heard a hiss and let out a breath. Seva turned and looked directly at her. The light from the second bonfire reflected in his eyes and sent a beam out into the sky. She couldn't look away. His face showed no emotion, but his presence warmed her as he closed the distance between them.

She stepped back. Tears of joy slid down her cheeks and she stopped breathing. She felt the heat of the fire, the cool ocean breeze, and his powerful energy. He reached her, whispered, "All is well," and opened his arms. She nodded and exhaled. He enclosed her in a hug. When at last she stopped crying, he released her and extended his left hand to her right. "Come with me. Into the circle." His voice was as soft and powerful as his energy. Feeling stronger and more peaceful as if a long held pain had burned away, she took his hand.

Nora grasped her left hand and the circle was complete. All the graduates turned to Seva. He began to chant.

Standing at his side, Sandy felt taller, expansive, as if the breath that flowed through her body had expanded every single cell. She joined the chant and glanced at Seva on her right. His head, slightly bowed, bore the strong nose and cheekbones of a Native American, a Tibetan, or some prehistoric shaman. His thumb pressed the center of her palm, strong, warm, and moist. Instantly she responded by sending energy from her heart into his hand.

Mystic power moved around the circle back to her through him. Her divine destiny was to be on this spot at this moment as the breeze from the ocean, the fire's heat, and the vibration of the sand spiraled together. In an instant, the hundreds of hours of training and the myriad teachings merged and burned together and she was filled with the powers of a healer.

When the chanting softened to a whisper, Seva bowed his head and raised his arms. "May the power of Spirit, Energy, and friends forged by this fire and connected by the shared learning of the arts of healing bless this circle. Go forward along the healing paths you have chosen."

As the others dispersed, Sandy turned to Seva. "Where do I go next?"

"Your hands are your path. And Alpha is the beginning."

II. 2. New Hampshire, 1992

Jeff

Jeff had returned from Virginia Beach to Fallon, New Hampshire determined to work hard designing Yippeedotcom webpages. A month later, discouraged at his slow progress, he walked to the carriage house to visit Martin, the seventy-year-old owner of the Victorian house Jeff shared with six other artists.

He listened while Martin talked about his favorite subject, the lovely old house. "When my daughter Martha was in art school she insisted this old gal, with a little restoration, would make a fine art gallery." Martin noticed Jeff wasn't listening and observed, "You seem distracted, young man."

"This high tech stuff is hurting my head. I know how a webpage should look—colors, fonts, graphics—but getting the code right takes forever."

"Maybe I can help."

"It's technical." Jeff tried not to sound condescending. He didn't think this old man could help him with state-of-the-art computer stuff, but to humor the old guy, he handed Martin the instructions the Yippee kids had scribbled on a handful of McDonalds' napkins.

Martin put on his glasses and studied the grease-stained notes. Then he took out pencil and paper. "Simple as pie."

"You understand this?"

"There's nothing new under the sun. This code, as you call it, is similar to the language old printers like me used to set type for their printing presses." He drew squares on a piece of paper. "Imagine this is a wooden box of metal type. Say I want the pressroom kid to reach for an uppercase T instead of a lowercase t." Martin kept drawing boxes. "So I say <u>t and he reaches into the upper box. Same way if I want italics or bold—"

"Yes!" Jeff hit his forehead with the heel of his hand. "I get it." He let Martin show him a few more examples, then hurried back to his room. During the next two hours he completed more work than he'd done in the last two days. At noon he looked out his third floor studio and saw Christopher, the tall skinny guy from Houston, Ariel, and the two other artists getting into Jake's old red Wrangler. Jeff hung out the window and called, "Where're you guys going?"

"Lake Winne… winnie… winniepesaukee for a… a picnic." Christopher, who often seemed depressed, stumbled and almost fell out of the Wrangler's back end.

"Come with us." Jake, dressed in overalls, like the Nebraska farm boy he claimed to be, stowed two six-packs in the cooler.

"Guys!" Jeff called. "Remember the art shows next month. You have to work. We talked about ideas to make money and sell our art." He'd tried with little success to teach them the tricks he'd learned from Sammie. Cast as a mature role model, he rose early every morning, spent a few hours at his easel and every weekend drove off to art shows and flea markets selling arts and crafts. It was hard work. He'd never been happier.

"It's a nice day. Don't be an old grump," Ariel teased.

Jeff did feel like an old man trying to get his over-thirty kids to do their chores. Since they all owed him money, he felt like a dad handing out allowances and setting rules. He remembered what an immature kid he'd been in art school. Everyone said he had talent but he took his talent for granted. He'd done nothing with his gift and his irresponsible behavior drove Sandy away. He cringed every time he thought about his drinking. Her leaving him wounded him and he was furious with her. She'd been the only person who understood him. She understood all right. He'd been a lazy selfish prick.

Jake, during years of drifting, had completely given up art. Jeff supposed that if his own father had been a famous artist and his dead mother's sculpture displayed in every major museum in the world, he might feel the same about art as a career. For himself, being free to create felt like a second chance.

Jeff worried most about Christopher, who didn't have the same natural artistic talent as the others. When he wasn't depressed, his habit of dressing in women's clothes and his hyperactivity disrupted everyone.

Ariel, who said her best art was produced after trances, had stopped giving psychic readings at Alpha Camp, the spiritual center on the other side of Fallon Falls. Jeff teased her about woo-woo stuff, but admitted the effects of her predictions on folks were always positive. Her calm playful presence had a stabilizing effect on every person in the house, but she often retreated into her own world and didn't support his plans. He'd forgiven her for tricking him into the dolphin tattoo, though he often wondered at the coincidence that the design was identical to one he drew in college for Sandy.

Jeff watched them drive off, absent mindedly rubbing the spot above his heart and wishing he could find a way to bring this talented group together.

***

Sandy

Sandy drove through the sunny New Hampshire countryside, crested a wooded knoll, and followed a one lane road that dipped into a wall of torrential rain. Slowing at an unpaved drive, she rolled down the Datsun's window. The smell of fecund earth and dead fish wafted in. Needles of rain hit against her face as she read the flaking letters on a wooden sign. Alpha Camp—It All Begins Here.

Beyond the sign, visible through drizzle and fog, lay a small lake rimmed with rustic cabins. A young woman in a smiley face print sarong and yellow duck boots splashed down the drive and tipped a tattered black umbrella. "Welcome," she called with an impish smile, eyeing the car's Virginia plate. "You must be Sandy. Follow me. I'll show you to your new home."

The woman walked her past freshly painted cabins and down a gully. Despite her guide's cheerfulness, Sandy's spirits sank when she saw her assigned tent—awash in three inches of mud. The letter she'd received promised that in exchange for providing two massages per day to Alpha Camp guests she would receive comfortable living quarters, healthy food, and forty percent of the charges for additional massages. She pulled a soggy envelope from her pocket and demanded, "Take me to Gaia O'Hara."

The duck-booted girl led Sandy to an office door, then took her smile and ragged umbrella off to greet another arrival. A soggy paper tacked to the door announced that Staff Orientation was cancelled and that all week one workshops except 'Running for Chi' and 'Out of Body Sex' were also cancelled.

Weighted down by her sodden denim jacket, Sandy entered a cluttered office where a middle-aged woman with aggressive blond hair talked into a phone. The desk sign read Guest Registration, Staff Assistance and Guidance—Gaia. The name on the sign appeared to have been crossed out and rewritten many times.

Hesitant to track mud onto the floor, Sandy kept her sandals on a worn rag rug and looked at the jumbles of papers covering Gaia's desk and the adjacent floor. What appeared to be years of dusty memos layered a bulletin board above a typewriter buried in paper. Three file cabinet tops held more papers than could have fit inside. Sandy's librarian sensibilities ached to straighten out this mess. Alpha Camp badly needed a computer system—or any system.

Stacked next to the door, tied bundles of this season's workshop catalogs blocked a copy machine with a tattered out of order sign. Sandy knew, without opening a catalog, it would be as unreadable inside as the ugly dark cover and weird typeface. AC also needed a decent artist and graphic designer.

Sandy took a breath and reminded herself that she was here at this spiritual center to work as a massage therapist. She wanted to touch people and help them, not solve these obvious computer and marketing problems. She hoped this summer would integrate the teachings she'd absorbed and give her time to meditate and perhaps discover an artistic outlet for the feelings rising up, calling her to create.

"Sandy Shellborn?" Gaia looked up, her expression neutral, her tone flat. "Peace and love. I thought you'd be younger. You just finished massage school."

Sandy responded equally abruptly, "Tent 5 is underwater."

Gaia sighed. "Young ones don't care. So be it. I can move you into a dorm. Rainbow, Windsong, and Mountain Dew's room can hold another cot." She pushed masses of electric blond hair over her shoulder. "Don't sit down. Your test appointment will be here soon."

"Test? I thought I had the job."

"There's always a trial. Like an audition. Probation. You give a massage to one guest and one senior staff member so we can see if you'll fit into our community of Peace and love."

Sandy's mouth tightened. She'd expected to stay here all summer while deciding where to go next. Now she had to pass a test.

Sandy was still speechless when the office door opened and, in a spatter of muddy water, a yellow slicker burst in. She watched a wet hand draw back the hood and cried, "Lisa?"

"Oh my god, Sandy." Lisa lunged forward and hugged her old college roommate. "What a coincidence. Daddy and I came to Boston for a law conference. He's sailing on the Cape with friends. I signed up for 'Running for Chi.' What is 'chi' anyway? You wouldn't believe how stressed I am. What are you doing here? I got my law degree and run the firm's library. Are you still with that hi-tech company in Texas? Barry Kohl was there, right? Heard about some wicked scandal."

"I—" Sandy began.

"Ms. Fitzpatrick," Gaia interrupted. "Are you ready for your massage?"

Fifteen minutes later, Sandy knocked on the door of the Massage Hut, slipped off her sandals, and walked in. Lisa lay face down on the table. Sandy pushed Yanni's *Dare to Dream* album into the cassette player and began to oil the skin around Lisa's athletic bra and nylon running shorts.

Lisa cried out. Sandy stopped.

"Do me harder," Lisa groaned. "Like my masseuse at the country club."

"You are a bit tight." Sandy pressed her thumbs into trapezoids as unyielding as steel cables. Sandy massaged. Lisa talked. And by the end of the hour Sandy was exhausted. Every deep tissue technique she'd learned in school had failed. Lisa's muscular body was still rock hard.

Returning to the office, Lisa told Gaia, "Great massage! Charge everything to my credit card and add a nice tip for Sandy. I'm moving to a motel in town near the high school track. Can't get traction on these muddy trails." She hugged Sandy. "Great talking to you. Keep in touch," and plunged out the door.

Lisa was as driven and focused as Sandy had been before Pagosa. Sandy closed her eyes. Visualizing her old Texas persona—minus expensive running shoes, she shivered, remembering how badly she'd treated people. She, like Lisa, never slowed down long enough to notice.

Sandy was still reeling from Lisa's frenetic energy when two men entered. The first with obviously dyed black hair strode in as if he owned the place and everyone in it. He was followed by a tall, tanned man with shoulder-length silver hair, dressed in a loose white tunic and pants. Sandy smiled at Seva. After the ceremony on the beach, Seva had disappeared and she'd begun her drive to Alpha Camp, believing she would never see him again.

Gaia introduced the first man as Clayton Clifton, AC's Director.

Clay appraised Sandy. "Older than the usual massage therapist!" He winked at Seva as if sharing a private joke.

"She won't be staying unless she passes the staff member audition." Gaia winked.

Seva watched the winking and stepped forward. "Clay," he said his voice soft, "I've just driven in from New York. I'd be most grateful for a massage. I'd be happy to see if she meets your AC standards."

Clay looked disappointed, then clapped Seva's shoulder. "Sure, why not. I had two yesterday." Another wink. He turned to Sandy. "Sandy, meet Seva, this season's premiere resident staff presenter and healer. You take good care of him."

Seva smiled at Sandy. "We've met." He turned to Gaia. "Sandy's had excellent training. I'm sure this massage is just a formality."

Fifteen minutes later Sandy knocked on the Massage Hut door. She heard "Om Namah Shivaya," the peace chant imprinted on her mind at the bonfire. She'd thought about Seva often since that night, but seeing him here so unexpectedly unnerved her. She walked in and found Seva had lit incense and candles. She took a breath of scented air and centered herself. Her fatigue vanished as she approached the table. He lay face up, eyes closed, completely naked under a thin sheet.

Floating her hands above his body, she felt his energy field. Each chakra beamed perfect vibrations into her palms. She repeated the scan, sure she'd misread his energy. No. He really was perfectly balanced.

She gently stroked his face and smoothed his silver hair. Their breath synchronized. She moved on to the warm pliable muscles of his neck and shoulders. She inhaled the peaceful, energizing lavender and eucalyptus that still lingered in her dreams.

She asked him to roll onto his belly and worked his back, hips, and legs slowly, but felt no need to linger. Her talent finding and working to dissolve blockages was not required. He was her first client totally free of physical tightness and blocked energy.

Still looking for Seva's Achilles' heel, that weak spot every human body possesses, she finished with a foot reflexology session. All areas of his feet showed perfect, balanced health.

***

After two weeks at Alpha Camp, the roof of Sandy's cabin collapsed. Her roommates moved into a apartment behind the kitchen and Seva asked Sandy to share his trailer. They'd been working together almost every day and she was sure she'd learned as much from him as in her entire time at the massage school. Their unspoken communication as they worked with each client amazed her. Sometimes she performed a massage while Seva guided her mentally and added his own energy healing. Other times Seva's hands brought relief from pain, while Sandy stayed close holding the energy and supporting his spirit as he searched for deeper causes.

Sandy repacked her damp wardrobe, soggy books, and personal items and left the cabin. As she walked across the campus doubts rose. Moving in with Seva seemed so serious. She'd lived alone for so long. During her marriage to John, they'd both worked so much, his presence seldom encroaching on her space. And in Texas, Barry had only been the occasional secret visitor to her condo. Living with Jeff in college had been easy and natural, but they'd just been kids. She was used to being alone.

Seva was the most incredible and inscrutable man she'd ever met, but he didn't seem real. He was beautiful and kind and understood her. Often he seemed to be not of this world, certainly not someone to share a bathroom with. She'd been stunned by her attraction to Seva when she first saw him in Virginia Beach. Meeting him at Alpha Camp seemed like destiny. Every day here confirmed her deep connection with this man she hardly knew. She wanted to be close to him, closer than she'd ever wanted to be to anyone.

Sandy knocked and stepped up into the trailer. The incense that always clung to Seva, sandalwood and frangipani with a touch of evergreen and sacred native tobacco, enveloped her. Her fears evaporated, almost.

Seva, sitting cross-legged on the couch reading, smiled at her. "Don't be nervous. All will be well."

She looked through the door to the only bedroom and for a minute wanted to tell him she'd be happy to sleep on the couch.

"Put your things in there. We have time for a cup of tea before our day of healing work." He gestured to the bedroom. When she didn't move, he added, "Do you doubt we are meant to be together?"

Sandy and Seva performed two morning massages and a reiki clearing, ate a quick lunch, led a staff meditation, and finished the day with three more massage healing treatments. Gaia had decided that if they insisted on working together, they still had to treat as many clients as if they worked alone.

By the time they sat in the dining room offering gratitude for the turnip soup and garlic pizza, they were both exhausted. Finishing an apple cranberry compote, Sandy realized it was time to go home. And home now was with Seva. In that small trailer. And tiny bedroom. As nervous as a young girl on her first date, she suggested they take a walk.

They strolled silently around the Alpha Camp campus avoiding moonlit puddles and ignoring the scuffling of woodland creatures. As they reached the trailer the second time, Seva took Sandy's hand, pressing his thumb into her palm as he'd done the night of the beach bonfire. And like then, Seva's powerful energy surged through her.

"There's nothing to fear." His soft voice soothed her doubts as he led her into the trailer and the bedroom.

He sat on the bed and gestured for her to join him. When they sat cross-legged facing each other, Seva closed his eyes and began to chant. When he finished, they sat on the bed clothed only in the loose tunics and drawstring pants they wore for sessions.

"Slow your breathing," Seva told her, "and bring it into sync with mine. Become one with me. As in our healing work, our union together honors the sacred shakti, the cosmic feminine. Together we will open to the power and joy of the kundalini rising. This is your path of healing. Our path of healing together. Duality. Beyond love. Join with me in the path of *brahmacarya*, chastity and abstinence."

Sandy took a choked breath. Not what she had expected.

***

Jeff

Jeff held the paintbrush tight, leaned around the porch railing, and hummed along with the radio playing Harry Chapin's 'Old College Avenue.' This brush wasn't a tiny art school sable or the acrylic airbrush he'd used at the Denver ad agency. He wielded a four-inch all-purpose exterior polyester from Aubuchon Hardware. Dipping the bristles into creamy maroon paint, he transferred his design to the Victorian's clapboards.

He set down the brush, checked the colored sketch he used as a model, then switched to a two-inch brush and navy-blue paint to edge the gingerbread porch trim that for the last hundred years had been covered in layers of dirty white. After two weeks of laboriously scraping and stripping flaking paint, another of repairing and priming rotted wood, inch by inch, the artists were turning their home into a splendid painted lady. When they hung the sign for their co-op art gallery, sleepy Fallon, New Hampshire, would never be the same.

Thanks to Martin's help, Jeff's webpage design work had become a breeze. Jeff spent his days renovating the house and art gallery and nights producing webpages for the Yippee kids. Their checks provided money to pay his rent, buy art supplies, and loan money to the others. Every envelope from Chip and Mike contained photocopied cartoon character certificates which they claimed represented company stock.

At first Jeff's artist housemates laughed at his ambitious plan to turn the parlor and front hall into a gallery. One at a time he convinced them. Jake was the easiest. He liked to work with his hands rather than anything related to fine art. Leaving a job as Alpha Camp's handyman assistant, he now worked at Jeff's side. Ariel's psychic visions confirmed that Jeff's plan was auspicious. And depressed Christopher agreed without enthusiasm. Although the group voted down Jeff's suggestion for a no alcohol or drugs house rule, at least they were working together.

Jeff put the final touches of maroon and navy on the porch newels and stepped back onto the lawn. He'd made this group project a reality. And, other than that unfortunate incident with the wasp nest under the eaves, all had gone smoothly.

Christopher, the tallest, stood on the second floor window ledge, wearing his favorite fuchsia cutoffs and a tight 'I Enjoy Being a Girl' t-shirt, while painting the gable a pale shade of lavender. Jake, the most athletic, was on the tall ladder applying purple trim. Ariel balanced on rented scaffolding painting clapboards pink, while Martin painted porch window trim.

Jeff called to everyone, "She's beautiful!"

Christopher turned and waved to Jeff. His left foot slipped off the ledge. Body twisting in mid-air, he slid headfirst down the side of the house as lavender paint splashed up from the bucket and arced down the wooden wall.

Helplessly Jeff watched as Christopher, brush still firmly in his hand, fell onto the slanted porch roof, rolled down over the gutter, and dropped through a lilac bush and hit the ground with an ominous thud.

***

Thirty-one days after the fall Christopher was still unconscious. Jeff sat next to his Fallon General Hospital bed. Jake, Ariel, Martin, and lots of other local artists visited, but Jeff always seemed to be with him or working on webpage design in the visitors' lounge. When a doctor suggested brain damage, Jeff told the unresponsive Christopher not to hear one negative word.

Every day, Jeff talked and read to Christopher. He described progress on the house and gallery and told him how much everyone missed him. Hospital rumors reported Christopher had been admitted wearing women's clothing and his 'brother' stayed, talking to him and massaging his limp body.

Jeff whispered to Christopher, "You've got to pull through this. A teacher in Colorado told me we meet people who seem familiar because we're part of the same soul group and it's easy to offer unconditional love to members of our own group. You and I must be part of the same group."

Jake stuck his head in the room. "Pssst, Jeff. The coast is clear. The nurse finished her rounds. Take this box of Lake Champlain chocolates to the nurses' station and entertain them for a half hour. Ariel's ready."

"Are you sure this is okay?" Jeff asked, hesitant to leave Christopher alone with a strange woman from Alpha Camp.

Despite Ariel's recommendation, he didn't want to take a chance of hurting Christopher.

"Absolutely. Ariel meditated to verify this woman was the one. We aren't doing anything wrong. Think of her as an unofficial hospital consultant."

"Consultant?"

"Actually, she's a massage therapist."

Jeff was still unsure. His neck began buzzing. It had been his idea to find an alternative practitioner, but now he doubted the decision. New Agey stuff might be dangerous to a guy in a coma. Finally, he nodded. "What harm can it do? Are you sure I can't watch?"

"Ariel says the woman insists on working alone. Stay at the nurses' station. Keep them entertained. Ariel's in the Linen Room. Just knock on your way by and she'll bring the healer to Christopher. I'll make sure no one gets off the elevator. Everything will be okay. Promise."

An hour later Jeff was back in the room. The air felt charged with electricity and the scent of lavender. And when the nurse checked Christopher's vitals, his fever was down and his breath came more easily.

Jeff remembered the week back in college when he'd had that awful flu and Sandy sat at his bedside, missing her midterms. Why had that come to mind?

He turned off the light, nodded, and sank into a dream. When Sandy's face floated before him, he woke with a start. Christopher pulled at Jeff's sleeve and pointed to the tubes which prevented him from talking. Jeff stood, leaned over the bed, and hugged him.

***

Sandy

Sandy and Seva sat before a campfire near the trailer they shared enjoying the clear midsummer evening. She loved the peaceful starry night skies. And being alone with Seva. Nights like this made her feel as if Seva's energy was turning her into a new woman.

Seva named stars. "There's Pisces. Your constellation."

Sandy leaned closer and stared up.

"Look left and lower. There's the Sculptor, like you, a constellation two hundred and fifty light years away."

"I'm not a sculptor." She sat back.

"Perhaps not yet. The stars chart your destiny. When we journey west I'll show you my favorite constellation—Delphinus, the Dolphin. Native Americans call the dolphin A'LUL'QUOY which means to go in peace and protect. Our journey will bring peace to many."

All summer they'd talked about traveling west as soon as the season ended. She wished they could leave right now. She broke the peaceful silence with a question she'd thought of often, but had hesitated to ask. "That night on the beach in Virginia, what did you throw into the fire?"

"A peace amulet. To heal old wounds. I established that school to teach healing. My partners wished a more mainstream path. I used methods I was not proud of in hopes of securing my position. I failed. I'd left with anger in my heart and bitterness on my lips."

"You could not be dishonorable." Sandy laid her hand on his.

He nodded. "I was angry. It took 50,000 miles of travel before I learned I must allow talented healers to find me, wherever I might be." He intertwined his clasped hand with hers, but didn't lean closer. "Like you."

"I want to do so much more."

"Your work's wonderful. You helped that comatose man in the Fallon hospital."

She smiled. "He only needed rest to sort things out. I felt good about that, but it was hard working on him. My neck was buzzing like I swallowed a swarm of bees."

"Your massage work allows bodies to open and accept healing. And you infuse my healing sessions with creative energy. And your grounding energy keeps the person's spirit peaceful."

"Alpha Camp makes me crazy," Sandy confided, "I do want us to leave," hesitant to bother Seva with her impatience. "That Gaia woman and Clay are not good people. Clay covered up the Lyme disease scandal. He called the ticks by their scientific name, *Ixodes scapularis*, and referred to them as an endangered species. You helped everyone get tested."

"Some spiritual leaders do not walk the walk. Others can't even find the road." Seva smiled. "You are learning to tell the difference. Clay is where he needs to be now. Gaia's different every year. You should have met her in '75. Did you know she spends her winters teaching high school math in Atlanta?"

"She talks about world peace and is surly to everyone. She even asked me what it was like to sleep with you."

Seva looked down and poked the dying campfire. "What did you tell her?"

"To take the Remote Viewing workshop."

***

Jeff

Jeff brought Christopher home from the hospital the day of the gallery's Grand Opening. His doctor wanted to keep him a few more days, but relented when the small town hospital became inundated with another Alpha Camp Lyme disease epidemic.

Jeff had named the gallery Martha's Folly, after Martin's daughter. He sent her photos and she'd called that morning to wish them all well. "The photos you sent are more beautiful than I ever imagined," Martha told Jeff. "I wish I could be there, but a soybean farmer's wife has to stay home during harvest. If Oscar or I can help, let us know."

Jeff assisted Christopher up the porch steps, pointing out the lavender splash down the front which added a quirky abstract touch to the house's exterior. They toured the gallery. New artists, a sculptor, a wood carver, and two watercolorists had joined their co-op. Jeff had been too busy with promotion and final details, but Ariel made sure Jeff's best work was on prominent display.

Martin and his housemates praised Jeff's talents, his leadership, and most of all his loving care of Christopher. Embarrassed, Jeff brushed off the compliments, but when Jake and Ariel presented him with a 'No Drugs or Alcohol' sign, he considered the gesture to honor his hard work.

An entire wall was devoted to Jake's photography. He'd begun taking pictures of the house renovation, then moved on to local landscapes. Jeff was sure Jake had found his true talent behind a camera lens. Jake showed Christopher every one of his house restoration photos, including the *Fallon News* story chronicling the house's history illustrated with Jake's photos.

"Too bad you didn't get a shot of my fall," Christopher teased. "That would have been a prize winner."

Ariel's surreal art covered the back parlor wall. Just looking at her whimsical paintings of fairies, elves, and lots of dolphins made Jeff feel good. He wasn't sure if it was the subjects, the peaceful colors, or Ariel's magic.

Martin and the other artists mingled with locals and offered a selection of wines and cheeses in the old dining room. Jake, in bib overalls, passed hotdogs and mustard and churned ice cream in the backyard. Ariel had wanted to read palms, but Martin advised her that an art gallery was unorthodox enough for old-fashioned Fallon locals. Martin introduced Jeff and Christopher to Milton Fallon, the Major, Chief of Police, President of the Chamber of Commerce, and owner of the town's only gas station. Milton took another hotdog from Jake and said, "Nice party. Your pictures are damn nice and that whittlin' guy's stuff is pretty good. These artsy-fartsy folk are okay. Not like those woo-woo palm readers over at that Alpha Camp place."

***

Sandy

The last week of the Alpha Camp season another presenter cancelled and Gaia expected Seva to cover the 'Spiritual Ice Hockey Workshop' in addition to his 'Chakra Healing.'

"Clay and Gaia always take advantage of you," Sandy told him as they walked through the trees from their trailer to the lake. "You must stand up for yourself."

He just smiled. By mid-summer, it had become clear that because advertising had been nonexistent, Alpha Camp attendance was unusually low. The spiritual grapevine passed the word and the bad season became worse. Presenters feared they wouldn't get paid. Many like J.J. McCorry, who cancelled his 'Spirit of Art' course, saying he needed stay in Nebraska for the hay harvest, clearly did not want to present a workshop to one or two or no participants.

"Look!" Sandy pointed to tents and booths along the lakeshore where scattered clumps of people stood watching ominous clouds approach. "Clay's idea of a Psychic Festival to end the season is a bust. Gaia went into a trance and neglected to send out the publicity."

He laid his hand on her shoulder. "Be peaceful, Sandy. Let it pass. We cannot make them other than the fools they choose to be."

"They have not fulfilled the terms of your contract. And—"

A pair of Harleys roared through the gates drowning out her words. The bikers stopped and a tall man took off his helmet to reveal a face more like an accountant than a Hell's Angel. "Is this the Festival? Ah saw a sign on the road. Is there food?"

Seva pointed to a large tent. "Pizza and chou'da down there."

The lady biker in tight leathers and a pink helmet drawled, "We're touring New England to see Fall. There's no Fall in Texas, y'all know." They propped their bikes under a tree and walked stiff-legged towards the tents.

Sandy grinned. "You didn't tell them it was tofu pizza and tempeh chowder."

Seva took her hand and led her toward the lake. "Lighten up. Or as they say here Enlighten Up."

Walking closer to the tents, they heard a plunking guitar and a girl's voice singing 'Let's Get Metaphysical.' Mountain Dew, who had changed her name to DhishuRaga sometime during the summer, sold copies of *Silence*, Clay's audiotape series. One empty booth held only a small sign that read 'Out of Body. Call My Spirit Guide.' The largest display belonged to a guy called Crystal Man, who spent most of yesterday unloading crystal boulders from his pickup truck.

Staff members carried aluminum foil cushions as protection from Lyme disease ticks, but Clay had refused to offer them for sale to visitors, saying tick fear would keep paying guests away.

The lady biker from Texas picked up one of Crystal Man's pink crystals. He told her it cost two hundred dollars because of its excellent vibration. She put it down. "I can buy a vibrator for four bucks." She walked off, asking everyone she met if they'd seen Shirley MacLaine.

When the crystal guy asked Seva and Sandy if they worked at AC, they nodded and he railed, "I passed up a New Age flea market in Portsmouth to come here and I haven't sold squat. Do you know how much these babies weigh?"

They walked on. Seva smiled, but Sandy's mood darkened. "This isn't a joke. All summer we fought the administrative pseudo-gurus just to do a little good. Instead of just giving massages, Clay wants me to organize workshops and illustrate and write next year's catalog. Gaia ruins everything I do. I worked so hard with no results."

Seva raised his hand to quiet her protests. "Two new students found me. One has come here for five summers looking for a teacher and the other got stuck on the muddy road in front of the gate. Remember we've brought peace to many truly ill beings."

The entire summer's frustration flooded into Sandy's voice. "The administrators need to be healed!"

"They are doing good work, even if they don't know what good work is," Seva soothed.

"We can't stay here any longer."

Seva smiled. "Yes. It's time to leave."

***

Jeff

One month after the gallery opening Jeff organized the town's fall festival. His maple leaf crown, proclaiming him Fallon's Foliage King, slid askew as he jumped off Jake's borrowed tractor. He waved to the crowd, thankful for the perfect New England postcard weather, and climbed to the porch of their resplendent Victorian gallery, draped with a Fallon & Fallon Falls Foliage Festival Headquarters banner.

Jeff joined Christopher on the swing to watch the rest of the parade as Jake led the procession on down maple-lined Main Street. His tractor pulled a wagon filled with hay and Fallon's Mayor and Board of Selectmen in denim and plaid, followed by the Fallon Falcons High School Band and the Chamber of Commerce float.

Christopher complained, "The Chamber's taking credit for everything you did. The whole Festival was your idea. You did all the organizing and publicity."

"Our gallery will benefit most." Jeff indicated the framed art hung in the wraparound porch which today doubled as the reviewing stand. On the lawn, Ariel in full-length skirt of hand painted leaves sold Jake's hayride tickets for $20 to tourists and $5 to townsfolk. Shoppers filled the inside galleries. Two men in suits loaded one of Ariel's life-sized dolphin paintings into a station wagon with New York plates.

A couple with two children, dressed in shades of New England tan and khaki, inquired about hayrides. "Yes," Jeff told them, "one cup of cider and a piece of apple pie free with each ticket. And our church ladies' Buy-A-Pie booth sells whole pies to take home."

A blond woman with voluminous hair marched up the stairs flourishing a red and yellow Foliage Festival schedule.

She pushed in front of two elderly ladies and backed Jeff against a cornstalk.

"This," she spoke loudly into his face. "This is good! Who designed it? One of those expensive Boston ad agencies?"

"Hold on." Jeff nudged her back. "I did it with a computer program I wrote. And our local newspaper printed it for cost."

Before she could respond, a woman with three cameras and flimsy high-heeled shoes interrupted, "Where can I pick apples that are five feet off the ground? I drove all the way from the City when I saw your TV promo." She whined, "Red, yes, red apples would be the best."

Jeff directed her to Ed's Apple Picking Map booth, then turned his attention back to the manic blonde.

"This is very good." She read, "'Come to Fallon for Fabulous Foliage and Fun. Enjoy hayrides, spicy hot cider, and steaming apple pies. Pick your own luscious apples from our trees and pick up something from Martha's Folly, the newest, most exciting, art gallery in New England.' Who planned all this?" the blonde demanded as a dozen cloggers clogged by and a cacophony of bagpipes drowned out her words.

Christopher stepped up next to Jeff and yelled, "Jeff did it all. He organized the booths, the kids' face painting, the all-day music program, even the pie-eating contest and the 5K road race."

Noticing Christopher had changed into a red-checked ruffled petticoat and Mary Janes, Jeff asked, "Why are you dressed like that?"

"Miss Fallon Foliage fell off her ladder giving the Apple Picking Demonstration. I'm her stand-in." He flounced off the porch and let Ariel help him into a candy apple red Model T

Laughing Dolphins

truck filled with apples and a sign: 'Miss Fallon Foliage—
Fairest in Fallon and Fallon Falls.'

Jeff began to apologize for Christopher's bizarre getup.

"Never mind," the blond woman told him and put out
her hand. "Gaia O'Hara, Director of Media Services, Alpha
Camp. My assistant is threatening to take off with our guru. I
need a graphic designer and a computer expert.

II. 3. Cross Country, 1994

Sandy

Sandy grimaced, bit her lip, and hit the accelerator. The jeep rocked, then slid back in a slurry of slushy mud. For the fifth time. Only dynamite was going to budge the old trailer out of the snow-packed ditch. Working at Alpha Camp had taught her what she called "patience" and Seva called "surrender." Multiple delays to Seva's teaching tour confined them to life in this cold, drafty trailer much too long. The first winter Clay and Gaia went off to some tropic island leaving Sandy responsible for planning and management. More delays kept Sandy and Seva at Alpha Camp another summer season. Seva seemed to never notice the temperature, but by this second winter Sandy despised the cold.

Leaving Alpha Camp on New Year's Day, they drove through steadily falling snow from New Hampshire to the New York state line. Seva insisted on driving and seven hours and three hundred miles later, he detoured onto a country road to contemplate the beauty of snow on the Hudson River and got them lost for the third time. When he pulled over to meditate on snow-covered tree branches and misjudged the road's width, the bald tires slipped and the Jeep hovered half in the ditch. The attached trailer tilted and settled against a fortuitously located sign. A loud crack told her that she didn't need a mechanic to tell her the trailer's axle had broken.

Sandy stepped from the jeep. Her clogs sank a foot into wet snow and she said some not very contemplative words.

Seva followed, bare sandaled feet impervious to the cold. "Be peaceful."

"Just unhook the jeep," she snapped, trying to pull her right foot out of the snow without losing her shoe. And failed.

"All will be fine," Seva told her, undoing the hitch. "I'm going to meditate."

She knew yelling would do no good. In the last months Seva had seemed to grow more and more out of touch with the real world. He trusted her to fix things, then gave the divine plan of the universe all the credit. She dug in the snow and retrieved her clog. Surrender wasn't working. Stomping to the jeep, she crawled into the driver's seat and started the engine by pumping her frozen right foot on the gas petal. Loose from the trailer, the jeep leapt up onto the road. Sandy checked her map. Sixty miles to Poughkeepsie. No point in trying to talk to Seva when he was meditating. She left a note.

The second year of living in that tiny trailer had strained her happiness with Seva. Gaia, knowing Sandy would stay with Seva, assigned more and more tasks. In her spare time Sandy planned Seva's cross country tour, scheduling New Age festival lectures, workshops in spiritual centers, and sanghas in private homes. Due to their mechanical delays, she'd canceled December commitments, but was determined to get them to the January dates in the Midwest.

Vowing never, never to go back to New Hampshire, she gunned the jeep and sped off down the road spraying mud and slush onto a white SUV.

Six hours later Sandy steered a giant Winnebago down the road narrowed by the most recent snowplow pass and braked next to their old trailer. Even pulling the jeep, the brand new motorhome handled like a dream.

Seva sat inside the lop-sided trailer drinking a cup of chamomile tea. "Have a nice ride?"

She took a deep breath. His peaceful smile melted her anger. As always, he'd trusted her to find a way. She kissed his forehead. "Help me get all the stuff into our new home."

He looked out the window. "That's a big rig." And without questions began gathering his books and papers. If he asked, she wasn't sure she'd tell him she'd bought the monster Winnebago with the last of her Megga settlement money.

They transferred kitchen supplies, then books, and finally carried clothing and arranged possessions in the RV's roomy compartments. Seva never asked how she'd managed this miracle.

When all was loaded, Seva transferred the yellow diamond Guru on Board sign to the RV's back window and announced, "I'll drive."

Sandy hugged him. "No way. This one is mine." For the rest of this trip she planned to keep them solidly on the right road.

He climbed into the passenger seat. "Let us begin this journey."

Sandy detected a hint of sadness in his voice, but that wasn't possible. Not from the man who always sounded happy and optimistic.

***

Jeff

An early season blizzard turned southern New York State into a glorious winter wonderland. Jeff drove his new white SUV and sang along with 'Only Wanna Be With You' from

Hootie and the Blowfish's new album. He slowed to let a dirt-colored jeep speed past. Windshield now spattered with mud, he continued to the end of the road, turned around, and drove back past an old trailer tipped into a ditch. It wouldn't take a mechanic to see the trailer's axle was broken.

He re-checked his scribbled directions. The turnoff to Storm King Art Center should be here in this hilly, wooded area. The five-hundred acres of monumental sculpture park closed in winter, but he hoped a few of their larger sculptures might be visible from the road. He made one more pass, abandoned hope of finding a sign, and turned towards Pough-keepsie to meet Christopher at the Culinary Institute in Hyde Park and Jake at the regional airport.

After giving in to the Yippee kids' pleading proposal to train artists across the country to create webpages, Jeff was determined to savor every mile. At the end of this tour, he'd be finished with Mike, Chip, and Yippeedom. Last winter Yip-pee's public stock offering hit the NASDAQ, causing a bid-ding frenzy that raised the opening price from $10 to $60. Within a month the price soared, split twice, and surged high-er. Searching through his desk trash, Jeff found he owned 50,000 cartoon shares valued at $3.2 million.

On a trip back to his old Boston haunts, half hoping to see Sandy, he ran into Jerry's sister Corin from the old pub. She now owned her own investment firm and advised him to diversify his finances. She began selling Yippee shares and moved his money into solid high-yielding investments. Once a month, he drove down from New Hampshire, took Corin to dinner and listened to her financial report.

When it finally sunk in that he was rich, he bought Mar-tin's house, and then the old Fallon train depot to turn into a second gallery. He paid for Jake's flying lessons and bought him an airplane. After helping each of his friends, he set out in the SUV on this Yippee road show to teach webpage design workshops. He'd carefully plotted his cross country trip to allow visits with friends, stops at sculpture parks and art museums, and attendance at a few Mensa regional gatherings.

Jeff pulled into the Culinary Institute lot in the late afternoon and parked next to a van with the words, Frozen Dolphins—Wedding & Bat Mitzvah Specialists on the side. Following a line of people into a striped tent, he walked past a row of crystal clear ice sculptures, swans of all sizes and colors, and, in between fountains and punch bowls, a few leaping dolphins.

Christopher, in a form-fitting fuchsia snowsuit, waved a Black & Decker drill. "Over here!" Setting down the drill, he stepped over a pile of chisels and ice shavings and hugged Jeff. "Look, I'm an artist."

Jeff stood back to inspect Christopher's sculpture. "How long will the chicken last?"

Christopher rolled his eyes. "It's a swan. It'll last for the judging and reception," then added with a shrug, "tomorrow... a puddle."

Jeff indicated an older man demonstrating techniques for smoothing the skin of an ice dolphin with a gas blowtorch.

"That's the judge. J.J. McCorry."

Impressed, Jeff considered complimenting the artist's work, but didn't want to disturb him. Instead, he turned to Christopher. "So, do you like chef school?"

"Oh yes. But I'm thinking of specializing in performance bartending."

Jeff smiled. "If that makes you happy."

***

Sandy

Sandy watched a line of women exit the Flint Convention Center's Grande Ballroom. Inside, all venues looked the same and most ballrooms were far from grand. These attendees, leaving Seva's lecture with peaceful glows, all appeared to be Ann Arbor college students. Where were the spiritual seekers of Flint?

A familiar looking woman, dressed in white with long silver hair, blocked her way. Their eyes met. Before Sandy looked away, she noticed a crescent birthmark on the woman's left cheek. When she glanced back, the woman said, "You have beautiful energy."

Sandy wanted to move away. New Age trade shows were filled with kooky extremists. This woman did not seem dangerous crazy, but she did not move. Just as Sandy was about to ask the woman in white if she did tattoos, the woman said, "My gift to you," and handed Sandy a plastic Wal-Mart bag and disappeared into the crowd.

Sandy poked the two-pound bag. Her finger bounced out as if she'd punched a baggy of pet shop goldfish. She hurried back to their booth, trade show jargon for rented space even though this was only a rickety table with the old sign with the logo some Denver artist created for Seva ten years ago. Sandy laid the jiggling sealed Ziploc bag on the purple-skirted table.

From the adjoining space, Picasso smoothed his messy red hair and asked, "What's in the bag?" as he climbed over piles of large smooth rocks to look.

She removed the baggie from the plastic bag and held it out to him. The gray mass inside squirmed away from her fingers and her nose wrinkled at a faint odor of vinegar. "God, it looks like a placenta—or some alien afterbirth."

"You've been attending too many New Age workshops. This is not a demon's spawn."

Sandy stared at the mottled glob. "Then what is it?"

"A kombucha—a fungus kind of mushroom." He pulled a folded sheet of paper from the Wal-Mart bag. "Here's instructions." He read silently, then summarized, "You get one as a gift. Then you grow two more in bowls in a dark closet. The two grow into four. You're going to need a lot of bowls and sugar and tea."

"I live in a motorhome."

"The juice is an elixir. Vitamins, stuff like that. You grow kombuchas like sourdough and give them away."

"I can see why." Sandy put the thing back into the bag, hid it under the table and began inventorying Seva's pamphlets and tapes. She'd need to find a copy shop soon to replenish stock. Seva always gave away more than she sold.

Picasso interrupted her. "My truck needs repair—you know—because of the rocks. Could you and Seva give me a ride to Flintstone Farms? It's an eating resort fifty miles from here. Not much quality, but lots of quantity, and lots of snow. I've got a gig giving massages during SnowShow."

"I don't have snow clothes."

"I'll loan you a snowsuit. A friend left it in my truck. He said fuchsia was getting just too boring."

"Who'd want massages at an eating resort?"

"Bobsledders and snow wrestlers love my hot rocks massages. And you and Seva should check out their cheap conference facilities."

She shook her head. "We try to stay away from strictly commercial venues." Then switched to the new jargon. "I mean, we prefer to connect with spiritually aware soulmates with higher light consciousness."

***

Jeff

Jeff taught the Poughkeepsie workshop, then dodging snow squalls, left New York State and drove on to Michigan. In the center of the state he pulled off the main highway and drove under an arch of ice blocks and a flapping 'Flintstone Farms Frozen SnowShow' banner and followed hand signals given by a blue grenade-shaped parka. The hand grenade's hands directed him to park between a trailer that proclaimed 'Saskatoon Snow Carving Team' and a new Winnebago with an old jeep in tow. He'd considered buying a big rig like that, but since Yippee paid his travel expenses, hotels with warm jacuzzis would do just fine.

Walking to the show grounds' main entrance, Jeff heard an engine, looked up, and saw Jake's biplane trailing a 'Let It Snow' banner. What a coincidence all his friends from New Hampshire were following the same winter cross-country path. Jeff training artists. Christopher in cooking school. Jake taking flying jobs. His old Boston buddy Picasso was happily working as a massage therapist at this resort and selling some kind of special rocks. And Ariel was traveling the winter New Age psychic show circuit. Each on their own journey. It pleased him to think his Yippee money was helping them.

Inside the gate, a twenty-foot-tall lump of shiny packed snow loomed before him. A purple rosette proclaimed it 'Best in SnowShow.'

As Jeff stared at the sculpture, Picasso rushed up with a hug neither could feel through layers of down and suggested, "Let's go get a mug of... coffee." Strong from giving rock massages, he easily lifted Jeff's duffle and led him around the giant glob, explaining it represented a dumpling. The resort served over one million pounds of the hefty hunks of dough each year and a dumpling sculpture always won the ice sculpture contest.

In front of them a tall blond couple in fur-trimmed white jackets faced a skinny teenage girl in a tight black ski outfit. "Ginnie, we thought you'd like the art?" the woman said.

The girl sneered at the big lump. "Pirogues are not art."

Picasso led Jeff past snow sculptures depicting Barney Rubbles, Pebbles, and lots of food items. Farm animals outnumbered swans and dolphins. The last sculpture baffled Jeff. "Picasso, what's that one?"

"The State of Michigan," Picasso yelled above the rhythmic oom-pah-pahs of a German band. "The Upper Peninsula broke off during a period of unexpected sunshine."

They settled at a picnic table in the Warming Tent, its roof sagging with snow. Steaming styrofoam cups of coffee defrosted their hands while they ate slices of frosted stolen dotted with raisins and nuts. Jeff had felt weird since entering the parking lot. He decided the bone-numbing cold was responsible for his body humming like a stuck doorbell.

Their server handed them each a broom. "Guys, help me poke the roof. Got to get that morning snow off the canvas before the afternoon flurries begin."

"Flurries?" said Picasso. "Six to eight inches every day are not flurries."

The three poked the canvas until an avalanche of snow broke loose and began to slide. They heard a whoosh and then a shriek as snow buried a woman up to the hood of her fuchsia snowsuit.

"Come on. There's more to do." Picasso pulled Jeff in the opposite direction, leaving the Warming Tent guy to brush off the woman. "The frozen chicken bowling tournament is about to start."

They watched the competition for a while, but instead of bowling or joining the ice cream eating contest, they purchased plates of world famous hot dumplings doused with beige chicken gravy.

At noon Jeff left Picasso and headed into the hotel lobby to locate his seminar room. Preparing to check in, he removed his parka. The Michigan map fell out and as he turned to pick it up his duffle swung around and smacked into a woman in a fuchsia snowsuit talking on a lobby phone. As he hurried away towards the elevators, he heard her say into the phone, "The manager called us New Age goo-goos, I got snow dumped on me, and just now some jerk hit me with his duffle bag. I feel weird. My head is buzzy like I'm coming down with the flu."

***

Sandy

Sandy drove the motorhome into a level spot in a grove of snow-covered trees. The icy surface of Little Muskego Lake sparkled through a spiderweb of branches. "We could travel further north and camp in the Winnebago next to Lake Winnebago."

Seva laughed. "After I meditate, let's go for a walk and find the sweatlodge."

"That's a beautiful idea. Afterwards I'll heat up some hot chocolate. I'm stiff from driving in the snow." She referred to the folder marked Little Muskego Lake Adventures. "The contract with Olaf and Stosh was for you to lead a sangha after the sweatlodge." Sandy looked out the RV window and didn't see any fires. "Wonder where the lodge is?" She put on the fuchsia parka Chris had given her and new tall shearling boots and walked down the steps into the snow.

Sandy stepped high into two feet of fluffy pristine snow and walked to a spot between two trees, turned to face the RV, and with a laugh fell back into the snow. Keeping her body flat she swept both her arms in an arc between her head and her waist, and moved her legs apart and back. Gingerly, she got up without spoiling her snow angel, jumped to another spot, and began again. Here with a warm RV close, the cold felt invigorating. Or perhaps it was the freedom of traveling.

By the time Seva came out Sandy had created three perfect snow angels and was putting the finishing touches on a snow Buddha. He placed his hands on her waist and swung her around. "Snow is a perfect vision of purity, reminding us how crystals surround us and heal our lives."

She smiled up at him. She loved moments like these when he was happy and excited to begin teaching.

Two men, a tall one in camo gear and a short guy in blaze orange, penguin-walked across the clearing, their snowshoes creating prehistoric bird prints. The tall one called out, "Move on. This spot's saved for a guy called Steva." The other, carrying fishing rods like cross country ski poles, added, "Don't want no trespassers in our campground."

Seva smiled and moved towards them. "I'm Seva. Peace and love."

The men stopped in their bird tracks. "Yeah, peace and love," the tall one echoed. "I'm Stosh Armandsdatter. He's Olaf Klepinski."

The short guy with the poles pointed at Seva. "Look. A real Injin."

Seva smiled. "Lakota. Whitehawk Clan."

"Don't care what kind of an Injin you are, we need one real bad." He skewed up his face and studied Sandy. "She one, too?"

Seva shook his head. "Why do you need Native Americans?"

"A party of Menominees was supposed to come down to set up a sweatlodge. They got snowed in. We got reservations for a bunch of folks who want to sweat. Can you do the sweat thing and then your songfest?"

"I'd love to help and also perform the sangha. Do you have the necessary supplies?"

The tall guy grunted and pointed through the trees. "Lots of wood and rocks." He led the way through the snow closer to the lake and they surveyed the carcass of a dome-shaped structure, a pit of stones, two cords of split wood, blankets, and evergreen boughs.

Seva picked up an oak log and nodded. "Good wood makes a hot fire." He threw it into the pit.

"You all set?" Olaf turned. "We got to take a party ice fishing."

"Before the lodge?" Seva frowned. "That's not a real good idea."

"No. These guys are from a gun club in Pewaukee. The bus of Waukesha customers should be here by sunset." The two turned and walked away.

Seva placed his hands on Sandy's shoulders. "We'd better get busy."

Sandy's mouth dropped open. "We're going to set up a whole lodge by ourselves? Make the fire. Cover the lodge. Carry stones inside. The whole thing?"

Seva nodded. "That way the energy will be pure and it'll be a highly spiritual experience for all who come. Even for some who are close, but not inside."

Sandy sighed and gave up thoughts of a cozy day inside the RV reading and sipping hot chocolate.

Sandy and Seva worked all afternoon, tending the fire and sorting and preparing stones. Sandy melted snow and added herbs for the participants to drink during the ceremony and cut up the fruit for breaking the fast. She tied bundles of cedar, rather than desert sage, for the purification ritual each would go through before entering. She must remember to explain all the rules. No jewelry to heat and burn the skin. No menstruating women allowed. Drink water. She hoped they'd all been fasting.

Late in the afternoon, she leaned back against a tree to rest, sweating despite the cold and giggled. "The blankets are all Packers lap robes."

"They'll do. Virgin wool and sacred to the natives. At least the lodge structure is not PVC and duct tape." Seva looked towards the finished lodge and the setting sun. "Olaf was not happy when I told him he could not charge his guests for the experience. They'll arrive soon. The stones are glowing red. Please hold the flap. I'll carry the first seven inside."

Sandy picked up the flap and watched Seva remove his shirt and strip off his boots and jeans revealing a deerskin loincloth. His skin glowed bronze in the fire light, as he picked up the pitchfork and slid the tines under a black stone.

He approached the entrance, bowed acknowledging the east, the direction of the rising sun crawled in, and said, "*Mitakuye Oyasin*. All my relations," the traditional words that acknowledged universal kinship.

Sandy anticipated the feeling she would experience after the fourth round when she led the participants, crawling on hands and knees like babies, to emerge reborn from the dark heat of the earth's womb. She craved that exhilaration and wished that this rebirth would also symbolize a rededication of her work with Seva.

The long-awaited trip had grown more and more stressful with every mile. Seva took less and less responsibility and she resented being the serious one, keeping them on schedule and handling all the details. Seva's name meant pure service, but she felt as if she'd become the servant. In Texas she'd been completely selfish. Somehow her life had turned in the opposite direction. She placed her right hand over her heart, attempting to still the pulsing vibration of her tattoo.

After Seva placed the seventh rock inside, he took her hand. "Enter sacred space and pray with me."

Sandy changed into a modest white cotton dress that reached below her knees. She whispered, "All our relations," and followed Seva back inside, moving in a clockwise direction. The flap closed the entrance and her eyes focused on the glowing rocks as Seva's drumming turned the interior into a beating heart. Lifting the pitchfork, she moved the stones into a harmonious arrangement, then laid branches in a cross, pointing precisely in the four directions. The damp cedar boughs hissed and spit their moisture into the domed lodge. North symbolized the direction of dreams. West the end. She desperately wanted this westward journey to end. She yearned for the south. South represented words, words of healing, harmony, happiness, and health.

***

Jeff

After a day of SnowShow activities Jeff was ready to move on. He didn't feel quite himself and blamed it on the start of a winter cold. Three more presentations got him through Gary, Indiana, Chicago, and Evanston, Illinois. As he crossed the Wisconsin border an avalanche of snow enshrouded his SUV. He pulled into the parking lot of a cheese-shaped drive-in, denuded his roof, de-iced his windows, and checked his map. The Mensa Mind Melt hotel was on Little Muskego Lake and he looked forward to a weekend filled with interesting people and no web design.

By three o'clock on Friday he'd settled in his hotel room. He parted the curtains and peered out into the courtyard. A heated pool steamed and he considered a quiet swim until a dozen large bodies cannonballed in. He read the weekend program and noted the Icebreaker Happy Hour. He checked off lectures and workshops that looked interesting, everything from chocolate tasting and forensic pathology to sushi rolling and crossword puzzle design. Duct Tape Origami sounded like fun. He'd skip the tour of a Kopp's frozen custard plant, the brewery side trip, and dairy farm cross-country skiing.

Mensa Mind Melt was a large Regional Gathering, but drew attendees from all over the country. It offered food, games, as well as mental and social stimulation. The whole weekend looked just like what he expected, a conference with no theme other than activities and conversation to stretch his mind. He'd stick with indoor events, play games, and maybe discover what he wanted to do for the rest of his life.

Entering the elevator, he saw posters for room parties and marathon game sessions for Trivia, Balderdash, and Sheepshead, whatever that was, and a request for an accordion player for a polka band jam session.

He found the registration desk and a table filled with t-shirts and books. As he pinned on his plastic badge, a man in a cheesehead hat and red t-shirt that read 'Head Cat Herder' threw his arm around Jeff. "I'm Fritz. How's by you? Your first RG?"

Jeff nodded and the man walked him down the hall. "Come to the hospitality suite and have a drink."

"I don't…"

The man made a sharp left turn and elbowed Jeff into a hotel room. "Donchaknow, there's a Non-Drinking Hospitality Room. There's also the Drinking, the Hugging, the Non-Hugging, Non-Talking, the Thinking, and the Non-Thinking Rooms. An RG this size has to have rooms open twenty-four hours. Some folks circulate between them and never go to a program. Word gets out where the best food is. Right here," he pointed to a kitchenette, "is where they bake cookies. I think I smell a batch. Pour something soft from the bar and we'll wait. Smells like double chocolate chocolate chip. Later there'll be brat pizza and since it's Friday, of course, fish fry."

When they'd settled on one of the sofas, Jeff asked, "Where are you from?"

"Right here. I'm the RG Coordinator."

"What do you do?"

The man hesitated. "A lot of us don't like that question. Jobs are just too confining to explain who we are or what we're interested in. Some of us have jobs around people who think if we use big words, we're weird." He leaned close. "I'm a brain surgeon. I usually say I work in a hospital and let folks think I'm an orderly. What about you? I promise not to tell."

Jeff kept the conspiratorial tone. "I'm an artist who teaches website design."

Just then a couple entered. A woman in a fuzzy red sweater with a black Mensa logo led a man in a black Mensa logo sweatsuit and matching hat. The woman hugged his companion, then turned to Jeff. "Hey, you look familiar. I'm Sharon from Cincinnati," she cried as she pressed him into a bone-crunching hug.

Jeff pulled away from the red-breasted woman he'd met ten years ago.

"Meet my husband, John Olson. I'm the Cincy LocSec now, that's like local president, and he's running for AMC, that's the Mensa equivalent of the US Senate."

Jeff searched his memory. "Weren't you a librarian?"

"Sure." Sharon giggled. "And John was married to one. Now we travel to RGs in an RV." She giggled again. "John has a PhD in math and provides investment advice. I design Mensa fashions, like the 'Thinking Makes You Smart' t-shirts and the 'Pi Shop' coffee cups. Get it? Pi, like the math thing. That was John's idea. He loves my creative artistic side."

John shook Jeff's hand, while his gaze skittered around the room. "I'm looking for people interested in a sweatlodge. I met this guy who told me he had room for a few more since the bus from Waukesha got snowed in near Mukwonago."

"Sounds good." Jeff had never done one of Seva's sweatlodges in Colorado and the thought of steam seemed fantastic. He got his coat and boots and met Sharon, John, and a dozen others at the registration desk.

"This will be so much fun." Sharon bounced in her Mensa logo boots. "Come on." She noticed Jeff rubbing on his neck. "What's the problem?"

"Just a tingling thing I get once in a while." He pulled on his jacket.

Sharon stepped closer. "Maybe the sweatlodge will help your bombinating neck. They say sweating is healing."

Jeff looked confused. Fritz walked by. "When you're with Mensans it's all right to ask a word's definition. Bombinate means make a buzzing sound."

Jeff nodded his thanks and followed Sharon, who led the group like ducklings through revolving doors and out past the pool and through a gate toward the lake. His boots squeaked on the snowy path until, within sight of the lake, they reached the lodge and a fiery pit of rocks surrounded by a circle of benches.

Sharon pointed. "That's where we strip down to t-shirts and shorts before we go in to get steamed up."

Jeff smelled wood smoke and evergreen boughs. He heard chanting from inside the green and gold lodge and hoped a spiritual leader like Seva would lead the sweat. A man and a woman's voices blended into 'O Great Spirit.' He took off his jacket and boots and noticed an increased buzzing in his neck and shoulders. His tattoo felt hot and he hoped the sweatlodge would help, not make the discomfort worse. As he unzipped his jeans, he heard someone from the direction of the hotel calling his name.

"Jeff, Jeff," Fritz huffed. "Glad I caught you before you went into that infernal cooker. I found a room for your workshops and hung signs in all the hospitality rooms."

"Workshops?"

"I've set you up to teach website design all weekend. Mensan geeks are really excited. You betcha, you're going to be the hit of the RG. You can't let us down."

***

Sandy

Sandy drove the Winnebago across southern Minnesota and stopped at the first truckstop outside of Sioux Falls. She left Seva in the back. She wanted some fresh, albeit frigid and windy, air and to check her map. Walking through the store, she entered the women's restroom. Grunts and groans came from every stall. Like Sandy, in this part of the country women dressed in cumbersome layers of winter gear almost impossible to remove in narrow cubicles.

178

As Sandy finished washing her hands, a six-foot tall woman in a miniskirt and angora sweater walked in. The bulge in the front of the mini was not particularly feminine and the grapefruit-sized breasts looked quite unnatural. She looked up at the man, trying not to stare at his five o'clock shadow, grabbed her purse, and pushed out the door.

Discovering she'd left her map in the restroom, she entered the travel kiosk to calculate driving time to Rapid City on the giant South Dakota map. A woman in a purple faux fur jacket pointed and said loudly to her companion, "My god, Marge, how can anyone get lost in South Dakota? Rapid City is still hours away. You refused to stop for directions—just like a man. When Jeff was my driver he never got us lost." The stocky Marge turned and walked away mumbling, "Crazy artists."

"Sammie?" Sandy asked the purple-furred woman whose rhinestone necklace spelled out "Sammie" across her chest. "The artist who did a mask workshop at my massage school in Virginia?"

"It's great to be a celebrity." Sammie dug into her purse. "I don't have a pen for an autograph, but my next masterpiece will be wrapping Mount Rushmore and Crazy Horse. I'm sure you've read about that. Big outdoor art—like Christo!"

Sandy nodded. Actually since Alpha Camp discouraged newspapers and TV, her contact with the outside world had been pretty meager for the last two years.

"The only month Jerome, my very classy French art promoter, could get a permit was January. He said there'll be lots of tourists in North Dakota in January. My construction will only stay up for three weeks. Imagine miles of blood red gauze floating between Crazy Horse and the Presidents. You know I made my name with my famous Yoni Chalice Tour, but now I'm doing universal political statements. Cha-ching!"

"Didn't you get closed down in Cincinnati?"

"Girlfriend!" Sammie hugged her and handed her two tickets to the opening ceremony. "We'll talk later. I'll tell you about my next tour. Do you think I should lose weight?" Then she grabbed the attendant to ask directions to the Rapid City Airport.

Sandy began reading brochures. Suddenly a woman in a white wool cape stood at her side. "I saw your RV. You're traveling with Seva."

"What if I am?" Sandy was tired of women following them from city to city. This one looked familiar. "Were you in Flint?"

"Right, I gave you the—"

"Kombucha. And the tattoo in Virginia Beach," Sandy finished. "Sorry, I had to give the kombucha away. I live in an RV."

"So do I. That's why I gave it to you. I'm Ariel Starwind. We've met many times. Once I took you to heal a man in New Hampshire. "

"Why are you following Seva?" Sandy placed her hand above her heart where the tattoo itched.

"Seva's a truly spiritual man, but I'm more interested in you."

Sandy backed up ready to excuse herself when she spotted the manic purple artist heading back her way. Trapped between two women, she chose the woman in white as the less dangerous and whispered, "I've got to hide."

Ariel said, "The ladies' room."

"No. There's a man in there wearing a fuchsia mini."

"My RV is right out in front."

Sandy followed the lesser evil to a dented Airstream. The interior was neat and cozy, filled with crystals and smelling of rosemary and incense.

Ariel made tea while Sandy enjoyed being waited on. "Nice rig. Where are you going?"

"Actually, I am following you. I'm a psychic."

"I don't need a psychic."

"I know you're not one of those women who sleep with gurus, cause scandals, and become suburban housewives."

Sandy shook her head.

"You're helping Seva now. Change will come. Soon you'll need my help."

Sandy stood. "I have to go."

Ariel blocked the door. "You've learned much from Seva, but now you must teach others."

Sandy pushed past her and jumped down into the snow-scraped parking lot. Strange people hung around truckstops, but this was ridiculous. She crawled up into her Winnebago and pulled back onto the highway.

***

Jeff

Disappointed at missing out on the Mensa activities and sweatlodge, but with pleasant memories of the enthusiastic Mensans who attended his workshops, Jeff had continued west, stopping in Madison to pick up Christopher, who was on his way to California.

At a truck stop in South Dakota, Christopher, now dressed in jeans and a red crewneck, got back into the SUV. Only a slight limp remained from his fall. "Thanks for changing," Jeff told him as he pulled back onto I-90 Westbound towards Rapid City. "Your fuchsia mini was getting way too much attention from truckers."

"No problem. Minis aren't right for my figure. And don't keep my legs warm. After bartending school, evening gowns will be my trademark." He handed Jeff a Rand McNally Road Atlas. "I found this in the ladies'. Its owner is probably halfway to Denver by now. Removing pantyhose, putting on designer jeans, and repairing my makeup takes me so much time."

Jeff opened the well-worn cover. The map book felt warm and his hand tingled. He flipped pages while Christopher talked and turned to the two-page US spread.

"I'm so excited I got accepted into the Performance Bartenders' College of America in San Francisco. So much to do."

"Can I help?" Jeff asked, paying more attention to the careful zigzag of lines mapping out a route across the country from the Fallon, New Hampshire freeway exit all the way to San Francisco. His exact route. Christopher was probably right that the owner was far from here by now. It was a little spooky, but how many east-west routes were there? He stuffed the book into his bag.

"You've been way too generous already. Besides tuition, I'll need electrolysis, laser treatments and a little lipo or botox."

The word botox drew Jeff's attention back to Christopher. "I'll help, if that's what you want." Jeff tried not to frown. "Is this like a sex change thing?"

"No way. I'm just an ordinary guy who wants to look good in women's clothes."

"Christopher, I just want you to be happy." Jeff looked for the next exit, wondering if the atlas's owner was traveling east to New Hampshire or west to California.

"Please, call me Chris, that name fits the new me."

"Sure. Chris. We'll make the arrangements when we get to Rapid City. Jake's already there meeting some weirdo artist who hired him to fly about a million yards of red cloth between Mount Rushmore and the Crazy Horse Monument."

"Who'd call that art?"

Jeff shrugged. "Art can be almost anything. Some people think a webpage is art."

Five hundred miles later, Jeff filled the SUV with gas and pushed a large coffee, a Snickers bar, and his credit card across the scratched formica counter. The attendant ran the card, waited, then grunted and tossed the card back to Jeff. "No good." Jeff handed over his personal credit card and slipped the Yippee corporate card back in his wallet. That card had never been rejected before.

Back in the SUV he remembered the atlas, pulled it out of the bag, and examined it again for a name or identification. Christopher was probably right, the owner was far away by now. His fingers touching the pages again felt warm in the chilly vehicle.

***

Sandy

Sandy pulled off I-25 just over the Colorado State line and parked the jeep next to the Winnebago in the Roaring Bear RV Park. After a two-day blizzard, she'd driven to buy food and a new road atlas, feeling stupid for losing the one with all their routes marked out.

When she returned, the RV's door was locked and the shades drawn. What could Seva be doing? Maybe one of those women from the Taos sangha had driven up for a special session. Spiritual-seeking women drove her crazy. One claimed Seva burned the clothing off her body during a healing. Others ordered Sandy around. Seva turned away those who only wanted attention, regardless of how much money they offered.

In her opinion, neediness was not an affliction Seva should work on. She trusted the handsome charismatic Seva, but women in flimsy goddess outfits who threw themselves at him could be tempting. She believed that he truly loved her. In his way. Everyone assumed she shared hot sex with the gorgeous guru. That was far from the truth. He said twin flames came together for a purpose and their true path lay in teaching. She'd argued that they could be both, but he insisted they focus their energy on healing others.

She listened at the door. Not a sound. Maybe he wasn't even inside. Thinking he could have gone for a walk, she used her key and, expecting the space empty, walked in. Soft music masked her entrance. She recognized 'Dream of the Dolphins' from *Cross of Changes*, the new Enigma CD she'd bought for him in Flint.

Seva sat on the bed with his back to the door. "Sandy?" He jerked his arm to cover a spiral pad with his meditation blanket. His expression reminded her of a deer frozen in a car's headlights.

"What are you doing?" She'd never seen him surprised or agitated.

"Just peaceful time." He stood. "Ah... let's take a walk."

"I want to see what you're doing." She'd never questioned him. He actually looked sheepish, his head bowed and his shoulders hunched forward.

"Please, Sandy." He looked into her eyes and hesitantly he reached under the blanket, pulled out a sketchpad, and offered it to her.

Sandy opened the pad and flipped through page after page of portrait sketches—each one more perfect than the last. Many were of her, Alpha Camp staff, and visitors. Others were people who'd come to him for healing.

Her belly tightened and her face grew hot as she realized what she was seeing. "Why are you hiding these? You're a really great artist." She hadn't drawn since coming to AC. Not a sketch nor doodle while slaving for Gaia. She'd focused her talents on supporting Seva. Now she discovered he'd hidden his talent from her. She felt betrayed, but wasn't sure why.

"I'm not an artist. Drawing merely helps me see people." He took more pads from his storage chest.

She paged through one book, then another. Each drawing was amazing. Some people had eyes that shone with life and excitement, other eyes were flat and dull, but always the eyes drew her into the picture.

Seva relaxed. He didn't look at the sketches, but told her, "Once a drawing is complete, it's like looking inside that person's soul. I don't like anyone to see them. Please understand." He handed her another sketchbook. "People I met in Colorado."

She opened this one, pausing at a group of people in front of a hot air balloon. A man standing off to one side looked familiar. Like Jeff... from college. Impossible. Jeff wouldn't be in Colorado with Seva. "I do not understand why you're hiding these."

"Your rejection of art is so adamant, I feared you would call these art. My path is healing. I use drawing to help. Your path is art."

"I don't need art." She shook her head. "I heal with my hands."

"Art is a part of who you are. Without art you cannot be complete. Without art you can never find peace. Art is your soul's purpose."

Sandy tightened. Seva was right about one thing. She hadn't wanted to know he was an artist. He was another man who was a more talented artist than she was.

***

Jeff

Jeff faced ten artists, in front of ten Farmington-Shiprock High School computer lab computers. He explained web design basics, showed samples of his favorite pages, then switched from overheads to the terminal hookup to demo website development techniques and finally passed out the handouts attendees loved.

An art teacher in the first row, a slight man in his mid-twenties raised his hand. "So, tell me again, how much money can I make doing this part-time?"

Jeff shrugged. "You can go offer to set up and run websites for local companies and call your own shots."

"But the companies in this part of New Mexico build pipelines or sell stuff to the guys on the lines," one woman told him.

"There's tourist stuff," the art teacher said, "and Native American art is getting hot." He became quiet, then started scribbling notes.

While his students worked on the practical exercises, Jeff walked out and down the drab hallway. Locating a payphone, he called the Yippee corporate number using his personal calling card. "What's going on?" he asked when Mike answered.

"Nuttin." Mike giggled and Chip picked up on another phone. "A little trouble. Advertisers suing us. Sorry about your credit card."

"You guys have tons of money."

"Actually, Mom cancelled our cards, too."

"Your mother, the Chairman of the Board?"

"Yep. Mom fired Mike and me. And we don't get any spending money—not even for techie toys—unless we go to grad school. Oh, you're fired, too. She and Mike's mom are taking the company in a new direction. They say internet shopping for housewives will be the new growth business. Makes no sense. Kids don't let their parents use their computers, so how can mothers shop online?"

Jeff sighed. "What happened?" Working for kids was not for grownups.

Mike giggled. "We made one little mistake. Those ads for growing your penis and the ones for taking off weight. Well, we kind of mixed them up. We forwarded orders to the wrong companies. 'Weight No More' and 'Wait No More' ads look pretty similar and I guess some buyers weren't such good spellers." He giggled again. "We got sued, big time."

Jeff hung up and dialed Corin's office.

Corin assured him there was nothing to worry about. "I dumped the last of your Yippee stock at the first rumors of trouble. The price plummeted. Now I'm starting to buy again."

"Why?" Jeff had begun to think he understood the stock market.

"There's a rumor the Yippee moms are reinventing the company." She paused. "Now that you're through with Yippee, you can cancel the rest of your trip and come back to Boston. I miss our dinners."

"No," Jeff said slowly. "Not yet. I think I'll just keep on following my map. My friends are going all the way to San Francisco. I'll fly back from there as planned."

***

Sandy

Sandy sat wrapped in a blanket on the edge of the Shiprock, New Mexico Campground on Highway 64, watching stars flicker over the Ute Mountains. After the Taos workshops, she insisted Seva take this side trip to Chaco Canyon and Shiprock. These sacred places had restored her peace and lightened Seva's heart. They hadn't talked about his furtive art and she again felt close to him.

He joined her on the bench and pointed up. "Delphinus! Remember, I promised to bring you here." They sat in silence for a long time before he spoke again. "The spirits and the stars are sending us each on separate paths."

Often Seva's words didn't mean what they seemed. Surely he did not mean separate paths. Not on this perfect night.

Early the next morning he drove the jeep to Farmington. When he returned he showed her his one-way ticket to India. She longed to rip the ticket in pieces and stomp them into the snow. She wanted everything to return to the way it had been at Alpha Camp. She shook her head and pinched her eyes shut. If she couldn't see him, maybe she'd be able to ignore his words. "You can't leave me. We aren't finished. You said we were twin flames."

"Some teachers believe each of us is a part of a soul group of fifty, one hundred or even one thousand people with the same light consciousness. Twin flames, twin souls, or soulmates are terms used for relationships between group members. There is no reason to be sad to part from a member of our soul group. We are always connected."

"I don't believe you." Sandy wanted to cry, not discuss spiritual philosophy.

"Let me demonstrate. Where were you in 1980?"

"Boston, graduating from the Art Institute and beginning my Masters."

"I was studying at Harvard Divinity School and cutting grass at the DeCordova Sculpture Park."

Sandy was amazed at the coincidences but wasn't about to let him know that. "In 1982 I worked in Ohio. Where were you?"

"I ran a home for troubled boys in inner city Cleveland."

"That's just a coincidence. In 1984 I was in Texas."

"See, it doesn't always work. I lived in Denver trying to start a retreat center and spent time in Pagosa Springs with hot air balloons."

"Pagosa!"

Seva smiled. "Convinced?"

She turned away.

"Do not be sad. I will always be close to you. I feel other soul group members are close. Roles may change, but we are always teaching each other and learning from each other. After every parting, we are more spiritually aware." Seva shook his head. "Our time together was perfect. Now you're ready to move forward. And I must go."

Holding back tears, she spun to face him. "Let me go with you to India."

"You've learned to heal and have experienced peace. Now, heal yourself. You need to be Sandy again." Seva's eyes were peaceful and moist. "Find yourself, my love."

"I want to help you. You. Without you I don't know what my path is." Sandy held her breath willing him to change his mind, to understand he needed her. That she needed him.

"It would not be a true journey if you knew the path before you put one foot forward." He swung his bag into the jeep. "Make peace with your art." He reached for her.

She relaxed and exhaled. "I would never have left you."

He held her close. His chin rested on the top of her head. "You helped me. Now we both can go on." He moved back, held her away from him, and got into his old jeep. "Be peaceful and accept coincidences."

She watched him pull onto Highway 64 and disappear down the road. Now only the Winnebago, Ariel's battered Airstream, and a purple van driven by that crazy artist remained in the campground. Sammie had caught up with them after the EPA tested the red dye in her gauze, determined it was toxic, and confiscated every bolt of fabric before she executed her massive art work.

The next morning Ariel, in a fuzzy white robe, knocked on Sandy's door. Sandy, puffy-eyed and blotchy-faced, opened the door. Ariel handed her a cup of coffee. "Blessings."

Back inside, Sandy sat at the tiny table, took a sip, and choked, "We'd been together for three years. I thought he needed me." Tears streamed down her cheeks. "He left me. He really left me."

Ariel nodded and sat next to Sandy. She put her arm around Sandy's shoulders and pulled her head close.

Sandy looked up into Ariel's calm face. "What do I do, my psychic friend?"

"Take the next step." Ariel held Sandy's hand, turned the palm up, and closed her eyes. "You've allowed four men to hold you back from being who you really are. You needed each one for a while. Two had their own agendas. Seva told you to be yourself, but you could not hear. You tried to be what you thought he wanted."

Sandy felt miserable but listened, focusing on the dolphin birthmark on Ariel's cheek and counted. Besides Seva, her husband John and Barry had both had agendas that weren't good for her. "You said four?"

"The young man from your college days."

"You know about Jeff?"

"I'm psychic." Ariel smiled. "You two were young. Not ready."

"I haven't seen Jeff in fifteen years. If he remembers me at all, it's as the stupid girl who left him."

"Be patient." Ariel stroked her head.

"But now, where do I go? I have no plan."

"Surrender. Let others help you. Let me. I promise this time you'll get top billing."

Sandy looked out at the swirling snow. "Please, make it someplace warm!"

II. 4. Virgin Islands, 1997

Jeff

A salty Virgin Island breeze played over his face and ruffled his pony tail as Jeff leaned against the rail of the magnificent sailing ship Mandalay and looked back at the coast of Virgin Gorda. The luminescent Caribbean Sea, full moon, and tropic isle looked exactly like the ad for this Windjammer Singles Cruise.

The woman next to him shifted her hips. The bottom of her dolphin printed t-shirt rode up to show off a silver thong bikini bottom. She gripped Jeff's tanned arm in one hand and a rum swizzle in the other. "Let's go for a little swimmy in the pool," she cooed, swaying to a steel drum rendition of 'New York, New York.'

"There is no pool." Jeff turned away from the sweet smell of rum and Hawaiian Tropic. She'd sat next to him at dinner and later found him sketching the First Mate and a group of deck hands and dragged him away to the first night party. He knew he should be social, but he was content watching waves.

"So, what do you do back in the real world?" She craned her neck to see his face. Scrunching her body between him and the rail, she began to trace the dolphin tattoo on his chest with one painful fingernail.

He flinched away from her touch. "Not much."

She cocked her head. "My friend from Newark told me you're in the Admiral's Suite. She said you look like that guy who made a fortune in Yipdeedoo stock?" She leaned closer and breathed, "Got a girlfriend?"

That was enough. He waved a punched card that served as money on the ship, mumbled something about a drink, and moved off towards the bar for another virgin swizzle. Did he have a girlfriend? The last time he talked to Corin, she'd hinted she was ready for commitment. She wanted him to stop bumming around the Caribbean and return to Boston. When he continued to make excuses, she booked a week for two at a luxury resort on St. Croix. He decided to take this cruise out of Tortola in the British Virgins and meet her plane in St. Thomas. After traveling alone for a year, a singles cruise had been a big mistake. He was too old for crab races and drinking games and the scheduled toga party filled him with dread. He'd imagined one last taste of freedom on the high seas, not drunken silliness.

After his cross country trip he'd spent time in Boston, getting reacquainted with the city. With his new financial freedom, Corin introduced him to a new lifestyle. He funded an art school scholarship and was invited to cultural fundraisers. He bought his mother a Florida condo in an art community and he and Corin entertained his dad and Jennifer for a holiday visit including front row seats at the Christmas Revels.

After the second winter nor'easter blew in, he flew to the Caribbean.

Maybe Corin was right. He needed structure and purpose. Goals. She'd suggested he become a partner in her investment firm and he was considering ways his accidental windfall could aid the Boston arts community.

Jeff searched the bridge until he located the First Mate, a tall elegant black man with the inscrutable face of a drill sergeant. Convinced to retrieve Jeff's passport from the Purser, Samuel promised to get Jeff off the ship and make everything quite fine with the BVI Customs Agent on Virgin Gorda.

An hour later, the ship's launch docked with a soft thud against tires tied to the Spanish Town pier. White teeth, starched shirt and shorts gleaming in the moonlight, the black officer gracefully jumped up, tied a quick hitch, and offered Jeff his powerful hand. He passed Jeff's duffle and dive bag to a tall figure in neon yellow jellies and told Jeff in a British public school accent, "My nephew will take you in his taxi to my sister's guesthouse near Devil's Bay," then switched back to island patois, "Ah haf tu gat back before da sails go up."

"Sorry to be a problem."

"No problem, mon," Samuel replied with a wink. "This was not the ship for you." He waved and shoved off as a bagpipe rendition of 'Amazing Grace' drifted across the water from the ship.

***

Sandy

The boatman, ebony black with a frosting of sea salt, helped Sandy from his open boat onto the Spanish Town dock. Working in paradise was not a perpetual vacation. Ariel had arranged this early morning charter from St. Croix to Virgin Gorda because she knew Sandy loved the famous cove called The Baths, so unlike any place in the Caribbean. Sandy thought the giant round boulders looked like Ariel's surreal New Age paintings showing cross sections of tranquil undersea life, flying birds, and leaping dolphins.

A taxi took her to The Baths and she stepped onto the beach. She left her bag and cover-up near the rocks and slipped on a snorkeling mask. Walking into the water to waist level, she dove below the surface and entered a water world with sixty feet of visibility in all directions. A school of blue tangs parted around her and a French Angelfish blinked a welcome. Sand, shells, and patches of coral and seaweed stretched before her.

She arched her back and let the natural ocean buoyancy raise her body. Her head surfaced and she spouted seawater. The near body-temperature water and the gentle waves soothed her like a watsu massage. Back underwater, rays of sunshine penetrated the surface and warmed her back, as she pretended she was a dolphin alone in her private marine milieu.

Though she loved the silky feel of saltwater directly on her skin she got out briefly to pull a t-shirt over her bikini. Today, her dolphin tattoo itched. Ignoring a few morning swimmers, she imagined she was alone in this tranquil fantasy world—until a scuba diver fluttered ten feet below her and bubbles from his regulator rose to tickle her belly.

Near noon, she carried her bag and copy of *Island of the Blue Dolphins* to one of the flatter boulders, ate her mango, read, and felt completely serene for the first time in weeks. These islands were truly a paradise. But locals had little time for pleasure. Everything was so expensive and Ariel scheduled back-to-back workshop groups throughout the short winter and spring tourist season. She believed Sandy wanted to be constantly teaching—like Seva.

Yesterday before Ariel left for the mainland, they visited the Gargantuan Princess cruise ship to give psychic readings to passengers too jaded to shop on St. Thomas. Drawing a dolphin in the wet sand with a palm frond, she wished she had more time for creative work.

A horn broke her peaceful world of ocean and sun with a blast, one of those beep beep codes only locals understood.

This sequence meant her friend Samuel's nephew and his taxi had arrived to take her back to the dock. The time had passed quickly. She wanted to spend another day with the taxi driver's mother, making nutmeg jam and mango chutney, as she'd done on her last visit. Carrying her bag and rubber sandals toward the taxi, she curled her toes deep in sugary sand.

The young driver waved as she approached and she smiled at his shiny black van. Despite Virgin Gorda's dusty roads, the taxi looked freshly washed. As advised, he'd named it Tamarind Ting. Sandy's meager psychic abilities had led her to fame as a taxi-namer for Caribbean drivers. When recognized, she never paid a taxi fare.

She offered psychic massages to tourists and created art as part of her readings. Like many in the islands, she worked at more than one job and felt part of a community as an artist.

The driver's neon yellow jellies tapped out the beat to a local radio station as Tamarind Ting swept her away, its fringed skirt sweeping the dusty ground.

***

Jeff

Jeff sat on a wall in front of the sunshine yellow government buildings near the Christianstead docks and sketched St. Croix taxi drivers leaning against their bright painted taxis. He admired the fanciful taxi names, like Sunrise Enchantment and Papaya Peace, painted on bumpers above low hanging fringe.

Jeff's fingers flew, choosing pastel crayons, exchanging cadmium yellow for chromium green, then in quick succession leaf green, vermillion, and cobalt turquoise to capture the Caribbean blue of the harbor. Early in his year-long island idyll he'd visited Martinique to purchase spiral sketchbooks with paper fine as linen and a supply of French-made pencils, charcoal, and pastels. This book was his last. The others he'd sent back to Boston with gifts of shells and spices for Corin. In his travels he only needed to swim, walk on the beach, read, draw, and talk to islanders.

Packing his art supplies into a waterproof case, he headed towards the hotel. He noticed a blond man in pressed shorts and short-sleeved shirt wave a clipboard at a thick, middle-aged American couple. "How about a free dinner?" the eager young man cajoled. The stocky man replied with a snort, "Not if we have to sit through one of those timeshare pitches. If I want dinner or a condo, I'll pay for it."

"Well then, how about a Buck Island tour? Free snorkel gear supplied and lunch on the beach!"

"We did that yesterday," the woman said with a smile. "We love the ocean. We're from Kansas."

The Kansans walked on and the young man turned to Jeff. "How about—" then looked closer at Jeff's tanned body and relaxed manner and mumbled, "sorry, you live here," and hurried to catch up with a couple in spandex biking shorts and matching 'I Conquered the Beast' t-shirts. From the back, the perky blonde reminded Jeff of Lisa, buff and intense, talking a mile a minute to her muscled companion.

Caribbean solitude and sun had given Jeff more than a new physical look, he had a new outlook. He even walked slower. Corin had flown in two days ago and kept him busy shopping and eating at the best tourist resort restaurants. This afternoon she'd gone to the hotel spa for a massage, wrap, and some kind of an artificial tanning treatment package. Tonight, she'd signed them up for a Hawaiian luau featuring Maine lobster and Norwegian salmon next to the hotel pool. He'd rather sit on the beach, snorkel with fish, and eat at a local café.

Corin needed more time away from the city and her business. Maybe he'd buy an island. A small island.

Even in the heat of late August, the streets of C'stead were crowded with cruise ship passengers, resort visitors, and athletes and media people from the Iron Man Triathlon.

He met his friend Christopher for a quick lunch of conch burgers and pineapple juice. Chris was studying moko jumbie training, that African stilt-dancing from Trinidad. Chris believed jumbie training would help his performance bartending and chattered on about costumes and stilt walking.

As Chris left, he'd begged, "Please come to the Festival tomorrow and see my first jumbie performance."

"Sure. Maybe Jake will come, too. He's flying down to take aerial photos for some artist stringing balloons between the three US Virgin Islands."

"What fun!" Chris laughed. "Artists just get crazier."

Jeff wondered if he would ever go back to doing art seriously. Right now, he told himself his sketching was purely recreational. He didn't judge his work, just loved doing it. Remembering Seva's teachings, he'd become content enjoying and experiencing the world. With his new outlook he believed he could live authentically anywhere. He felt ready to settle down and planned to ask Corin to marry him before they left St. Croix.

***

Sandy

Air thick as honey made Sandy's morning a solitary delight. Already sounds of Carnival wafted from the fairgrounds. Shaded by a trellis overflowing with magenta bougainvillea, she savored a cup of lavender tea and read Jean Rhys's *Wide Sargasso Sea*. Ariel was off-island—meaning anywhere but St.

Croix—at the Texas New Age Business Conference workshop schmoozing for Virgin Island tourism. Her friend's latest idea to bring spiritual bliss to 1990s yuppies centered around a chain of Caribbean retreats called 'Holistic Huts' featuring rotating gurus. Ariel planned to convince big name teachers to spend winter vacations leading sessions.

Sandy and Ariel's apartment above Christianstead's Indian restaurant in the downtown tourist district included a deck where they gave psychic readings. The wood building was painted lavender, yellow, and blue in the tradition of Caribbean cottages and Indian spiced cooking smells blended with salt air and frangipani blossoms. The pink and green sign, Sandy, Virgin Goddess of Synchronicity—Find Your Future, Follow Your Path, was Ariel's idea.

Ariel was by far the better psychic, but Sandy's quirky taxi-naming side business, started as a favor to a local driver, had grown. She intuitively offered auspicious names to be painted on taxicabs, like Bluebird of Evening or Sunrise Glory, by telephone all over the islands. And all the drivers recommended their tourists visit the American psychics.

Ariel's knack for putting together spiritual retreats and advertising them in New Age magazines and on their new website had paid off. Sandy's five-day workshops, held at a local plantation, did well. The Zen diving, meditative snorkeling, beach ball yoga, and Atlantean mountain hiking made great ad copy, but, once a client was on the island, Sandy's healing massages made sure each participant left relaxed and happy.

Sandy's Soul-Art drawings, the most sought-after of her talents, created during psychic readings, combined subconscious soul work and art. Each became a personal inspiration for the client and a treasured original art work.

Sheltered behind bougainvillea, Sandy watched an athletic woman about her own age walk up the steps and knock on the railing. A large floppy hat and sunglasses hid her face. "Is this the place to get a psychic reading?" the woman whispered, pulling her hat lower over her eyes.

Sandy slipped into her reading robe, draping a gauze veil over her face and sun-bleached hair. Most tourists preferred readers with gypsy hair. Real Rasta dreadlocks scared them, but a few corn rows brought better tips. She came out from behind the flowers and gestured for the woman to sit at the crystal-strewn table.

The gaunt-faced blonde wearing the I Conquered the Beast muscle shirt looked familiar, like Lisa, her old roommate with the running obsession, yet thinner and... Before Sandy could ask her name, the woman demanded, "Will I win?" Sandy closed her eyes. She never saw pictures or visions as Ariel did, but she let her mind be free as she sketched then read her drawings for answers. Now she quickly drew geometric shapes with sharp angles in red and orange. She studied the drawing and said, "You won't lose."

The woman gasped, "Oh-my-god," slapped down bills, and left.

As the woman rushed down the steps, a tall, thin white man walked up. He wore the striped shirt of a jumbie student over baggy fuchsia shorts. Despite an easy smile, Sandy immediately sensed sadness.

He looked into her eyes and relaxed. "I'm Christopher. Call me Chris."

"Do you want a psychic reading?"

The man just smiled, this time a genuine friendly American smile. "I guess I just want to talk."

"We can do both." She took out a fresh sheet of paper.

He took a breath and began his story while Sandy drew. "My life has been a series of accidents. I almost got married in a hot air balloon. I lived with some artists and fell off a roof. One guy made a lot of money and paid for me to go to chef school and then performance bartending school, plus the botox and stuff."

Sandy noticed his soft beardless skin.

"Now I'm in jumbie training. I haven't made any friends here. I just don't fit in anyplace. I'm thinking of becoming a blonde. What do you think?"

Sandy let a bit of a smile cross her lips. "Different hair won't make your life easier." Drawn to this confused young man, she took his hand and studied the drawing full of rainbow colors and connected circles and lines. She explained that his soul couldn't be confined to one piece of paper or one life. "You have to be yourself."

They talked for over an hour and when he stood to leave, he told her, "I feel we've been friends for a long time."

She watched him go, feeling she, too, had known him for a long time.

Yesterday, a woman in black, who talked without moving her lips, had asked, "Will I marry Jeff?" and Sandy told her, "Yes. You'll marry your Jeff." That time the drawing had included a sketch of a man's face. It must have been the name 'Jeff' that brought to mind the face of the only Jeff she'd ever known. From the woman's shocked expression Sandy knew she'd toss the drawing in the trashcan at the bottom of the stairs.

***

Jeff

The next morning Corin sipped a mimosa and looked out the window of their Harbor Resort suite and sighed, "I love the Caribbean. The food, the weather, the water. So perfectly romantic."

"You've only eaten in air-conditioned hotel dining rooms and swam in chlorinated hotel pools." Jeff really wanted to show Corin the things he loved about the islands. "How about some sightseeing?"

"The concierge said we could tour that big cruise ship."

He picked up the *St. Croix Avis*. "Let's go to this carnival." He read, "Food, jumbies, horse races, fortune telling, livestock—like a good old county fair!" He avoided mentioning that Chris would be there. Corin didn't get on well with Chris or his flamboyant wardrobe.

"St Croix is part of the United States," Corin admitted.

A taxi took them to the fairgrounds and before they walked through the gate Jeff was singing along to a steel drum band's 'Island in the Sun.' His tanned body, longish sun-bleached hair and cut-offs blended into the crowd of locals of all colors and sizes. He'd picked up enough of the dialect islanders called English to joke with the vendors while Corin's black cruise wear was a magnet attracting roving timeshare salespeople.

Tempted by the heady aroma of roasting goat, Jeff ordered a juicy sandwich. Corin dabbed at grease running down his chin onto his red Windjammer t-shirt, but refused to try a bite.

He finished his sandwich and turned to the next booth where hairy coconuts floated in a galvanized vat. Corin skewed her face, but he ordered one. A steely-haired old man chopped the top third off a coconut, stuck a straw into the top, and handed it to Jeff with a wide-mouthed grin. Jeff turned to offer Corin a sip of the cool coconut water, but she backed away from the cooking smells and stumbled out of the way of two Crusians, bareback on sleek horses, trotting towards the racetrack. A fuchsia-suited clown on stilts holding a sign advertising the Limbo Bar wobbled into her path and she jumped sideways. Jeff had told her mocko jumbies symbolized ghost healers. She skittered away and disappeared into the crowd.

Jeff plunged after her, but ended up in the middle of a line of racegoers. By the time he extricated himself and found Corin in the vendor area, she threw herself at him.

"It was terrible. A runaway goat butted me. I stumbled and fell. Knocked over a table filled with crystals. A black man in some naval uniform rescued my purse from the dirt. A woman with an American accent told me she'd done a psychic reading for me yesterday. She had a dolphin tattoo just like yours. It was frightening."

Jeff patted Corin's back and held her close until she stopped panting.

"Do you want to go," she said in a tone that was a statement not a question.

"Sure. I'm ready," he lied. "I saw the jumbies. Everywhere I turn, I think I see people from my past. I thought I saw Sammie, that artist from Boston, and Lisa, the lawyer from Denver. I swear I even imagined a little dark-haired teenager with blond parents looked familiar." And he thought—and Sandy, his college girlfriend, as if she'd be wearing braids and selling crystals at a Caribbean festival.

Corin interrupted. "How silly! Why would any of those people be here? Let's go back to the hotel and get ready for dinner. Tonight is Italian night."

Jeff's head buzzed. The music and the smell of rum and over-ripe fruit must be making him light-headed.

***

Sandy

Rhythms of steel drum bands and shouts and whistles from Carnival games of chance swirled around Sandy's fortune-telling booth. One hand held crystals and a bit of sage and the other the tall black woman's long-fingered hand. Closing her eyes, she blocked out the sweet island smells of overripe fruit, roasting goat, and ocean. When she opened her eyes, the elegant woman in a madras turban and giant gold hoop earrings looked hopeful. Sandy smiled. "No need for me to make a drawing. Go have a fine visit with your daughter in Chicago. Tourist business will be slow during hurricane season."

"But, Sandy, will a hurricane hit dis island? Ah worry about my baby on that wooden ship." She smiled up at Samuel, handsome in a starched white uniform. "I was on my knees in church all day on Hurricane Supplication Day. Please tell me what winds are coming."

"Weather is not part of my prediction talents."

"Tu bod. Dat would truly be a blessing, if you could do dat." She hugged Sandy to her proud body. "And keep my son safe."

"Go back to your shop," Sandy told her. "The President of the Business Association and our Legislature's new Senator should not be lollygagging at Carnival when the Gargantuan Princess is in port. Didn't they teach you that at Harvard's Business School?"

"Shush, mi fren, you blow mi cover." Her ebony eyes sparkled.

Sandy and the tall man watched his mother walk away, hips swaying to the drums, and disappear into the crowd, a curious mixture of locals in Sunday rayon dresses, straw hats, hose and stiff shoes and very blond ladies from the ship dressed for tennis in appliquéd linens and Nikes. A few cruise passengers stopped to look at Sandy's sign, but didn't step too close. When she and Ariel went on board cruise ships, these same ladies lined up for Ariel's readings and Sandy's soul drawings and tipped generously for glimpses into futures of self-created boredom.

Sandy looked up at Samuel. "So, Mr. Mandalay First Mate, enjoying your day off?"

His inscrutable face softened as he looked down at her. "I am so very tired of these American singles cruises. I came to see if my favorite fortune teller could tell me how to avoid the winds that make my passengers as green as the green flash. Winds are tough on ships and the tourist businesses. The National Weather Service informs me this will be a bad season. What do you say?"

"As I told your mother, weather is not my talent."

"If it were, I'd be promoted to Captain." He moved his hips to 'The Girl from Ipanema.' "I need to see all is shipshape on the Mandalay, but then I will return ready to dance all night with you at the soca." He kissed her cheek lightly.

"You know for sure that will happen?" She cocked her head and flipped her braids. "I hear they call you the psychic sailor?"

"That they do." Samuel grinned, showing beautiful white teeth. "I have seen visions of you as queen of the Festival, a mermaid emerging from the sea."

"I'll help you become queen," a voice came from over their heads.

They looked up at a fuchsia-clad mocko jumbie. He pulled off his mask and jumped down from the stilts, untangling expertly from the long pants. "Just stopped by to thank you again for your advice."

The officer nodded and rested his hand on Sandy's back. "So, this beautiful lady read your fortune?"

"She told me to be myself," said the jumbie. "Now she has to read my fortune and help me figure out who that is."

Sandy smiled. "That, Chris my jumbie friend, like weather, is too difficult for my small talent. I don't even know who I am. When I draw my own Soul-Art drawing it is always the same—endless circles."

***

Jeff

Corin was in the shower getting ready to catch the ferry from St. Croix to Charlotte Amalie when the phone rang. Jeff put down Herman Wouk's *Don't Stop the Carnival* and answered, anticipating another emergency call from Corin's office. Instead, he heard Jake's hurried voice. "The weather's getting bad. All flights to the Caribbean are cancelled. The Triathlon people packed onto that big cruise ship headed back to Puerto Rico. I've filed a flight plan to get you, me, Corin, and Chris out of here."

Jeff looked out the window at the cloudless sky and calm ocean. "Dive boats are going out to the reef. Corin and I are taking the ferry to St. Thomas."

"Listen to me. Pack and drive to the airport. Now."

"Wouldn't flying be dangerous?"

"It's a lot safer than a ferry boat." The phone line went dead.

"Corin," Jeff pounded on the bathroom door. "Hurry. We have to pack. A hurricane's coming."

By the time Corin opened the door, wearing the hotel robe, Jeff had pulled their luggage out of the closet and was stuffing clothes into his duffle.

"Don't be silly. The hotel would have told us if there was a hurricane threat. The concierge predicted today would be a perfect day for shopping."

"I don't think so. Jake insists there's a big storm heading this way. He's going to fly us out." By now, Jeff was throwing Corin's clothes into one of her matched leather bags.

She shrugged. "I want to go to St. Thomas. Besides, we have dinner reservations."

"This is more important than shopping." He tossed an armload of black dresses on the bed.

"Stop that. If you're going to act like a crazy man, I'll do it myself."

"Corin, please hurry!"

As soon as Corin finished packing, Jeff carried their luggage to the hotel lobby and, with the help of the doorman, pushed Corin into the nearest taxi. Halfway to the airport, the rain began. The fringed skirt of the taxi in front of theirs had Laughing Dolphins painted on the back. It fish-tailed from side to side throwing sheets of water up from the already flooding road.

"I hate these taxis and their silly names," Corin said through pursed lips.

Jeff said nothing. By now the rain fell more horizontal than vertical and their taxi hydroplaned sideways. Corin's thin body leaned toward him and flinched when a coconut hit the windshield. Their driver turned into the airport, swerved, and came within inches of hitting a woman on a bicycle.

Corin moved closer to Jeff. "I want to go home. Now." Jeff put his arm around her and silently hoped he could get Corin safely off the island before the hurricane hit.

***

Sandy

Sandy pedaled her bicycle towards St. Croix's Alexander Hamilton Airport, ducking her head against the stinging winds. The Laughing Dolphins taxi passed her, splashing cold sandy water on her legs and dress. The driver signaled his apology with two beeps. The next taxi also splashed her, then jumped the curb heading for the gate reserved for private planes. Her denim jacket was soaked and her batik skirt pasted to her legs. She turned into the parking lot and laid the bike down against a coconut palm.

Just an hour ago, Ariel had called from the Texas conference and told her to get to the airport. A combination of weather reports and intuition told her a momentous hurricane was moving towards St. Croix. She told Sandy to leave everything and not expect to return.

So, Sandy carried only a small bag with cash from the apartment and her passport. In her gut she knew Ariel was right, but how was she to get off the island?

She ran to an airport guard who'd just put the last shutter on the open front terminal windows. "Airport closed," he yelled into the wind. "All commercial flights have left 'cept that charter from Kansas."

Sandy leaned against the wall and watched her bike blow across the parking lot and skid against a taxi. The Laughing Dolphins driver lifted luggage onto the curb next to a solid couple in St. Thomas t-shirts. The woman yelled, "Hurry, Oscar. That's our plane."

Behind her a voice yelled, "Sandy. Is that you?"

She turned and saw Chris, still dressed in fuchsia jumbie shorts. "I need to leave."

"How...?" he began. "Never mind. I can get you out of here. My friends have a plane." He put his arm around Sandy's waist and pulled her, fighting the wind, toward the gate. She tried to talk, but her words were blown away by the knife-sharp wind.

The airstrip was empty except for a red and white twin engine shifting in the wind. From the cockpit the blond pilot yelled, "Hurry, Chris. Only room for you."

Chris yelled up, "She comes or I stay."

The pilot did not hesitate. He jumped down the slippery steps, opened the luggage compartment, reached in, and pulled out all the dive gear and five pieces of matching black leather luggage. "Who cares about Corin's luggage anyway? In here," he screamed over the wind and boosted Sandy into the compartment. "You'll be okay," he assured her, "until we stop in Key West to refuel. Hold on tight. If I have to fly high, use these." He lifted two air tanks and regulators back in. "Put on the BCs for protection."

Chris crawled in after Sandy and helped her into one of the half-inflated BCs. "You'll be fine. It's like a cushioned life jacket."

As the plane taxied, Sandy braced herself between the side of the luggage compartment and Chris, distracting herself by thinking of the coincidence that led her to meet this jumbie at the airport. Seva taught her to accept. He said coincidences explained why she noticed the same people over and over. He said sometimes people come into your life for brief but intense periods and sometimes they come for an entire lifetime. This was no doubt one of those intense times.

The plane lifted and bounced in heavy turbulence. Holding tight to a bracket, she remembered asking Seva if all soul groups had high goals to accomplish, like a cancer cure or world peace. He'd laughed that sweet laugh and told her all depended upon what the group needed and the level of the group. He insisted it was the lesson that was important, not our concept of good or bad. She could understand soul groups working on philosophy, sports, or medicine but she'd been shocked when he suggested a group could have crime as their common goal or just need to help others find themselves.

***

Jeff

Jeff propped his elbows on a scratched Formica table in the crowded Key West Airport coffee shop. The strong steaming coffee had begun to revive him while he waited for Jake's plane to be refueled. Despite the noise, Corin slept curled up next to him in the booth. The air was heavy with adrenalin, as pilots talked about the Category 3 hurricane battling the St. Croix coast with winds up to 120 mph, heading towards Puerto Rico and possibly Florida.

Jeff gripped Jake's arm. "You were great, man!" he said for the twentieth time. "You flew us through a hurricane."

"Just some awfully high winds. I kind of skirted the worst."

Jeff shook his head, recalling the last few hours. "You saved our lives. Corin was terrified. And Chris was so grateful you let his girlfriend stow in the luggage compartment. You got us all out. As soon as we landed, Chris carried that girl off the taxiway. He came back to say they're going to stay here in Key West for now."

He looked around the café at patrons holding prized possessions like refugees. One man clutched golf clubs, a teenage boy protected his boombox, a woman held her makeup case, and a little girl hugged a red and white toy chicken. A blond couple sat with a dark-haired, big-eyed teenager gripping a sketchbook tight to her narrow chest. A stocky couple held hands across their table. The woman told the man, "Oscar, I wish we were home in Kansas."

Jeff said again, "You saved our lives."

Jake grinned. "Everyone's safe. That's the important thing. Chris was amazing, choosing to ride in cargo with that woman. Your investment in my flying lessons paid off. For all of us." He poked Jeff's shoulder. "But wait until Corin finds all her luggage and shopping treasures got dumped on the tarmac. She'll kill me."

"I saved this." Jeff drew a tiny white velvet box out of his jacket pocket and flipped it open. Jake took in a quick breath. The waitress refilling their cups almost dropped the pot.

"So, you and Corin are getting married." Jake raised his eyebrows. "Opposites attract, I guess."

"Corin can be a pain with her ambitions and pretensions. But I knew her when she poured beer in O'Brien's Pub for drunken college boys. Despite her tough ways, she really needs me." And marrying Corin was what he needed to do.

PART III

*"Do you think the universe fights for souls to be together?
Some things are too strange and strong
to be coincidences."*
Emery Allen

III. 1. Key West, Florida, October, 2000

Jeff

Jeff smiled as he examined the cruise ship tickets, then stuffed them back in the pocket of his tux and looked out at the clusters of artists sipping champagne in the courtyard garden. Corin had rented the Isabella Stewart Gardner Museum for their wedding reception. The board members and supporters of their Delphinus Foundation to help young Boston artists, all Corin's friends from the financial community, and every successful artist in Massachusetts were there.

Jeff's parents attended, both happy for their only child, for different reasons. Even Corin's twin Jerry, who Jeff was learning to call Jerome, flew in from Paris for his sister's wedding and to rub shoulders with the cream of the art world. But that thought was uncharitable and today Jeff felt good will to all, even Jerry.

Jeff had looked forward to the wedding. His new life felt good. He was no longer a young artist. No longer an artist. He was done with forks, painting walls, and designing websites. He didn't feel as if he'd sold out, just moved on. Now through his good fortune and Corin's expertise he could make it easier for others to follow their dreams.

Jerome walked up chatting with a premier Boston sculptor. The muscular artist clasped Jeff's shoulder. "Congratulations. Pleased a philanthropist is giving back to the arts community."

Jeff grimaced. "Actually, I went to art school here in Boston."

The sculptor cocked his head. "Really. I heard you made a ton of money in the dot com world. What galleries show your work?"

"I'm not in any galleries. I've been working in the financial world recently." Jeff still disliked artists' attitudes toward money and success, but he wasn't going to irritate this one. After the sculptor's latest big commission, Jeff hoped that he would write a large check to the Foundation.

The artist leaned close. "Perhaps I should apply for one of your Delphinus grants?"

Jeff bit back the sarcasm in his reply. "Thirty is the cut-off age for our young artists' grants."

The artist narrowed his eyes. "Aren't you the same Jeff Sandler who had that ridiculous Pricknic tour?"

Jerome snickered and Jeff turned away. "Time to return to my bride." He took a breath and walked towards Corin. She looked gorgeous in a sleek black satin gown copied from one worn by the museum's founder; its severe lines reminded him of bygone glamour, perfect for this Renaissance setting. With a single white gardenia in her hair, she stood, antique champagne flute raised, no trace of the pub waitress from his college days in this elegant woman. In addition to her financial practice, she'd made a name for herself in the feminist community by establishing a non-profit to assist young women professionals. She was smart, successful, and respected.

She smiled, red lips in a line, as a newspaper photographer took her photo, then turned to Jeff as he kissed her cheek. "Isn't the day glorious." She pointed to a couple near the silver punch bowl. "The Smiths are considering donating a former mill building to be divided into studios."

As the photographer snapped another picture, Jeff hugged her and whispered in her ear, "Wonderful news. And I can't wait to start our honeymoon cruise. The airport limo will be here in a few minutes."

Behind her back, people often described Corin as unfeeling, but they were wrong. She was goal oriented and lacked the sensitivity of an artist, but she'd worked hard to come so far. With Corin's business skill and his ability to recognize truly talented artists, their Delphinus Foundation was known as one of the best run in the country and brought in donors from all over the world. Her hard shell hid the girl who smashed the tray of glasses and escaped that Boston pub. She cared about him in her way and she'd done so much for him. Now that they were married, he felt she'd relax. Helping more young artists would bring her out of the cold world of numbers and into touch with creatives and non-profits who put people first.

Seva taught him to trust himself, honor commitments, and most of all love. He loved Corin and would make her happy. They'd create a good life together. He would never leave her.

And a leisurely Caribbean cruise was going to be the perfect way to begin.

***

Jeff smiled, closed his eyes, and let the thick, salty Key West air, buoyant music, palm trees, and sunny outdoor cafe bring back memories of carefree days in the Caribbean islands.

"If I never hear another Jimmy Buffett song, it will be too, too soon," Corin said without moving her lips.

"Sorry this hasn't been a great honeymoon." Why did he say that? He wiped sweaty palms on his khaki shorts. When Corin spoke with her mouth closed it was a sign she was annoyed and he needed to tread softly.

"Jeffrey. A Caribbean cruise during hurricane season! Every hour here reminds me of leaving St. Croix in that dreadful hurricane three years ago. We could have been killed. A Windjammer first mate lost his life trying to get back to his boat." She shook her head. "If that wasn't bad enough, this cruise ship is filled with Midwestern yokels taking advantage of off-season rates."

"I'm sorry—"

"I can't believe you booked this trip because you thought it would be fun. Beginning in Key West. During this Fantasy Fest thing." She leaned across the small restaurant table. "Nude people covered with paint parading in the streets. Disgusting!"

"Corin, I said I'm sorry." She seemed set off by the Key West homosexual community. When some lesbians in Boston financial world were good colleagues and friends. He checked his map. "Let's go see Hemingway's house."

She wrinkled her nose.

"Well, how about one of the historical tours?"

"The founding fathers were wreckers. Besides, I'm sweating." Corin patted her pale cheek with a tissue and re-applied a magenta layer to her lips. Leaning away from blaring speakers, her shoulder brushed the iron fence that separated tables from sidewalk.

Further down Duvall Street, Jeff noticed the back of a woman riding a pink bicycle pulling a two-wheeled cart piled high with painted coconuts. Sun-bleached hair swirled as she swerved around a scooter driven by a bikinied teen.

A Harley's roar blocked the blare of yet another chorus of 'Margaritaville.' A leathered biker leered through the fence and Corin hissed, "That's it! I'm going back to the ship." Standing, she smoothed her black silk blouse over unwrinkled black slacks.

In Boston, Corin looked sophisticated in black. Even her wedding dress had been black and Jeff had chosen a black dinner jacket and cummerbund, hoping to disguise his bulging girth.

City life had softened him. Taxis, meetings, and rich restaurant meals. He was proud of their work, but no longer recognized the man whose face looked back at his every morning.

Here, where every building, flower, sign, and tourist was a riot of tropical colors, his wife looked as out of place as a penguin in a rainbow cotton candy factory.

'A Pirate Looks at Forty' blasted from the restaurant speakers. Jeff mumbled, "Right, Jimmy. I'm forty and forty pounds too fat."

He caught up as Corin stepped into the path of a six-foot tall blond woman with a five o'clock shadow. Corin grabbed Jeff's arm. "The men and women here all wear pink."

On the corner of Duval and Southard, a salmon-haired girl handed Jeff a folded flyer. He offered the pink sheet to Corin. "Look. You could get a massage."

Corin pushed the advertisement back at him. "Here? I'm going back to the ship and book a real massage."

Jeff stared at the logo. Two dolphins and the words 'Laughing Dolphin Massage Therapy.' He sputtered, "I drew that."

"Don't be silly." Corin kept walking.

"I did. In art school. Look. My initials JS on the tail of the dolphin on the right. And on the left SS. Sandy Shellborn."

"Don't be silly. Though it does resemble that ghastly tat-too you refuse to have removed." Corin turned away and waved to a stocky couple in billowing Mickey and Minnie t-shirts.

"You said you dislike Martha and Oscar Weatherhill," Jeff whispered, as their two Nike-clad shipmates bore down on them.

Corin smiled a pinched smile. "They speak English, bathe, and are heterosexual."

"Hi Ho!" Oscar snorted and yelled, "You young honey-mooners having fun?" with a wink at Jeff.

Martha called, "Oscar saw two guys holding hands and he's dragging me back to the ship." Reaching into one of her shopping bags, she pulled out a painted coconut and a stack of postcards. She handed a postcard to Jeff and another to Corin. "Look. I bought the entire stock." Each card had a sketch of a haystack. Bold red letters printed diagonally proclaimed "Ain't in Kansas Anymore! Greetings from Key West!"

"That's silly," said Corin.

"Positutely!" said Oscar.

"Sure is," said Martha. "I'm sending one to everybody back in Kansas."

"May I walk back to the ship with you?" Corin asked. "I've had enough of this bizarre place." She waved an arm through the air dismissing Jeff. "See you on board."

Corin walked off between the two Kansans. Jeff knew he couldn't follow her back just yet. She was in a pissy mood and he felt... wonderful. He touched the right side of his neck. A sensation like the foam on good beer tickled down to his shoulder. He felt absolutely great.

Jeff unfolded his map and walked down Southard Street away from the crowds and traffic, past the square white Tru-man Annex buildings, and through formal gates into Fort

Zachary Taylor Park. He continued until he reached the old Civil War fort and climbed onto a parapet wondering where, exactly, the Atlantic and the Gulf of Mexico met.

The walk had been longer, hotter, and more strenuous than he'd expected. Sweating, he stripped off his forest green polo shirt and tucked the damp cotton into the waistband of his Bermudas. The slap of waves against rocks reminded him of that perfect Virgin Gorda beach. He climbed down and hiked out to the breakers. Settled on a rough rock, he allowed his mind to drift as surf lapped rocks and salty mist sprayed his face.

From the moment he got off the cruise ship in Key West, thoughts of Sandy had flashed through his mind. Now, excitement like being a young art student stirred his entire body. From time to time over the last twenty years memories of her had come into his mind, but this was much stronger. He closed his eyes, leaned back, and imagined the smell of oil paints and pizza in their old Boston apartment.

Sandy shared his dreams and passion for art. One night she told him about a trip to Florida with her dad. When she swam with wild dolphins, one had become sexual. While she talked, Jeff drew the two dolphins. They'd made love laughing and vowed the laughing dolphins would be their totems forever.

He shook his head with regret. Ten years ago when he lived in New Hampshire, he'd tried to find her. He discovered that after college she'd married and moved to Cincinnati. Returning from the Caribbean, he had again searched and found she'd divorced and moved to Texas. He searched the Internet and even considered hiring a private detective, then admitted he was obsessing over a lost dream. Telling himself to let it be and go on with his life, he married Corin.

Then, damn it, why did Sandy feel so close right now? This cruise was setting Corin's temper on edge and his distracted behavior made it worse.

That pesky tingle again. The result of too much sun? He looked down at his red blotchy chest and, bright against his pasty skin, the dolphin tattoo Corin hated. He put on his shirt to cover the spare tire that bulged over too-tight Bermudas.

He'd admired Corin's financial wizardry that turned his dot-com money into a fortune and built their non-profit foundation. After giving up his computer work and a try at a leisured Caribbean idyll, he settled down and helped her expand her investment business and run their foundation. They were already good friends and partners and he'd proposed after their hurricane scare. Swept up in her dreams, he enjoyed their busy city life. And last month after living together for two years, they married.

But here in Key West, his thoughts were hugger-mugger. Was he crazy enough to consider becoming an artist—again?

He crawled back up the rocks and followed the shady path between the beach and the pine trees. "I'm no college kid," he said aloud. The sooner he got back to the ship, the better.

***

Sandy

Sandy leaned her pink bicycle against the wooden stockade fence. The Healing Garden sign wobbled as she opened the bamboo gate. She smiled over her shoulder at the dark, handsome man lounging in the classic pink Corvette. "Sorry I'm late." Her best customer was always on time.

"I missed you." Jerome Oberon tilted his sunglasses down as he slid long legs out of the sports car and followed

Sandy through the gate into the palm-shaded tropical garden. Red hibiscus, as big as his hand, brushed their arms.

She shrugged, pulling back sun-streaked hair. As he strode behind her, she felt him watching her push the bike and wheeled cart of coconuts. Jerome was different than the laid-back locals. His manners were formal and he often slipped into French, although at times she imagined she heard a hint of a South Boston lilt that reminded her of her college days. He even looked a lot like that Guy from the bar Jeff liked. But she never had the nerve to ask him if he had relatives in Boston. Inhaling the scent of hibiscus and orchid, her body relaxed. "Most locals are on Key West time."

"Not quite a local, *mon cher.*" He laughed and raked his fingers through his styled hair. "I have been here on this almost-island only three months setting up my gallery. I love your peaceful style, so refreshing compared to the affected artists who hound me to exhibit their work. Your magnificent talent is wasted painting dolphins on coconuts."

She shrugged off his compliment with a toss of her head as they reached a Bahamian style cottage painted coral, blue, lavender, and lime green. Propping her bicycle and cart against a coconut palm near a pyramid of coconuts, she knew Jerome's words held truth. Three years of painting coconuts was long enough.

Jerome stepped close and swept her into an enthusiastic hug. "I missed you all the time I was in Boston for my sister's wedding and the boring business trip to Paris. Now, Fantasy Fest brings *beaucoup* patrons into my new gallery. And soon you will be crowned Queen." He set her down. "I love you because you lack anger and fear. And are filled with beauty and kindness."

She kissed him lightly and pulled back from his seductive good looks. "Just take off your clothes. Or, would you rather go inside?" She gestured to her bright cottage.

"You know I like it here next to the water. Just you, me, and the birds." With a Gallic shrug, he unselfconsciously removed his Key West business attire: flowered shirt, white shorts, sandals, and sunglasses.

"You don't have to strip naked," she reminded him, taking her bag from the bicycle basket.

"I keep hoping." He grinned. "Everyone thinks we're sleeping together."

"Why would they think that?" Her flirtatious glance was bold, but her gaze didn't drop lower than his dark eyes.

The day Jerome first arrived in Key West, he took one glance at the city's coconut painter and fell madly in love. Sandy enjoyed his company and stories of the art world. He was undeniably charming, sexy, handsome, and lonely. She'd gone enthusiastically to his bed, but soon realized his personal energy, though giving, drenched her creativity. When she ended the intimate side of their relationship, he pressed her to stay friends. Unfortunately, Jerome held hope she'd change her mind.

Sometimes after a swim in the ocean she'd emerge with saline tears as well as salt water on her cheeks, remembering how Samuel carried her into the warm surf to swim together in the crystal clear waters like two fish. His ebony body sliding through the water next to hers. Maybe she was jinxed in love. Losing Barry had been a shock. Losing gentle Samuel Bahani Merton in the hurricane had been a tragedy. Two men dead. Her ex-husband John was starting a new life. She hoped he'd find happiness. And Jeff, she wished his dreams had come true in the twenty years since she'd walked out of his life.

She felt a flush and then a tingling under her skin on the left side of her neck, from her earlobe down to the dolphin pair tattooed above her heart. She'd never discovered an explanation for this unpredictable sensation like bursting champagne bubbles. For all Jerome's charm, she didn't think he was the stimulus.

"They think we can't resist each other."

"Face down, please. I'll start on your back," she said with a laugh. She liked Jerome and she could see he was still smitten with her. "Try to relax." She slipped off her sandals and padded into the cottage to wash her hands and select oils and music for his massage.

Later that afternoon Sandy leaned forward over Chris. Her friend, who now called himself Christa, lay back in a tube-top and fuchsia capris, one of his more conservative outfits. He had many friends in Key West, but only Sandy knew his history. They looked out for each other like siblings. When Chris worked a split-shift bartending at The Golden Cockatoo, Sandy tied her massage table atop the coconuts and bicycled to massage him in the bar's patio.

"*S'il vous plait*, Sandy. You may even call me Christopher. When I feel your magic fingers massage my neck, I fall in love."

She pushed the tall man's shoulders down away from his head. As requested, she had put Helen Reddy's *I Am Woman* album in the bar's sound system. Now 'Love Song For Jeffry,' one of her favorites, played.

"Come back to my place and I'll show you my secrets."

"What secrets?" Sandy laughed as she pulled Chris's long bleached platinum hair forward and worked her fingers deeper into his trapezius.

"In a sealed garment bag I keep a charcoal Brooks Brothers suit for emergency trips to the mainland." Looking up, he raised the back of his hand to his forehead. "Now, you know my secret, you must marry me."

Sandy laughed so hard she stopped kneading his neck. Bright, funny, and incredibly loyal, Chris had been her best friend after they fled from a tropical hurricane and landed in Key West. She'd never forgot that Chris and his pilot friend saved her. Pushing his face back into the padded ring, she replied, "I do love you, but you'd wear my clothes."

"Your clothes are *très* conservative." Chris waved long tapered fingers.

"You have to take better care of your neck," Sandy said, working his spinal vertebrae.

"I need to practice." Without raising his head, he pointed behind the bar. An eleven-foot tall object resembling an Eiffel tower covered with feathers leaned in a corner. "*Très phallic! N'est pas?* Boom-Boom promised to wire it with flashing lights."

"*Très* too heavy for you." Sandy shook her head as she performed the final strokes of the massage.

"I must win. It will be so fabulous. You'll be the Fantasy Fest Queen and I'll win the Headdress Ball Contest. And a gig singing at Diva's. I'm more beautiful than those drag queens."

She helped Chris slide off the table. "You are a drag queen. And more."

"Performance mixologist!" Chris moved back behind the bar. "The sexiest bartender on Duval." He grabbed two bottles of rum and struck a pose.

"Pina colada, virgin," Sandy requested.

"No problemo. Jerome and I think you must be the only innocent in town. But regardless of your un-Key Westy ways, you'll be our next Fantasy Fest Queen."

"Jerome Oberon, the gallery owner?"

"You think I don't know your classy Euro friend? Jerome and *moi* are promoting your campaign. All you need is a few more donations and *voila!* You are the Queen. Jerome—that cutie." Chris paused and studied her with a cock-eyed grin. "Are you in love with *Monsieur* Jerome, *petit cher?* You can tell me, *moi* girlfriend."

"Jerome is wonderful… but—"

"No magic? I sensed it. *Quel dommage.* Were you ever in love?"

"A long time ago. Just a boy in college. But he's been on my mind the last few days."

"You wish you could find your soulmate?"

"I had a wise teacher who said that sometimes we experience detours, perhaps until we mature enough to meet our soulmate or twin flame. I believed Seva was my soulmate, but that was not to be. I think I'm one of those souls destined to never feel that kind of love in this lifetime."

"*Quel quel dommage.*"

She touched the side of her neck, enjoying the champagne bubble sensation. "Tell me about the contributions."

"Jerome says tonight's campaigning will put you over the top."

"I'm only doing this for charity."

"I know. Show me your publicity picture."

She handed him a flyer. "Ariel painted me and Jerome took photos. My pores still feel caked with gallons of paint." She tried not to look at the revealing image.

"Ariel, our good *amie,* the most psychic psychic in town, predicts your success."

"I trust her predictions and her advice. When I told her my strange tingling feelings returned, she told me to be careful, because there is someone in town I am not ready to meet."

"Don't worry about that. You have many, many *amies*. You will win. They all want to see the *masseuse* with the *magnifique* fingers who paints *quelle bien* coconuts win." He leaned closer. "Will you go *au naturale*?"

"Chris! You know I would not."

He wiggled his hips. "I will lend you one of my G-strings."

"Ariel painted only my face and torso... with my bikini for the pictures. She's trying to convince me that a complete body paintjob is necessary to make a good—pardon the pun—showing. I have seen the naked bodies of half the year-round residents of Key West. Perhaps I will take Ariel's advice."

***

Jeff

That night Jeff guided Corin through the Mallory Square crowd. A bagpiper crossed their path, tuning his raucous instrument. Corin covered her ears. A reggae band snaked past. The last drummer swung his hips to bump Corin and she yelped, "I smell pot!"

"Come on, Corin. This isn't so different from Cambridge crowds," Jeff pleaded. "Let's just enjoy the sunset. Mallory Square's Sunset Celebration is world famous."

"I made reservations for four at the Hyatt. Mickey and Minnie—I mean Oscar and Martha—will be joining us."

"Why those rude people?"

Corin looked happier than she had at any time during their honeymoon cruise. "Oscar sold an immense farm back in Kansas and wants me to invest his profits."

Her skinny black heels wobbled on uneven brick paving stones and she looked at the milling crowd with distaste. In a long black dress with a slit exposing a pale calf, she appeared to have crashed the wrong party.

"Just walk with me a little way. Then we'll head up Front Street to the Hyatt."

"Fine," Corin replied without moving her lips.

It was definitely not fine. "Look at the fire-eater. And a juggler on stilts is coming this way. Did you bring your camera?"

"I will remember this day without photos," she said, as a woman in a feathered costume dragged a leashed chicken across their path. The chicken pecked Corin's leg and Corin shrieked as loud as the chicken.

Jeff led her to a quiet spot where they could watch the cat tamer put his housecats through their act. He watched the cat act while Corin plucked chicken feathers off her dress. One cat jumped through a fiery hoop and Jeff whooped with delight.

"I've seen enough," was Corin's tight-lipped response.

"Look. There's Statue Man." Jeff pointed at a chalky-painted man holding his expression and body motionless as children tried to tease him into breaking his pose. Jeff lowered his voice, "I feel like I'm with Statue Woman." Yet even with Corin in this pissy mood, he felt exceptionally good.

Martha and Oscar waved from the opposite side of the square and Corin said, "Let's go to dinner. I don't think Oscar enjoys this X-rated Disney World any more than I." She sneered as a woman in a string bikini, both sunburned and drunk, swayed past. "I can see a sunset any night."

"I'll be there in a minute," Jeff stalled as Corin careened off, knocking against the stilted juggler who wobbled, swayed, and yelled an obscenity. Between Jeff and the Oscars, a woman, dressed in filmy white, blocked Corin's way and peered into her eyes.

"You may find your love far from here. Would you like your fortune told?"

"I certainly do not." Corin pushed by to the safety of her Kansas friends.

***

Sandy

Sandy and Jerome stood in the shadowed alley behind his Duval Street art gallery. If Fantasy Fest was Key West's Halloween, sunset was the Fourth of July—every night.

Sandy unbuttoned her flowered dress and felt it slide to the ground revealing her painted body. Already embarrassed, she bent down and picked up the dress and stuffed it into her bag.

"I'll put your things in the gallery." Jerome's eyes remained on her. "You look as frightened as a Key deer. Relax. You're beautiful."

The dimming light revealed how Ariel's talent had turned Sandy's body into a silky sea creature. Her breasts shimmered with painted abalone shells and her legs and torso appeared covered in iridescent scales. An ocean wave rose up behind the dolphins tattooed on her chest and crested along her collarbone. Her hair shone with oil and glitter, glowing around her face in subtle pastels like a mer-princess.

"Wow!" Jerome said softly.

"Thanks." She reached up and hung a necklace of plastic beads around his neck.

"Thank you. I think tonight you will need a bodyguard more than a money collector."

He opened a box of flyers. Sandy's photo showed through tangled strings of multi-colored beads ready to be given to contributors. "I want to keep you to myself." He kissed her softly, careful not to smear her paint. "I am sorry if I pushed you into this silly competition. You're so private. The parties I gave to raise money for your candidacy were also good publicity for my gallery. I am selfish, no?"

"I chose to do this. Raising money for island people in need is important to me. If I win I'll be able to select charities that will benefit the most needy. And the parties reminded me how many friends I've made in Key West in just three years." She swallowed. "After my finale..."

"Finale?" Jerome's eyes widened.

"I'm leaving Key West after the festival. Please don't tell anyone."

"But why?"

"Here in Key West, I'm no artist. I give massages and paint dolphins on coconuts. It's time to find a new place. Maybe in the West." Avoiding his gaze, she looked off down the alley to the crowds moving toward Mallory Square.

"Let me help," he said quickly. "Your 'This Ain't Kansas Anymore!' haybale postcards were silly, but gave me an idea. Would you like to travel and photograph hay?"

"Hay art?" She giggled. "Not very sophisticated."

"Haystack shapes are no different than outdoor sculpture. Envision a traveling Heartland of America exhibit featuring photos of hayfields and rural towns. I'd pay for your travel. And..."

"And?" She could see he was thinking as he talked.

"Come to my Los Angeles gallery for a grand show. No obligations. You could stay with me or find your place in the West, far from Key West and coconut dolphins."

"Your offer sounds too good to be true." She let herself imagine traveling alone across the country free to explore and create. It seemed like a dream.

"I'm a promoter. I know the business of art." He stroked her cheek. "But now, it's time to go to the Square." He took a handful of necklaces and began looping them over Sandy's head.

"What are you doing?" she laughed.

"Covering you up," he said, arranging the beads over her breasts.

***

Jeff

Jeff wandered through the crowd, absorbing the cacophony and riotous color and watching happy revelers. When he finally reached the Hyatt and joined Corin, Oscar, and Martha, the dinner conversation revolved around the decadence of Key West and, in particular, the disgusting Fantasy Fest.

"Everything here is tacky!" Corin complained.

"The guidebook says only *Le Oiseau Rouge* has quality art," Martha told her.

Corin sipped her sparkling water. "My brother, Jerry, has galleries in L.A., New York, and Paris. I've heard he's also opening one somewhere in Florida. Probably Palm Beach. But we're not close. We have little in common, but I'm sure his galleries are much more discriminating than anything here."

"This sure ain't Cape Cod," Jeff noted, remembering trips with Sandy to the Cape. Jerry, now successful, seemed to have turned back into a nice guy.

"Why do Key West's town fathers allow bikers and homosexuals to take over?" Oscar said for the fifth time.

"Did you ever consider the homosexuals might be the town fathers," Jeff asked, flatly sipping his rumless punch, "and mothers?" The others ignored him. Jeff was itchy and bored enough to say whatever he thought, even if he embarrassed Corin.

Restless, his gaze roamed the dining room and settled on a Scandinavian-looking couple at the next table. Their pale college-age daughter with neon green hair and black dress faced him. He heard the girl say, "Dad, like, get off my case. I came on this stupid cruise to please you and Mom, but you can't tell me how to dress."

"Ginnie, we let you study in Japan for a year," the prim blonde whined. "Now you must finish college."

"I'm an artist, not an art teacher." The daughter rolled her kohl-blackened eyes and noticed Jeff eavesdropping.

He looked away, but not before he saw her purposely flash her tongue ring. Embarrassed, Jeff excused himself and walked to the edge of the hotel balcony. Bagpipes, reggae, and Jimmy Buffett music swirled in the soft moist air. Mallory Square glowed as the sun slipped behind the horizon. The crowd applauded another spectacular sunset and with a sigh Jeff returned to the table.

Oscar and Martha ordered Key lime pie and coffee. Corin handed the dessert menu back to their waiter. "Oh, that's too rich for us. We're on diets."

Jeff snickered, remembering the frozen Key lime pie on a stick he'd enjoyed on the way back from Zack Taylor Park. Cool, creamy, and tart, and chocolate-covered.

Corin stood. "Since Jeff and I aren't having dessert, we'll just pay our bill and go back to the ship."

"Love birds." Oscar winked.

Corin's mood improved as they left the restaurant. "Tonight we sail for St. Thomas and this time I'll finally get to shop." She shook her head. "Unfortunately, we have to walk through this obscene circus to get back to our ship. I, for one, am ready to see the end of Key—"

"Remember me?" A veiled woman in white stepped between Corin and Jeff. "My friend is running for Queen of the Fantasy Fest." She handed Corin a flyer and dropped a necklace of cheap plastic beads over her head. "I'm a body artist. I painted her."

Corin's inscrutable face skewed. "No thanks." She crumpled the flyer and turned away to grab Jeff's arm.

Jeff jammed his hand into his pants pocket and pulled out three singles and a money clip with a hundred-dollar bill. He thrust all the money at the woman.

Corin jerked him away from the woman and dragged him up the cruise ship ramp. As soon as they boarded, she ripped the beads from her neck and threw them and the balled-up flyer into a trash container. "Why did you give that disgusting woman money?"

"I think you were supposed to make a donation in exchange for the beads," Jeff suggested, wondering why that woman had purposely ignored him. "The woman in white reminded me of Ariel, my artist friend from New Hampshire, but Ariel would have recognized me. Unless she was trying not to see me. Psychics can be even more peculiar than artists."

***

Sandy

Sandy watched the golden sliver of sun dive into the Gulf of Mexico. Hundreds of times she'd stood in Mallory Square as layers of clouds reflected a heavenly impressionist's palette. Tonight she felt as awestruck as any tourist seeing it for the first time as she joined the spontaneous applause cheering nature's art show.

Cat Man waved a salute to Sandy as he stuffed cats into cages, stacked pedestals, and packed up his whips. Fire-eaters stowed wands and fluid into carrying cases. She twisted a batik cloth around her hips as Jerome laid her old denim jacket over her shoulders, then packed up leftover flyers and beads.

Chris chatted with friends from the bar, unabashedly begging a few more dollars for Sandy's campaign. Ariel finished one last cruise ship passenger palm reading. From Ariel's sad expression Sandy suspected the psychic knew Sandy wouldn't be here for many more sunsets.

Tired and happy, Sandy felt the raucous energy dissipate as tourists and locals wandered off into lively bars. Key West had been great fun. In a few days, the parties and parades would be stored in her memories. These were her friends, her community—the scruffy boat people, water-addicted dive instructors, and wasted artists. "This sure ain't Cape Cod," she whispered aloud.

The free flavor of this Conch Republic made the Florida Keys feel like a foreign country. She'd hidden here long enough. Winning would be her gift to the home that had taken her in and loved her.

Jerome rushed up, hugged her, and swung her around. "The committee just announced that you won, *mon cherie*. By just $103! Come back to the Square to be crowned." He reached for her hand to lead her off.

Across the water the floating resort called a ship pulled out of the harbor. Soon she, too, would soon be gone. Another journey. Wondering if she would ever find her own place, she touched her neck, enjoying the intense tingling sensation. She remembered Ariel's warning. It was still not time? When would her time come?

***

Jeff

Jeff left Corin in their upper deck cabin and rushed back down the cruise ship passageway. He ran to the trash container stenciled Gargantuan Princess, where Corin had thrown the flyer and beads. Headfirst, he dove in and rummaged through layers of garbage. Unsuccessful, he crawled out, stood, and emptied the entire contents onto the spotless deck. In the dim light, he used his foot to separate greasy trash. Spotting the necklace and balled-up paper under a rum bottle, he pounced.

He moved to the rail directly under a light, smoothed the paper on the railing, and saw the dolphin drawing. And a photo of Sandy. Rainbow-hued scales flowed over the same beautiful body he'd known twenty years ago. He looked closer, squinting in the light, then noticed the printing: 'Vote Sandy from Laughing Dolphin Massage for Fantasy Fest Queen.' It was her. More beautiful than he remembered. She was smiling. At him.

The deck under his feet rumbled as the leviathan vessel prepared to pull out of the harbor. That feeling of exhilaration he'd experienced since docking in Key West began to dissipate. That tingle which had grown into a sting of sharp needle pricks meant she was here. He'd found her. And—was leaving her.

He slipped off his sandals and pulled himself up onto the polished rail. Standing, he stared at the phosphoresce wake of the giant ship and felt himself falling.

III. 2. Nebraska/Kansas, October, 2001

Sandy

Sandy lay on her belly in the middle of a Nebraska hay-field. Pieces of hay sharp as pins poked through her tight jeans and worn denim jacket. Ignoring the pain and the morning dew soaking her shirt, she angled her camera up at a pyramid of haybales, focused, placed her tongue to the side of her mouth, and refocused. Too late to go back for the tripod, she held her breath and waited for the sun to rise a fraction of a degree.

She loved the solitude of the prairie, golden hay as far as she could see. Leaving Key West she stayed off interstates and on back roads. Exploring the country one mile at a time, she pulled over and photographed any image that intrigued her. These early morning shots were going to be—

"May I help you?" a deep voice asked.

Startled, Sandy's Nikon slipped from her cold fingers. Recovering the camera, she protected its long, heavy lens, rolled onto her side, and pushed up into a sitting position. "Ouch! This hay is prickly!" Her khaki bush hat tumbled off into the damp dirt. She tossed her sun-streaked hair out of her eyes and looked up at a man silhouetted against the sunrise.

237

"I sure can't make the hay soft," the silhouette told her, "but maybe I can help. If you tell me what you're doing here?"

"I know I'm trespassing. I usually ask first. I saw the farmhouse. But the morning light was just so..." Sandy heard herself babbling.

"You're photographing... hay?"

She shaded her eyes. His hair, the exact color of the amber bales, shone in the morning light. She restrained herself from raising her camera and photographing this handsome farmer modeling bright plaid shirt against the golden sunrise. Instead, she carefully filed the bucolic image in her memory. His portrait would become her personal archetypal icon of her heartland show.

Aware his voice had sounded more curious than angry, she answered slowly, "Well, yes. They're beautiful. Like sculpture. But I suppose you wouldn't understand." She gestured at the bales. "You see your cash crop all the time."

He offered his hand. She took it and let him pull her to her feet. She brushed hay from her jeans, pulling out pieces that had pierced the denim and poked her legs and butt. She removed her denim jacket and shook it.

The man waited patiently for her to finish, then reached out his hand again. "Jake McCorry. Jake."

She clasped his strong warm hand. "Alexandria Shellborn. Sandy." She smiled up at him. "I'm a photographer."

Jake held her cool, damp hand until she pulled free. "I see that," he said as he retrieved her hat. "Sorry I spoiled your picture. I was on my way to work. Saw a body lying in the field. Thought I'd check it out."

"I guess I did look pretty silly."

"Not every day I find a beautiful woman under a haystack."

Sandy blushed and looked away from the intensity in his eyes. Behind her SUV and stubby travel trailer she noticed a red pickup and a green tractor next to the fence she'd climbed. "Are you here to plow?"

"You must be a city girl or you'd have noticed the combine baled the last of the crop."

"Nice tractor," she said, imagining Jake sitting on the tractor while she photographed his profile against this clear, blue Nebraska sky.

"Thanks, but it's my dad's. Tractoring's not my part of the business."

"What do you do?"

He grinned. "How about I give you a ride and show you?"

Sandy instinctively liked the slow talking farmer drawn to his quick wit and easy smile. "I'm on assignment to photograph hay—bales, stacks—all the shapes. Morning light is the best."

"Then we'd better hurry." Jake shouldered her camera bag. And before she could reply, was striding back over the lumpy rows towards the road. She ran to keep pace with his long legs.

She drove behind his pickup for a mile until he pulled up next to a domed steel shed and slid open its wide door. Sandy saw an airplane shadowed inside, grabbed her bag, and ran to Jake. "It's an antique plane!"

"My Stearman's a working cropduster," he told her in mock outrage as he pushed the red biplane out of the hangar. "I'll do a quick preflight and you'll be up in the air before the light changes."

"I could photograph the bales from the air!"

"You sure could, City Girl."

Two hours later Sandy looked down at thousands of acres of Nebraska hay. She loved the feeling of freedom in the open cockpit, but appreciated the security of the harness that held her snug in the seat. She was out of film. Four rolls exposed. The rest were in her car. She sighed and touched the silky white scarf Jake had tied around her neck. "Nebraska is so... so flat," she yelled into the mic. Even with the leather helmet and radio, talking in the air was difficult.

"And its hay is so prickly," he teased.

Jake landed and taxied back to the hangar.

She thanked him as he helped her to the ground. "This was perfect. The light was amazing. You flew so low and slow, it felt like hovering. I got great shots."

"Glad I could be of help. This baby's made for tight turns and low passes." He grinned. "But I was good. I didn't fly under any power lines."

Her eyes widened. She hoped he was joking. "What do I owe you?" she asked, untying the scarf.

"Well... I did use a bit of gas and I'm getting a late start on my schedule. The scarf is yours to keep. I'd guess you owe me..." He paused and his eyes looked up as if mentally calculating her bill.

She reached into her bag for her checkbook. She'd been careful with Jerome's advance money, but the photos from this flight would be wonderful. How much could an old plane cost for two hours? Yet, it looked nicely restored and had a small computer monitor and keypad in the cockpit, as well as a Global Positioning System—all very high tech. She'd never thought of chartering a plane and Jake had seemed to know instinctually the best angles for her shots. These photos would be the hit of her show. Whatever Jake charged would be well worth the bill.

***

Jeff

Corin called to Jeff from the kitchen window of their suburban Kansas ranch house, "Fire up the barbeque! Oscar and Martha will be here soon."

Jeff looked up from the metal on his workbench and removed his welder's hood. He smiled at Corin's happy tone. Still a driven businesswoman, moving to Kansas changed his wife into a supportive partner with a positive attitude. That same move allowed him to begin this bodybuilding art form. He'd grown to like good-natured blustering Oscar Weatherhill and enjoyed talking art with Oscar's wife Martha. They'd become kind and generous friends.

Jeff maneuvered the chrome bumper out through the studio door. Sunshine glinted off chrome, reflecting a shiny rainbow. He delighted in the feel of the heavy metal and enjoyed welding substantial hunks into fantastical objets d'art. Some called his work recycled or found art, but he'd paid dearly at auto junkyards for every piece.

His abstract pieces were popular but cows, pigs, and mules sold better around here than lions, bears, and hippos. Corin loved the chrome horse he'd made for her side pasture. His stock of car parts and rusted farm equipment didn't seem fitting for delicate nudes, but he'd experimented with almost everything else. Oscar had commissioned a draft horse and a tractor that once completed would take a crane to move, but he wanted to finish an eagle first. And he'd sketched a new series of whirligigs.

Taking a satisfied breath, he leaned against the half-completed dinosaur and watched Corin walk across the patio. He admired her strong stride and the way her black jeans hugged her fit body. The red shirt was a cheerful reminder she was no longer so serious and moving here had been a good

decision. Neither considered a return to city life. Her investment business was such a financial success, she no longer
needed his help.

Corin put her arm around his waist and they stood in
front of the barn that had become his fulltime art studio.
"Nice."

"Thanks. Just five more bumpers and I'll be finished."

"I mean you. You feel good. Healthy again. Trying to
jump off that cruise ship… I thought I'd lost you."

"I admit I was a little crazy for a while. Lifting auto parts
agrees with me." He leaned down and polished the chrome of
another bumper. "This one's from an old Dodge."

"I'm glad you're back to your arty stuff. I don't understand art, but that piece you sold for $4,000 was very nice.
Soon my brother will be begging to put your junk in his gallery." She looked at the abstract pieces that waited for buyers
in the sculpture garden in their side yard. "Don't forget you
promised to paint an art hayfield mural in my office."

"Just don't tell your clients I'm in the faux decorating
business." Corin's reconciliation with her twin brother had
helped both of them let go of a lot of anger. They had plans to
visit Jerome in Los Angeles.

"Let's get those steaks going." Jeff placed his arm around
Corin's shoulders and turned her back towards the house. "I
hear the Weatherhills' truck."

"Hi ho, kids," Oscar called, helped Martha out of their
Caddy SUV, and headed to the ranch house door.

Corin smiled at their matching red-checked shirts. "Come
on in. Drink?"

"Postitutely!" said Oscar as he strutted out the sliding
doors to find Jeff.

Martha followed Corin to the spacious kitchen and
poured three frozen margaritas while Corin got a root beer for

Jeff. "This ten-acre ranchero is precious. Can't believe it was once Oscar Senior's soybean field."

"Compared to Boston, real estate here is a bargain," Corin told her as they carried the drinks out to the men. "We have so much land."

Jeff expertly slid four thick steaks onto their built-in gas grill.

"To Corin and Jeff," toasted Oscar. "I'm pleased as a pig in petunias you two are here."

"How could I refuse?" Corin raised her glass. "All your friends as clients in my brokerage firm was too positutely good to pass up."

"Us dumb farm boys needed a hotshot to manage our money." Oscar clinked his glass against hers. "I'm sure Jeff was a fine broker, but his artistic constructions will make him famous. Turned me into a fancy art collector. A real a-fish-in-ad-oo." He nodded. "Got him away from all that liberal Boston thinking. No wonder he acted crazy on the cruise. I thought he'd gone round the bend when he flew back to Key West as soon as you two got home. But, you're here now, right here in Rancho El Rancho Estates."

"Moving to Kansas was the best thing that could have happened to us." Corin sighed. "Now Jeff and I have another surprise. Follow me."

The four walked to Jeff's two-story barn studio and Corin pointed to a wooden addition. Martha squealed. An elegant thoroughbred mare extended her sleek black neck over the corral fence to nuzzle Corin.

"She's just four years old," Corin said. "I'm re-naming her Osmara in honor of my good friends."

Jeff grinned. "I'm so proud of Corin and her riding lessons." He noticed Corin didn't even grimace at her horse drool-splashed shirt.

"Nice rig," Oscar said, admiring the shiny black and white horse trailer with 'Osmara' painted in elegant script on the side. "Calls for another toast."

Back on the patio, as Oscar refilled glasses, Corin's thin lips opened into a wide smile. "Riding is something I always wanted to do and Jeff loves being a full time artist. We don't miss Boston one bit."

"I have news, too." Martha snorted. "I know you city folk think I'm just an ignorant yokel. But I was an emerging artist when I met Oscar."

Jeff laughed. "Now that you're chairing the Delphinus Foundation board you have an important voice in the art community. And I have more time for art."

"And I thank you for that." She blushed. "An old friend is in town next week for a gallery opening. I told him about my brilliant stockbroker and her artist husband. Ta dah! Monday you two have a meeting with McCorry."

"You know J.J. McCorry?" asked Jeff, remembering his old friend's father.

Martha nodded.

"Who's J.J. McCorry?" asked Corin.

"Just an internationally famous artist with works in the National Gallery, the Met—every major museum in the world," Jeff explained.

"A painter?" asked Corin.

"J.J. has oils, bronzes, and stone sculpture in exclusive galleries in all the fanciest cities," Martha said proudly. "He even teaches ice sculpture."

Jeff stared at Martha. "He's your old chum?"

Martha turned her back to Oscar and whispered, "As they say, we were close. He's famous now, but in the old days we shared a loft. He went to Paris and I came to Kansas and became a decorator."

"He's coming here?" Jeff felt as nervous as a kid trying out for the major leagues. "I'd love for him to look at my sketches for future projects."

Martha smiled. "He has some local festival this weekend, but he'll be arriving by private plane Monday for a business meeting with Corin. And to look at your art pieces."

Corin nodded. "That's perfect. Sunday, we're taking Ossy to a country fair horse show. Nora, my riding instructor, entered us in Beginners Adult Class. Thank goodness, my Ossy is a pro."

***

Sandy

Sandy followed Jake into a long silver torpedo of a building called the Hay Country Diner. "When will you tell me how much I owe you for the flight?"

"First, we need food. We've both been up since dawn."

From behind the counter a hair-netted woman in a purple apron yelled, "Jake, you and your lady friend sit wherever you want," as she rang up a sale, "Cha-ching!"

He led Sandy to a booth by the front window. She couldn't stop thinking about this morning's aerial shots, certain they would be the best of her entire trip. The wall phone near the cash register reminded her she'd promised to call Jerome. For months she'd sent rolls of film to him in L.A. When they talked by phone, he praised her work and told her his gallery manager already sold enough images to stock photo suppliers to cover her expenses. In their last conversation he explained that her Heartland Show would travel to all his galleries and he wanted her to appear at each opening. She'd again discouraged his request to visit, saying she needed to totally concentrate on her work while the fall weather held.

Jake ordered corn fritters and buckwheat pancakes and while they waited for their food, she leaned back against the crunchy, red plastic seat. She felt comfortable with Jake, as if they'd known each other forever, and soon she was telling him more about her past than she'd revealed in years.

He sat quietly and smiled, not touching the food, watching her devour light corn fritters and steal bites of his pancakes.

Wiping her mouth with a thin paper napkin, she asked, "Why so quiet? What are you thinking?"

"Thinking I haven't been this happy with anyone, ever," he said softly.

"You hardly know me." The intensity in his eyes hinted that he did know her well.

"Some things can't be measured in ordinary time. Sometimes you just know."

Their waitress stepped up with perfect timing. "I'm Sammie," she introduced herself to Sandy and started rattling off the list of desserts starting with fruit cup, Jell-O, layer cake, yellow, white, and chocolate. She finished by reciting ten of the fifteen kinds of pie until Jake held up his hand for her to stop. Sandy ordered Key lime and he ordered the apple pie.

Sandy looked behind the counter at the glass fronted pie cabinet and noticed twenty-eight oversized decorated cups on a high shelf. She wondered if they were reproductions from that silly vagina show that made news ten years ago. Sammie resembled the artist she'd met in South Dakota, only older, heavier, and much happier. But famous artists don't run diners in Nebraska.

"Stop. I'll never get off the ground again." Jake looked at Sandy who made an I'm-full gesture. "Just the check."

Before Jake went back to personal thoughts, she said firmly, "Tell me the price of the flight!"

"The way I figure…" Jake scribbled numbers on a napkin. "Bring more film and meet me back here tonight and we'll be square."

"What?"

"I'd like to take you up again right before sunset. Would that light be good for pictures?"

"Oh yes, wonderful. But what do I owe you?"

"Another flight." His gaze pleaded. "Please stay in town. A town twenty miles north is having a hay festival. Opens tomorrow. Let me take you. A couple of years ago some yokel farmers started a hay sculpture contest."

"You're kidding. I thought bales were stacked in different ways for fun or because that was the way it had always been done."

"Not exactly. This year there are thirty-five official entries. And lots of farms have stacks and funny signs in their fields along Highway 88 into town. It's turned into a big country fair of hay." He winked. "Great local color for a photographer."

"Sounds wonderful!"

"Does that mean we have a date?"

"Where's the town?"

"I won't tell you. You might go without me."

***

Jeff

Jeff cheered with the rest of the horse show crowd as, with a flourish, the judge pointed to Corin on her smart black mare.

"Corin won! Corin won!" Nora screamed in Jeff's ear. She hugged him and jumped up and down. "Her first horse show. She won her class!"

"Huh!" Jeff's breath rushed out in a grunt. He wondered how many ribs the trainer had cracked.

Nora released Jeff, then ducked between the fence poles and ran to the center of the showring. Jeff watched the chunky horse trainer lope off in her tight jeans and floppy shirt. Reaching Corin, Nora grasped Ossy's bridle and yelled for a photographer.

Through a break in the crowd Jeff saw Nora pose horse and rider and help the judge attach the blue ribbon. The photographer hunkered down and threw a white handkerchief into the air. Ossy's head perked up and he snapped.

Nora led the horse and rider off while Jeff ran around the outside to the ring exit and followed them.

Back at the trailer, Corin squealed, "Oh Jeff. I really won. My first time."

"Congratulations. I'm so proud of you." Jeff hugged her, smelling musky horse mixed with her sweat.

"Ossy was perfect, just like Nora said."

***

Sandy

The next morning, Jake drove Sandy to the Haycock Fair in his truck. He'd flown the Stearman over earlier, but insisted he wanted her to see it all from the ground first. Five miles outside of Haycock traffic slowed. Sandy gawked at decorated bales lining the road. Stuffed jeans stuck out of one bale like the legs of an octopus. Next a sign propped below a giant fist read 'Haymaker Acres.'

"Wait 'til you see the official contest entries," Jake told her when she asked to stop to photograph the funny signs. "You can take pictures of these on our way back."

As they entered the town, a banner hung across Main Street: 'Hayseeds Gone Haywire—Haycock, Nebraska—Hay Capital of the World."

"Hey, Harry!" Jake called to a man in bib overalls with clumps of hay sticking out his pant legs and shirt sleeves. The scarecrow man approached Jake's pickup. "Howdy, Jake," he drawled, "who's the little lady?" looking in at Sandy and tipping his frayed straw hat.

"Visiting photographer," Jake told him.

"I thought you were the only daguerreotypist in these parts."

Sandy's mouth opened.

"Sandy Shellborn's in charge of this shoot. I'll help with ground shots this morning and later we'll take the aerials. All I do is fly the plane."

Sandy was still speechless when Jake pulled into the County Fairgrounds and parked next to a sign that read "Hay Rides—Adults $5—Children $2."

"Jake, why didn't you tell me you were—?"

"You didn't ask." He got out and reached behind his seat for a worn leather camera bag. "We'll have fun. Photograph the sculpture entries, some of the artists, and the crowd. Besides the usual colorful locals, city people from Omaha and Kansas City drive in, and there's tons of kids. Locals sell great pies, cakes, and produce in the big red barns. Artsy-crafty things in the back. The parade starts at noon and at one the mayor awards prizes."

"This is big." Sandy grinned. "No wonder you need an assistant."

The loud speaker blared, "Photographer to the show ring."

"I'm also one of the horseshow photographers, so I've got to check in with the judges. Why don't you look around?" He pointed. "I'll find you later."

She watched him walk away, great-looking in white shirt and long, snug jeans and much more than the simple farmer she had imagined. Being with Jake made her smile. His light happy manner made her as comfortable as if she'd known him all her life.

In the shadow of the grain elevator, she set down her bag and removed her camera, changed lenses, and clasped the bag closed with her carabiner key ring. She rubbed her lucky pink plastic dolphin, a souvenir from Virginia Beach. This had been a very lucky day.

She entered the nearest long red barn and passed jams and jellies, 4-H hay dolls in calico dresses, and baskets woven of hay. At the far end in the Fine Arts Exhibit she browsed the watercolor, quilt, and whittling sections. She walked closer to a group of matte black and white photos of barns and aerial shots to see the name, J.J. (Jake) McCorry, Jr. On the back wall she noticed a few small oil paintings. She stepped closer and read the name. Wasn't that the name of the artist who critiqued her student show in Boston? Aloud she said, "J.J. McCorry!"

"Yes," answered a voice behind her. She turned and faced the lanky scarecrow.

"You're J.J—? Jake's father?"

"At your service, ma'am." He bowed, sweeping off the straw hat to reveal silver-streaked blond hair.

"You're famous!" Sandy sputtered.

"Around here folks just think I'm crazy. 'Course during Hay Week, I'm ol' Harry Hayseed."

He led her outside to show her the sculpture entries. When they stood at a ship's rail made of hay looking at two breaching fifteen-foot whale tails, he told her, "This is what I call the seaside section. Some of us flatlanders miss the ocean so much we sculpt hay into water themes."

Sandy grinned. "Like a whale watch off Gloucester!" She closed her eyes and imagined ocean spray on her neck, then realized the tingling felt like evaporating moisture. She hadn't experienced this strange sensation since Key West. Her eyes flew open as two boys with squirt guns jostled past her toward the castle maze.

***

Jeff

When Corin and Nora began to groom Ossy for the next class, Jeff walked off to see the displays. The atmosphere of this fair energized him. Entering the Arts & Crafts Building, he wandered down the main aisle past 4H exhibits into the Arts section. He stopped next to a gangly teenager staring at a portrait of a young woman. A purple rosette hung from the corner of the canvas.

"Nice work," Jeff said softly.

The boy whipped around. "You think so, mister?"

"Yes, I do." Jeff smiled. "Your painting?"

"Yeah. My girlfriend, CarolAnn."

"Pretty."

"Sure is. Beautiful."

"You an art student?"

"Freshman at NU. The campus has the most amazing large—I mean really humungous—sculpture. I love walking around there. That's what I'd wanted to do..." He hung his head and his voice trailed off.

Jeff nodded, sensing what the boy would say next.

The boy set his jaw. "I'm switching majors. From Art to Ag. To run the farm. Dad says I'll never make any money doing art." Then added defiantly, "But look at J.J. McCorry! That's his stuff on the back wall."

Jeff stepped to the back corner and looked at three small oil paintings. The index card read 'J.J. McCorry. Exhibition Only.'

"He makes a lot of money. So does his son, J.J. Jr. Jake's a big time aerial photographer. Flies all over." The boy lowered his head.

Jeff smiled, pleased to hear his old friend had found his way back to Nebraska, his father, and his art. He turned to the boy, reached out and tilted the kid's chin level. "If you love art, find a way to make it your life." Jeff's advice to the boy echoed in his head. He'd strayed far from his original dream of art, but found his way back. Every step taught him something about life that would forever be reflected in his art. Right now his art was commercial, experimental, and so much fun to create. He'd never have been able to build these whimsical sculptures as a boy. That art student was too serious about art and too casual about life. He was beginning to get things straight. Corin had taught him financial success was not to be scorned, but put to use.

Yet looking at this young man, a part of him yearned to be that age again. To have the chance to hold on to Sandy, the woman he would forever think of as the lost love of his life.

The boy stared at Jeff, then asked, "You an artist?"

"It's in my blood. Don't leave it for too long." He paused, looking at the sad young man, "Or CarolAnn." Then he handed him his Delphinus card. "If you need a scholarship, call this number."

Jeff walked out of the barn considering the advice he gave the farm boy. He rubbed the side of his neck. That tingle was back, the one he felt in Key West when he'd thought he'd found Sandy.

He walked past hay sculptures to an enormous hay maze built like a castle. The bales were piled fifteen feet high and a sign stated the maze was constructed of fifty round and two hundred rectangular bales. He walked up the wooden bridge, over an imaginary moat, and through the arch of tied sheaves of hay.

Inside the maze, every turn he picked became a dead end. Like his life. He'd made choices and some choices chose him. He headed in a new direction and heard children's voices on the other side of the bale wall. With a laugh, he crawled into a hollowed cylindrical bale tunnel. Hay poked through his jeans into his knees. Two raucous boys brandishing squirt guns scrambled up behind him, sprayed him with water, and raced ahead. He chased them, laughing, tumbling, and rolling with the boys until all three reached the end, where the horizontal bale tunnel dead-ended into an upwards slanting hollowed bale. The boys scampered up the bale, scaled the wall, and with a kick of sneakers disappeared over the edge.

Jeff lay back, breathed in the sweet earthy scent of drying hay, and looked up at a circle of blue Nebraska sky surrounded by a round window frame of hay. Resting, his artist's eye savored the perfection of the picture.

A buzz disturbed his contemplation. A red biplane bisected his flawless circle of sky. It reminded Jeff of the old cropduster Jake wanted to own someday. Jeff stood and waved at the plane like a kid waving to a train engineer. As the plane turned and again passed directly overhead, an object spiraled slowly down and fell next to him. He bent down and dug into the hay and pulled out a carabiner with a plastic dolphin as the sole attachment. Rubbing the worn doodad, he felt inspired.

Jeff climbed up out of the bale and stood on top of the hay castle parapet. He saw the plane disappearing in the distance, the hay sculptures, crowds below entering the fair buildings, and the horse show ring. His neck itched like he'd developed an allergic reaction to hay.

He climbed down the outside of the maze and wandered through the hay sculpture competition, admiring light-hearted creativity crafted in a temporary medium. Some bales had been piled into shapes and spray-painted. Others, like the dolphin jumping out of a pig trough, were built on topiary bases. Sheaves of hay brushed into waves moved in the breeze around another very happy looking dolphin. The sign read 'Art today. Feed tomorrow.'

On his way back to the midway he saw the scarecrow man in front of a breaching whale surrounded by a crowd of giggling children.

As Jeff walked past, the scarecrow man waved. "Enjoying yourself?"

Grinning, Jeff pointed at the whale's fluke. "Haven't had this much fun since my last Gloucester whale watch."

***

Sandy

That night Sandy and Jake worked side by side developing fifteen rolls of film. She almost forgot the flutter building in her neck. The last time it was this strong was right before her life changed in Key West. A stereo played and Sandy hummed along with Elton John's 'Candle in the Wind.'

Finishing the work, they continued talking in the dark. It had been late when Jake drove up and led her into his dark-room. Excited to develop her photos, she hadn't noticed much about the tall narrow building. "Where are we?"

"The first floor of my new house. I renovated an old silo. An apartment is on the second and my studio on the third." He flicked on a light and pointed to his computer and software setup for digital processing. "I'll show you my silo. But first tell me more about your hay photographing travels. I never met a hay artist."

"A gallery's sponsoring me. I bought an SUV and a little travel trailer and started wandering from Florida. For almost a year Jerome, the gallery owner, has been developing and selling stock photos of festivals and farms. Small town stuff."

"An expensive trip?"

"Not with my own trailer. During 9/11, alone out here in the country's heartland, I felt as safe as I could be, by myself." She paused, realizing the initial solitude of solo travel had lost its allure. "It's been great. Only wished I had a dark room. With a setup like yours, I could do everything myself and send digital images to Jerome. I'd be in control of the whole pro-cess."

"It would be perfect. But tell me, Sandy." He placed a hand on each of her shoulders. "Where do you go from here? For the winter?"

"I'll head south and find a place to paint. My trailer's too cramped for an easel."

"What if…" He swallowed. "What if there was a place… a studio for you… here?" Jake pulled her close in the dim light.

She wasn't listening. All she could see were his sky blue eyes. She inhaled. As he held her, she relaxed and breathed out. As he lowered his lips, she turned her face up. His kiss enveloped her in a cocoon of warmth and happiness, excitement and contentment. He pressed her closer and ripples of pleasure flowed through her. For the first time in a long time she felt content.

"Come upstairs," he asked.

His voice sounded shy but she knew he meant more. If she followed him it would have to mean more to her, too. "I just met you." She picked up her bag, hoping to signal she was ready to leave.

"Sometimes, you just know," his voice teased as he replaced the bag on the table.

She took his hand. She didn't want to leave.

He led her to a spiral staircase and drew her after him into the dark. On the second level she saw outlines of furniture and a kitchen. He kept climbing. Halfway up the second flight, Jake whispered, "Close your eyes," and clasped her hand tighter. They reached the third floor. He drew her next to him and guided her across the wooden floor.

"Now?" she asked when he stopped, "can I open my eyes?"

"Yes."

Eyes open, Sandy stood next to Jake looking out into the night sky. She twirled. The round room's walls were all glass. She saw millions of stars, infinite layers, on and on, forever. "Is this place heaven?"

"It's your studio."

***

Three months later Sandy stood in the sunlight that streamed in through the silo's windows. Every morning she woke loving Jake more. After their breakfast she couldn't wait to begin work on her latest oil painting.

Jake understood her artist's heart. But he had the playful spirit of a man who experienced the world and had chosen his perfect life. His joy in flying and photography was infectious. Every day he reminded her that life and art should be fun and she'd discovered new ways of connecting with her creative soul. And rediscovered the joy in living. This stark Nebraska plain energized her in ways sunny island life had not.

Jake was so much in love with her. She wondered if he loved her too much. More than she could ever return.

From the window she saw him close the hangar. Minutes later he rushed into the silo and ran up the stairs. "What a wonderful day." Still cold from the frosty air he threw his cap on the chair and swept Sandy into his arms. He smelled like home.

Happy and safe, she pulled back and pointed to the oil painting on her easel. "See what I've been working on. The light from last night's sunset was surreal. I've captured the glow over the fields. I want to paint your plane into the painting."

"Told you you'd love winter in Nebraska. But first I have something for you." He fumbled in his jacket pocket. "My dad gave this to me. J.J. bought it a long time ago in Boston for an artist he loved. It's not much, but he said it's filled with dreams that need to be fulfilled." He handed her a small scuffed velvet box.

She opened the box and stared at a delicate rose gold ring with intricate gold filigree and a sparkling yellow diamond. She pressed her lips together, not trusting her words. It could mean a gift. A promise. Or more. Jake's grin conveyed the meaning very clearly.

"I love you," he whispered in her ear. "I've been waiting for you all my life."

***

Tomorrow would be New Year's Day. A new day and a new year. Working with Jake the artist and loving Jake the man the last months had been beautiful. They worked together with discipline and played with high spirits. Jake's non-competitive nature ignited her creative energy. She was crazy about the idea that this man who put her first was madly in love with her.

Jake too had turned his back on his artistic passion but returned to be a better artist. She was certain her work as a massage therapist gave her a deeper understanding of the human body and a feeling for human emotion she'd never have achieved strictly as an artist. And what of her life in the library and business world? Although painful to think of who she'd been during those years, stuck in a way of thinking that tolerated no space for emotion or art, part of that life reflected back in the discipline of her current work.

She cringed at the memories of her disastrous first marriage and her affair with Barry. Neither man allowed her to be a truer person. She'd needed to grow up before she could love someone. Jake was her soulmate who'd travelled a parallel path to find a joyful reunion with art. With him she'd be able to reconnect with that girl she'd been with Jeff.

She needed to go forward. She was an artist again, in love with an amazing man. Jake told her how he rejected art. He shared how his parents' obsession with art made him feel like a less important creation. But his own passion to create never left. He told her he even built sand sculpture. And later when life drew him to New Hampshire he lived with a great bunch of artists, but avoided doing art until one guy had an accident. Then Jake borrowed a camera from a friend. As soon as he touched that camera, he felt that it became a part of him, an extension of his imagination.

She loved his story about that friend who later bought him an airplane to combine his two loves. Photography and flying. When she asked if that was dangerous, he explained mounts let him control angles after barnstorming and cropdusting taught him to fly low with precision.

They'd traveled to museums in Kansas City and St. Louis, attended J.J.'s Chicago gallery opening, and visited her father in Boston. J.J. was a dear and reminded her of her supportive father. Both knew when to offer advice and when to just praise. She never asked him about the students he critiqued in Boston and he didn't seem to recognize her name. She only smiled when he criticized malevolent critics who threw cold water on promising artists' spirits instead of letting them bloom. The three artists energized each other. J.J.'s sculpture found renewed vigor. Jake began to paint again. And Sandy created a new media by mixing oil paints with natural materials. They'd begun to discuss collaborating on a three-person show.

The phone rang. She gulped a mouthful of air, fearing it was Jerome. He'd threatened to come to Nebraska and see what was holding her there, but when he found out she was working with the McCorrys, he decided the benefit to her career outweighed his concerns.

"Sandy, thank goodness you finally answered the phone." Jerome's voice was breathless, with no sign of a French accent. "I missed you over the holidays. It's New Year's Eve. I could catch a flight and be in Kansas City by midnight. Please, meet me there. We could—"

"Jerome, I truly care for you. You have done so much for me, but..."

"What's wrong?"

"I've decided to stay in Nebraska. Permanently. I'll come to L.A. for the opening and appear at your other galleries as I agreed." She could feel his pain over the silent phone. "I'm sorry." She felt sad, but free now the words had been said.

259

She didn't tell him she and Jake planned a spring wedding and. J.J. booked them a Paris honeymoon. "I'm happy. This is the life I've been meant to live."

He wished her well, but his tone lacked sincerity. She could tell he wanted to convince her he could offer more.

The phone line cracked. She saw a storm approaching. Racing black clouds formed a heavy front across the northern sky. Normally, she loved watching storms from the silo studio, but today Jake had planned to fly back from a shoot near Lincoln and she prayed he'd stayed safely on the ground.

As the ominous storm approached, she watched Jake's red plane appear over frozen wheat fields and smiled as it flew closer, bringing Jake home. Suddenly the plane wobbled and teetered sideways. Jake was struggling to keep the plane on a level course. A downdraft pushed the plane like a toy. It surged up again. She watched Jake's plane approach the landing strip. Almost home.

The plane was fifty feet off the runway. He would land and all would be fine. Jake would be home.

Without warning, lightning shot from a roiling black thunderhead. In slow motion, the bolt jagged towards the ground, then detoured sideways and hit Jake's plane. Sandy closed her eyes. The rumble of thunder and the explosion reached her ears at the same time. With a cry she dropped the phone.

III. 3. Los Angeles, California, 2002

Sandy

Sandy looked out the thirty-foot wide window of Jerome's Malibu beach house. A narrow strip of beige sand divided his deck from the indigo Pacific Ocean. Behind her, sand footprints trailed a path across white Berber carpet. She shivered. "This ocean is cold, that's all. I'll be fine."

"Sandy, *ma cherie*, I want you to be happy, like Key West, only better." Jerome came up behind her, folded his arms around her, wrapping a plush bath sheet over her wet bathing suit and nuzzled a shivering ear.

She pulled away and snapped, "This isn't the Keys. This is L.A. and the other ocean." Every time he touched her she remembered those few nights back in Key West. Jerome's neediness so different from her months of happiness with Jake. Both men had professed to adore her, but Jake truly selflessly wanted the best for her.

"Tell me what's wrong," Jerome pleaded. "Since you got here, nothing I've done has pleased you."

"L.A. just isn't my—"

"Try, *cherie*. Look. Your *magnifique* gown!" He held up a plastic garment bag, unzipped the cover, and revealed a gold metallic evening dress with a long stiff-pleated skirt and rigid strapless bodice.

Sandy turned away. Jerome even sounded more French in L.A.

"This designer is the absolute best in Hollywood. I told him I wanted you to look like the ultimate American golden girl. A golden sheaf of ripe wheat. And look." He opened a shoe box and held up matching shoes with one-inch platform soles with metallic Mary Jane ties.

"I'm an artist. Not a Tinseltown star. Or a damn bundle of wheat."

"I know. But this is the opening of your first show. Tonight you are the star. " He sighed. "Please smile, *cherie.*"

"Sorry. It's not your fault. It's me."

Jerome's eyes looked deep into hers. "You think of him? That guy in Iowa."

"Nebraska!" Sandy turned away.

"You refuse to talk about him. He was your friend, *non?*" Jerome nodded, reaching for her shoulders.

"So much more." Her eyes moistened. She would not turn back and let Jerome see her cry. Not again.

"You didn't know him long. Consider your career. J.J. McCorry wants to see you before the opening. I told him we would meet him for coffee on the way to the gallery, after you're finished at the salon. Having him attend is quite the coup. How fortuitous your friend in Idaho... Nebraska had a world famous father. You must help me convince him to let my gallery handle his works in L.A." He paused and laid his hand on her cool shoulder. "Don't you care?"

"It's not that." Sandy brushed off his hand and his words. She'd told Jerome little about her time with Jake and Jake's famous artist father. She couldn't expect him to understand how she'd found a man who loved her... and a home and family, only to see it explode before her eyes.

"And your friend, Chris, the cross-dresser guy called. She, or he, is in town with Ariel, the psychic body painter, and they'll be at the opening. Your Florida friends will lighten your spirits, *n'est pas?*"

Sandy shivered. "I need a hot bath."

***

Jeff

Jeff stood in line at the Ventura Boulevard Starbucks closest to his studio. Out the window he could see two more Starbucks. Only in L.A. The excitement some experienced here eluded him. This was the first place he'd freely chosen in all his life. When he and Corin split he could have gone any-where. He'd anticipated a fresh perspective and a new begin-ning. For a while it had been like that. But now, a year after leaving Kansas he felt stuck. He was producing interesting metal art but it wasn't enough.

"What side of the street is this?" a tall, older man in the front of the line asked the wispy boy behind the counter.

"Like, this side!"

"I mean east or west?"

The boy wiped his hands on his green apron. "Duh? I'm a barista, not a tour guide."

The man closed his eyes. His lips shaped the words, "One, two..."

Jeff stepped up. "J.J. McCorry?"

"Do I know you?" J.J.'s face softened and he reached out his hand. "Of course. You're that Kansas bumper sculpture guy. Exceptional chrome dolphins. Imagine meeting you in

L.A." J.J. shook Jeff's hand warmly. "I think I'm in the wrong Starbucks. The wrong world." He laughed at himself. "It's been a rough year. My son…" J.J.'s face skewed with pain.

"Sorry for your loss. I knew Jake when we shared a house in New Hampshire."

"He told me you helped him learn to fly. And bought him a plane." J.J. grimaced. "I should have given him that. It meant so much to him. And it ended his life, too soon. For so long I foolishly worried he'd waste his talent."

Jeff didn't let go of the older man's hand.

"An accident. They tell me I need to talk about it more. And accept." Then quickly added, "Who the hell are 'they,' anyway?"

Jeff held J.J's hand between his until a thin young woman with burgundy-splashed hair stepped up. "This is Ginnie Ostergard," Jeff introduced her, draping his arm around Ginnie's narrow shoulders and hoping J.J. wouldn't think he was just another horny middle-aged guy with a woman young enough to be his daughter. "She's a manga artist." Her look was pure punk, but there was a delightfully real quality about this savvy young artist. When they first met, the hip art student with too much eye makeup reminded him of Sandy, but this confident woman was an original. And what she'd done best was remind him of who he wanted to be.

"Japanese comic books?" J.J. looked back and forth between Jeff and the girl in the black tube top and thigh-high black boots. "In my day as an art student, only oil and bronze were considered real art."

The girl smiled, widening her dark eyes, which accented with smoky shadow appeared to cover half her face. "I studied in Japan. Now I concentrate on incorporating manga into monumental sculpture." Her mouth twisted into an engaging pixie grin, showing off a silver tongue ring. "Maybe just to make up for my size."

They laughed and J.J. asked Jeff, "What brings you to the Coast?"

"I have a studio here now." Jeff handed him a card.

"But your wife?" J.J. avoided looking at the big-eyed young woman.

"Ex-wife. Corin and I are still great friends. She'll be in town next week for the L.A. Horse Show. She's become quite a horsewoman."

J.J. still looked confused.

"It's okay, really." Jeff's head bobbed. "She needed a new life. We both needed a new life. She and Nora, her horse trainer, are happy, together. Corin's investment skills made the Delphinus Foundation a success and made my new studio here possible." He swallowed. "Ginnie and I call our studio Form, Fire and Furnace."

"That's great. I'd love to talk more. I'm meeting a…" He paused. "A friend at Starbucks. I'm late. And really need a cup of coffee." He looked out the window. "I think I'm supposed to be at that Starbucks across the street. L.A. is senseless." He patted Jeff's shoulder. "Come to my show," he said as he pressed two tickets into Jeff's hand. "I'll visit your studio."

Jeff and Ginnie took their coffees to a tiny front table. Jeff leaned his back against the window and sipped his venti low-fat cappuccino with an extra shot.

When J.J. crossed to an identical Starbucks and greeted a tall man in black jeans and turtleneck and a woman in a gold evening gown, Ginnie mused, "Wonder who they are? That woman must be famous. An evening gown in Starbucks in the afternoon! I love L.A.! The dress is ugly, but the guy looks hot. Think they're artists?"

Without looking up, Jeff replied, "Artists aren't famous like that." Coffee in his left hand, the fingers of his right rubbed his tingling neck.

"Artists aren't all anonymous! And don't have to be." Ginnie noticed him kneading his neck. "Are you okay?"

"Don't worry, just a tingle."

"I'll work on it later. You do too much lifting without enough stretching." Ginnie kissed his cheek and raised her espresso macchiato with extra whipped in a mock toast. "Jeff. This is not just hooking up. We were meant to be together. Like we've known each other for years and years." She wiped a dollop of cream from the tip of her nose. "Too bad there's someone between us."

"Don't be silly." He shook his head. "There's no one else. I'm just too old to fall in love, that way. You know artists, we only love our work."

***

Sandy

Sandy and Jerome met J.J. at the Starbucks entrance and guided him to a small table under blue painted pipes. Sandy took the most inconspicuous corner, hoping her gaudy gold dress would blend into the coffee shop's mustard walls.

"What'll you have?" Jerome asked.

"Just a small decaf. I am so wired." Sandy looked at J.J., who seemed older and more fragile among the too-thin-to-be-healthy black clad young patrons.

"Something strong," J.J. told him.

As Jerome walked to the counter, J.J. took Sandy's hand. "Are you okay?"

"I'm... I'm... I miss Jake so much." She pressed her lips together to keep back tears.

"Me too. He loved you. And I love you like a daughter."

Sandy willed back the tears brimming in her eyes. "I was truly happy with Jake. And then he was gone."

"Some people are only part of our lives for a short time. I lost my first love and I lost Jake's mother. And now, my son. But I believe they were in my life for a purpose."

"I learned to love from Jake. I learned love could be the grandest work of art. He was so real. So good. I think it takes a while to become a person capable of loving, truly loving. Your son…" She looked away from J.J., trying hard to hold back tears. She couldn't tell him she thought she hadn't loved Jake enough. That he loved better. That he gave more of himself than she gave back to him. "Here in this frenetic city with its flashy people and pretentious art scene, there seems no place for love. It's all just a stupid game. Oh J.J., how do you do it?"

"I choose to play the art game only with people who have a real streak. Then I run back home." He squeezed her fingers. "Come back to Nebraska. It can be your home."

"I know, but without Jake…" She rubbed her neck.

"I understand. You need to find your own place." He noticed her gesture and looked concerned.

"I'm fine. That hair stylist pulled and fussed so much she must have given me a sore neck. This show is important for Jerome's gallery. It's not just for me." Sandy carefully dabbed a tear. "I'm forbidden to mess my makeup." She rubbed the strange champagne bubble sensation on the left side of her neck.

Jerome returned juggling three cups. "A tall decaf Frappuccino with cinnamon and double whipped for the lady, a grande DoubleShot Caffé Americano for J.J., and a plain old venti latte *pour moi*."

J.J. took a sip. "Good strong coffee. Thank you. You speak the language."

Jerome grinned. "No harder than learning English or talking to women." He took a long swallow, then jumped up to greet an art critic at another table.

J.J. leaned toward Sandy. "Jerome's not a bad man," he whispered, "though I swear his Parisian accent is by way of South Boston."

"Jerome is fine," she giggled and whispered back as Jerome returned. "It's me. I'm not myself."

J.J. finished his coffee and stood. "I hate to rush off. I'm meeting friends. I'll see your show tomorrow, after the crowds."

"Bring your friends to the opening, today," Jerome offered.

"They're from Kansas. On their way to Disneyland."

Sandy hugged J.J. and leaned back against the gold wall while Jerome walked J.J. to the door, schmoozing until the last possible moment. Returning to find Sandy staring out the window, Jerome touched her shoulder. "What's on your mind?"

"I keep thinking about Dunkin' Donuts back in Boston when I was in college. You didn't need a menu or a translator there."

"Sandy." Jerome pointed to his cup with the familiar green logo, a long-haired woman with a crown. "Remember when you were queen?" He brushed his hand over her hair, swept up and sparkling with gold glitter, then trailed his fingers down her neck until they rested on the dolphin tattoo.

An involuntary shiver passed through her body. "That was so long ago."

✳✳✳

Jeff

As soon as Jeff and Ginnie left Starbucks and returned to their studio, Jeff lay down on the floor mattress. Ginnie noticed his discomfort and rolled him onto his belly. In minutes he sank into the thin mattress thoroughly aroused. Every inch of him became totally aware of Ginnie's naked body standing on his torso, her tiny feet massaging his back. A year ago she'd crashed a party at his gallery and stayed. The acts she performed unselfconsciously always amazed him. He'd never had a lover so concerned for his needs. But his needs were changing, again. "Where did you learn to do that?" he asked, trying to switch the focus from his body to his mind. He was grateful for her skill and loved her massages. She was so kind in her sexy young way.

"When I was a kid, I ran away from home and met a very cool massage therapist in Virginia Beach. I wondered what it would be like to give massages, so when I studied manga in Tokyo, I traded English lessons for Ginza shiatsu training." Ginnie swayed and repositioned her feet lower on the sides of his spine. "Breathe… Release… Breathe… Would you like me to talk to you in Japanese, Jeffy-san? I know the best erotic words."

"I bet you do! But I thought this was to relax me."

"Oh yes. I mean *ah so.* How does that feel?" She poked her big toe into his trapezius. "And that?"

When Ginnie stepped off and knelt beside him, his body between her thighs, rubbing ylang ylang oil into his skin, she worked from his tender back down into the gluteus maximus. "And this?"

"Marvelous. Absolutely," he sighed, wallowing in the sensations her fingers created along his spine. Yet instead of dissipating, the tingling in his neck now filled his entire body. This felt better than sex. He loved Ginnie. Loved helping her and sharing art with such a freely creative artist. But she was so young. Happy, talented, and enthusiastic was the plus side, but sometimes, like today, being with her made him feel old.

Ginnie slowed her movements, rolled him over, and slid her hands to his shoulders. Beginning with his dolphin tattoo, she traced her fingers down his chest. When she moved below his navel, he stopped thinking.

Later, repositioning him on his belly, she said, "I am so excited J.J. McCorry's coming to our studio. If he likes my work, this could be my big break. Do you know other mega important art people?"

"No one," he sighed and turned his head to looked at a tall mirror where a single string of cheap, plastic beads dangled from one corner. Ginnie's body slid down his well-oiled back. Her breasts pressed against him. He closed his eyes. She rolled off and lay down on the mattress, curving her body to his.

He felt great, but the tingling hadn't left.

***

That afternoon Jeff pointed up to their main gallery's thirty-foot high ceiling. "This vaulted room will be perfect for Form, Fire and Furnace's large exhibitions."

Ginnie danced in a circle. "We were so lucky to get this fabulous space. It has history!"

"History? Sea creatures and giant ants manufactured for grade B movies are historical?" He laughed. "I guess, since it's all done with computers now." After Jeff bought the studio at a bargain price, the owners sold off the sharks and killer whales, but couldn't be bothered to truck off tons of giant ant mandibles and octopus tentacles.

"We got to keep all this great stuff. I get inspiration just being here. If I weld ant parts to my monumental aluminum manga, the effect will be awesome. Jeff honey, think creatively. Imagine your auto parts with ants crawling up the bumpers."

"Too avant-garde." He knew it wasn't like him to be so closed minded, but since arriving in L.A. he'd become more traditional, not less.

She stopped dancing. "I thought you wanted to work on the cutting edge? What do you want to do? Sculpt horses and cowboys? Paint still life? Jeff, this is now!" Ginnie unconsciously tapped one thick-soled black shoe to a song whose lyrics Jeff would not repeat in public.

He blocked out the noise and raised his voice. "I use found materials."

"Yes. And we found these. We're saving them from the landfill or worse, a flea market."

"I like flea markets. I got a lot of good stuff at flea markets. But now, I need to return to traditional materials. Bronze. Stone. Wood."

"You just don't understand. I don't plan to be your Ginza Girl forever. Someday I will be recognized as a serious artist in the international art world. Not like that flash in the pan yoni cup artist you told me about. Artists have to change with the times. I thought that's what you wanted, too." She waved a tentacle over her head. "This space is *pāfekuto*, perfect. We can work here and have our own gallery space. Rent out the rest to wild energetic artists. Create our own art district. Our own trends."

Jeff nodded and rubbed his neck. The tingle, like beer foam, always appeared before a big change in his life. He was tired. Ginnie picked up her chainsaw and began dismembering a giant ant.

***

Sandy

Sandy stood in the middle of the rotunda of *Le Oiseau Rouge,* L.A., or LaLA as the art crowd called it. She crossed her arms over the ghastly gold dress and turned her back to Jerome.

"Claudio did a fabulous job setting up your show." Jerome forced a smile through clenched teeth. "He will be disappointed you are not pleased with the presentation of your work. But, perhaps it needs a petit tweak."

"Tweak? Tweak? This show needs a bulldozer, not a tweak."

"Claudio's a genius at showing an artist's work to perfection."

Sandy nodded. "Some other artist's work. Not mine."

"The show opens in a few hours. Nothing can be done."

"Can't you see? Those heavy rococo frames destroy the purity and cleanness of my hay photos."

Jerome spun on his heel to consider the entire display, his black silk suit hugged his body without a wrinkle. "Perhaps—" He heard a crunch and lunged toward her. "Sandy, stop!"

Sandy grabbed the closest photograph and ripped the print from its frame. "See." She held it up. "Looks much better this way."

Jerome anxiously examined the edges for damage. "All right, they'll be fine unframed. If you insist."

Sandy was already pulling the frame from the next hay photo. Perspiration misted her brow.

"Careful, you'll ruin your manicure and your hair. Claudio, come. Help Mademoiselle Sandy. *Vite, vite!*" Waving his arms, Jerome directed a bug-eyed Claudio to unframe the remainder of the photos.

Sandy watched. "Fine. That's a beginning. Now let's see what we can do about my mixed media." She untied those awkward gold platform shoes, gathered up the hem of her gown and rushed barefoot into the adjoining gallery.

By the time Jerome reached her, half her mixed media oils were off the wall. "What are you doing? This room is perfect."

His voice was more irate than Sandy had ever heard, but she held her ground. "They must all be hung lower. I want people to see the detail, the texture of the hay and the dirt."

"Earth, at least say earth, *cher*, not dirt. This is Beverly Hills, not Iowa."

Sandy glared at him. "Nebraska."

"I am sorry, but my clients expect a certain Old World ambiance in the presentation."

"Well, this is a New World exhibition and I want my small town festival shots displayed. All of them. They're full of humor and local color. And I want my prints and postcards for sale."

"Claudio thought—"

"I am sure Claudio thought they are tacky. Well, hay art is non-traditional." She pointed to the largest painting. "How many traditional European artists mix hay and dirt into oil paint?"

Sandy became aware she'd pushed Jerome to his edge when his face flushed an inelegant shade of aubergine. He purposefully took a deep breath and smoothed his unwrinkled suit. Ignoring his distress, she waved a gold parchment brochure in the air. "'…aesthetic cacophony of humanistic luminosity.' What the hell does that mean?"

"It is your Artist's Statement, *cher*." Jerome's tone was definitely sharp now.

"This is not what I wrote."

"Claudio tweaked it. He knows about such things."

"I'm the artist, not Claudio!"

She turned to read a large banner printed on the same deckled parchment. "'Heartland, a series of 28 photographs and 15 mixed media works that depict the sculptural impact of nature on the American prairie in its infinite varieties.'"

"Sandy!" a high-pitched squeal echoed through the marble rotunda.

Sandy was lifted off the ground and spun around by a tall, elegant blond woman in a fuchsia and green silk caftan.

"Chris, you look wonderful!" Sandy surveyed her old friend's dramatic outfit with matching turban and strappy heels.

"Ariel and I would not miss our beautiful friend's debut. We became, *aussi*, tired of Key West. Ariel desires to do more than paint bodies and tell fortunes to cruise ship passengers. And I need to be myself, the new Chris, in a place where no one remembers Christopher or Christa, the bartender. Time to strike out for new places."

"I missed you both. How have I managed without your fashion advice?" She looked down at her gown and giggled.

"Love your dress! Finally, a gown fit for a queen—not." Chris looked around. "And my, this place is a *très magnifique* palace." He snuck a look at the catalog. "No wonder. The prices are *très* high. Wow!"

"Jerome and Claudio insist the higher the prices, the more I'll sell."

Jerome stepped up. "Hi, Chris," he said tightly and stuck out his hand. Chris shook it in a very masculine fashion, then did an exaggerated swoon.

"Chris, listen to this crap." Sandy again began to read from the Artist's Statement. "'Alexandria Shellborn's premiere show has achieved an aesthetic cacophony of humanistic luminosity.'"

Chris rolled his eyes.

"It gets better. 'Her work as a photo-based artist is filled with passion. Truths become universal. Form becomes function. Conventionally-based techniques suggest movement in stunning, ethereal works. Her work deconstructs the American dream and expresses the fragility of the time and space continuum. Motivated by her history, Ms. Shellborn studied art and communications in Boston and enjoyed an illustrious career as an innovative information technologist, followed by work in the field of physical energy and intuitive artistry before coming home to the underlying core of her being. Her current work merges the academic connection of her past with the freedom of her present soul.'"

Chris made a pruney face. "Pretty pretentious." Glancing at Jerome, busy talking on his cell phone, he said, "Show me around," and steered Sandy into the adjoining gallery. Chris moved to a painting called 'Prairie Parthenon,' studying a silo floating like a glowing medieval tower over an endless flat plain. "I love it." Next they stood in front of Sandy's largest mixed media piece. Six by six feet, entitled 'Dream Flyer,' its label noted that it was not for sale. A red plane hovered in blue sky over a field of hay. Pieces of actual hay mixed into gold oils brought out the richness and texture of a Nebraska harvest. The plane's open cockpit was empty.

"For Jake," Sandy whispered.

"That guy in Nebraska you wrote me about?"

Sandy nodded. "They all leave me." The man she'd worked for, Seva, her first mate friend, and now beautiful Jake. Not true. Not every one. She'd left her marriage without a backward look. And she'd left Jeff, the man she'd promised to love forever. Leaving was hard. Being left was worse. "What's wrong with me?"

"Nothing's wrong with you. You told me that life is a journey with many side roads."

"I guess I did."

Sandy followed Chris and pleaded, "Please help me."

"Anything, *cher* Sandy. I won't leave you. And Ariel is also your true friend. We love you."

"Thank you." Sandy hugged him. "Do you have a car?"

"Ariel and I rented a Sportster."

"Good. Drive me to Malibu. My laptop is there. I need to rewrite my artist's statement. And change clothes."

"*Alors*, girlfriend."

Sandy led Chris to the gallery office and wrote Jerome a quick note. She scooped up the stack of statements and, carrying the ridiculous shoes, pushed Chris toward the door and out past the open-mouthed doorman.

***

Jeff

Jeff sat on the mattress in their studio and looked up at the tiny woman, hands fisted on narrow hips, without hiding the sadness in his eyes. He had tried to avoid this moment, but Ginnie deserved more than he could offer. She deserved more than a cliché. She deserved honesty. And he was being honest.

Ginnie glared at Jeff from in front of a tall mirror. "What's wrong with you?"

He hung his head. "I thought this was our dream and now…"

Ginnie grabbed the string of plastic beads hanging on Jeff's mirror and held them up to her vintage black dress. "These would be great. Tacky plastic next to satin and lace."

"No. Not those!" Jeff yelled louder than he'd meant to.

"They're just your old Fantasy Fest beads." She tossed them to him. "Here, if they mean so much to you."

Jeff caught them and changed the subject. "This L.A. scene—"

"It's the best. Parties, galleries, the cool international crowd. And Hollywood. I feel like I'm in the center of the latest art trends. It's like Paris must have been…"

"Like Paris was for us old guys?"

"I didn't mean that."

"I did. I'm too old for you." He looked at her pixie face and the kohl-rimmed eyes that reminded him of Sandy's goth makeup.

"No way. Lots of—"

"Lots of girls your age have old boyfriends?"

"No. Anyway, we're different. You're a cool artist, you know. We're a team. You're my wild man."

"Ginnie, you've been great for me. When my marriage ended, I needed a big ego boost. You walked into my life and I felt I'd found the perfect partner. You're the best. This last year has been—"

"Been?" Ginnie stopped primping. "Jeff, what are you saying?"

"It's time for me to leave L.A." Saying the words that had been in his head for weeks felt so freeing.

"I don't want to leave."

"You helped me to the place where I need to figure out the direction to take with my art. And my life."

"If you want shows, this is the place…" Her voice trailed off.

"You keep this studio. J.J. told me about a place near Shidoni in Albuquerque. I can work there. I'll sell at Loveland, Sedona, Santa Fe and some of the big western sculpture shows. I have contacts in Scottsdale, Taos, and Colorado Springs. I can move from studio to studio and experiment with new ideas using traditional materials without pressure to impress the L.A. market."

"I love you," she whispered.

"I love you, Ginnie, but I'll just hold you back."

Ginnie threw her arms around him. "No."

A loud bell rang. Ginnie kissed him sadly, pulled away, and ran to the window. "It's Heidi Van Hansdorf. She has an invitation to an opening at LeLA. Don't you want to go? It'll be a great chance to meet people. Gallery owners, the press, movie business people. Everyone will be there."

Jeff shook his head. "No. Not my thing. Whose show is it?"

"Some new artist, very avant-garde, I'm sure, or she wouldn't be doing a major event at LeLA. There's a rumor she mixes her oils with dirt. If that's not cool."

"Go on without me."

***

Sandy

Two hours later, Sandy drove her SUV up to the front entrance of Le Oiseau Rouge L.A. Cars lined Rodeo Drive, leaving no empty parking spaces, especially for a Grand Cherokee pulling an eighteen-foot Casita trailer. She nosed into the loading zone, leaving most of her rig angled out into traffic. Horns blasted and passengers in passing cars could easily read her Accept Coincidence bumper sticker.

The valet parking attendant marched to her window. "Miss, this is a no parking zone. We have a very important art event here. Lots of beautiful people, if you know what I mean. You will have to move that..." He looked at the stubby travel trailer, then with a Hollywood bad boy gesture with his chin, said, "that vehicle, if you know what I mean."

"I do know what you mean," Sandy said cheerfully, but instead of backing up, opened the door, slid out and grabbed a box from the front seat. She tossed him her keys. "Find a safe place for this vehicle. I *am* the important art event. And take care of my friend." She pointed to Chris's red convertible waiting behind the Casita.

The valet checked out the petite woman in denim jacket and jeans carrying a Kinko's box and muttered, "Go figure."

Sandy ran up the marble steps. The doorman, first expressionless, then disapproving, recognized her, grinned, and opened wide the etched glass door.

Inside, a chattering crowd preened and clustered around a champagne fountain. Half the women were dressed in black and the other half in this season's shade of beige. Older men postured, showing off the cut of their custom black suits while young men slouched in circa-sloppy designer fashions. Jerome oozed charm for the art press, a blonde in a black dress no larger than a tea towel tight to his side. On his left, a tiny young woman with enormous black eyes vied for his attention.

Jerome's arm moved in a dramatic arc encompassing the gallery rotunda. When he saw Sandy at the doorway, champagne sloshed from his fluted glass and splashed over the woman with the big eyes.

He began to laugh. "Sandy, Sandy!" He crossed the floor, leaving the blonde with her arm crooked out in space. The rotunda became quiet enough to hear the harpist as the beautiful people watched their host walk toward this woman who looked wholly out of place.

Sandy grinned up at Jerome. Her eyes shone and her face appeared relaxed and happy. She looked like an American farm girl in a white t-shirt, denim, and boots. Without sparkles or spray, her hair hung loose and clean, framing her tanned, sweet face. Her only accessories, a long, white silk scarf around her neck and a canary yellow diamond on her left hand ring finger.

He took her hand and raised her fingertips to his lips. The gold polish was gone.

Sandy touched Jerome's cheek and whispered, "Either they like my art or they don't." She handed him a copy of her revised artist's statement.

With a smile, he raised his hand for attention, then announced, "I am pleased to introduce Sandy Shellborn, the artist you have been waiting to meet. Let me read *her* statement to you." He began, "'I am an artist in transition and transformation. I believe in the randomness of fate and celebrate coincidences. Things are not what they seem. The creative energy of my core invigorates my hands whether I am holding a camera, painting in oil, or massaging an aching back. I pound oil paint into mashed hay and dirt to create my mixed media base. Highway maps and aeronautical charts add texture and interest...'"

As Jerome read, Sandy passed through the crowd handing out copies from the Kinko's box.

"'Along my journey I was a librarian, entranced with the world of books and technology and business. My life taught me the extremes of human emotions which led me to study, then practice, therapeutic massage. I translate tactile knowledge of the human body and soul into art. My next show will be called "Dolphins in the Desert," and will explore sculpture as the mystery of coincidence and soul.'"

When Jerome finished, Sandy stood at his side. He bent down and kissed her forehead. "They do love your art and love you." He whispered, "But you are still mine for a few more minutes," as he took her arm and guided her to the reporters. "Ladies. Gentlemen. Sandy Shellborn, the *artiste* whose work you have been raving about." He grinned. "I suggest you interview her quickly before she gets away. Again."

III. 4. Sedona, Arizona, 2004, Sandy & Jeff

Sandy

Sandy sat cross-legged watching the high desert sun reflect off the crest of Cathedral Rock. Disentangling from meditation pose, she stretched out her legs and released her shawl. Her arms reached high and she let out a contented sigh.

That familiar spiral of energy she now called her own personal vortex rushed through her body. Just now, here in Sedona, where everyone used words like 'vortex' and 'chakra,' the champagne bubbles had returned with an intensity greater than she'd ever felt. This tingling had always been the harbinger of change in her life. She'd felt it at her massage school graduation. Before the hurricane in St. Croix. The week she left Key West. Then not again until Nebraska when she'd met Jake McCorry. The last time was in Los Angeles during her show opening. Recognizing change was near gave her the courage to leave. Now two years later,, here in this peaceful land, the feeling had returned.

Like many Sedonans she'd been drawn here without understanding why. The red rocks and deep canyons pulled her from the L.A. chaos and she'd driven through the desert, skimmed Las Vegas, and turned south in Flagstaff. Driving into Sedona, she'd exhaled. And stayed.

Her massage therapy training had taught her much about the human body, but no healing modality explained these sensations. The phenomenon always felt good and no longer scared her, but right now, content in her life and fulfilled in her art, she resisted change. She'd lived several lives since her college days and each had taught her lessons of love and loss, pain and pleasure. Each person and place had touched her deeply and changed her. She'd lost touch with her art, then rediscovered it. Often she marveled at the coincidences that brought lost friends back into her life. From time to time she yearned for a man to come to share her joy. But it was a desire, not a need. Right now she felt complete.

She picked up her meditation cushion and sage bundle and walked to her outdoor studio's work table. Closing her eyes, she let her hands hover over two masses—one a two-foot piece of stone and the other a block of red-brown clay. Her left hand, the feminine, felt the cool vitality of the clay. Her right felt waves of warm energy rising from the pure white marble. Her fingers lightly brushed the stone and settled on the surface. Easily she slipped back into a meditative state, setting her intention to channel a vision from the rock and clay. Without conscious effort, an image formed in her meditation and the vibrations coming from her stone and the moist clay rose merged. And she clearly saw what they held hidden inside.

Excited, she opened her eyes, found her sketchbook and with sure strokes drew the picture lingering in her mind's eye. Her first lines shaped a smooth sinuous female back, strong, flexible, and sensuous. Instinctively she knew the approach her hands would use to bring the details of this torso out from the clay, the same techniques she'd used so often to massage tension from breathing human bodies. She visualized the torso cast in bronze with a rich golden patina.

Her fingers flew, sketching more strong graceful lines. A leaping dolphin arched against the woman's torso. Sandy already envisioned the precise strikes she would perform to cleave the surplus stone and free the sea creature.

She propped her sketchpad on a rock and stood, shaking red dust from her white dress. Divine inspiration had spoken. Life in Sedona held sunshine, happiness, good friends, and art. And peace. "Please," she begged the Spirits of the Canyon, "No change. Not now."

***

Jeff

Jeff gripped the wheel and held his breath as the heavily loaded four-horse rig plunged down the steep, twisting road. "Why'd I choose the scenic route?" 89A south from Flagstaff, Arizona was gorgeous, edged by pine trees and majestic gorges, each vista more spectacular than the last. He forced his wandering artist's mind and eyes back to the road. He needed to focus, watch the road, and control the long, hefty trailer swerving behind him—if he wanted to get to Sedona alive.

The best coffee he'd drunk since leaving northern Colorado spilled over his white shirt, both ruined by that last switchback. Pinion nuts bought in Hopiland lay scattered like pebbles on the floormat.

At last the road leveled and he was surrounded by Sedona. World class tourist shopping rimmed by postcard-famous scenery provided no place to pull over and check a map. T-shirted families with small children and polyester mountain bikers blithely crossed the road, uncaring that his truck pulling six tons of trailer and heavy art could not stop quickly.

Jeff drove past a hotel and into open hills. Certain he'd passed the entire town and come out the other end without finding a place to pull over, he scanned the roadside for an exit. Traffic was heavy and not one vehicle allowed the big rig to change lanes. In another mile he reached an area with more or less normal businesses, groceries, gas stations, a McDonalds without arches, and a Pizza Hut that looked like a pueblo. When he was again sure he'd passed through Sedona and would have to turn around or go against his gender and ask directions, he saw a large sign for the Sedona Cultural Park and a small one with an arrow: 'Sculpture Walk Exhibitors.'

He followed the signs. Rolling down his window, air, hotter and drier than Colorado, tickled his nose. As he waited for a parking attendant to direct him, he took a deep breath and looked around. Prettiest art show site he'd seen this trip. Not a bad place to spend a few days. He looked forward to camping among red rocks, moss green mesquite, and unbelievably blue skies.

Two years sharing studios to create art, traveling to shows, and easy comradery of artists was a good life. The best of several since college. A life he could never have dreamed for back in art school. He still cringed at thoughts of his self-indulgent youth and the detours he took. And blessed the friends who'd helped him along the way.

He never regretted putting all his Yippee money into Delphinus and hoped it was helping young artists find their way. He loved his independence and creative freedom, but sometimes longed to find a woman to share his life. Now with contentment, a measure of success, and a knowledge of who he was meant to be, he wanted to share it all. He wanted to recapture the feeling he'd had so long ago when he and Sandy

---

had freely created art together, blending paint and love into bliss. Having experienced that once, he now saw he'd searched but never again found it. He wasn't quite ready to give hope up as a youthful fantasy.

He held his exhibitors pass out the window to the attendant and noticed that funny neck tingle had returned. Maybe he'd get a massage in Sedona or try one of those New Agey cures.

"Drive straight ahead." The bald young man in peach robes looked more like a Buddhist monk than a parking attendant. He handed Jeff a map, pointed out the RV and truck parking area, then indicated, on the other side of the map, the show site. "You got space 155, next to Sedona Visionary Artists." He assessed Jeff's rig. "Can you like carry your stuff to the site?"

"Like, carry!" Jeff slipped back into L.A. slang. "No way."

"Okay. Okay. Don't blow your root chakra. Just move your vehicle out of the exhibition area before dark."

"What if I need help?"

"Hey man, this is Sedona. Ask someone to levitate your stuff."

Jeff drove on, his head buzzy from the elevation and the ripples of energy that had begun flowing through his body as soon as he'd arrived. Yet, instead of feeling disturbed, he felt like he'd come home.

***

Sandy

Sandy pulled into the Rouge Mountain parking lot to pick up four clients at Sedona's most expensive hotel. Her jeep tour business was successful and enjoyable. Even her mother, now married to a retired Scottsdale investment broker, brought her friends to Sedona for her tours. And her dad loved to trek back into the canyons with her when he gave poetry readings in nearby Jerome.

She waited. Guests couldn't miss the 'Purple Dolphin Jeep Tours' sign on her purple jeep. But often did.

Right on time, a stocky man in a Sedona Red Dirt t-shirt walked to the jeep. "Are you the vortex guide?" he snorted, examining the 'Purple Dolphin Jeep Tours' sleeve patch on her worn denim jacket.

"Will we photograph vortexes, spirits, and aliens?" asked a woman in an identical rusty shirt.

"That's why we're paying big bucks," her husband told her before Sandy could answer.

"Oh Oscar, seeing the sunset in the red rocks will be worth the price of this tour."

"Sunsets are free. But if you want a $500 sunset, Martha," he hugged her, "it's yours."

Sandy began her usual disclaimer. "A Vortex Photo Tour attempts to photograph 'spirit' in energy form, not spirits or aliens. That's someone else's tour," she explained to be sure there would be no misunderstanding. She'd been super-careful after one California tourist sued Ariel for not making his fortune fortuitous enough.

"Will it be like having your aura photographed?" Martha asked Sandy. "I had that done in a crystal shop."

"Not quite. I like to think that we capture glimpses of souls on film."

"That is so exciting. I love everything about Sedona. The mountains are spectacular. And there are so many art galleries. I'm an artist, myself," Martha told her. "We're here for the Sculpture Walk."

"We have free passes," Oscar added. "We're friends with one of the artists."

"You'll love it," Sandy assured them. "Now as soon as the other guests arrive, we'll get started."

"They're our friends from Kansas," Martha said.

"Lesbians," Oscar whispered. "Just so you know we aren't bigoted hicks."

"Oh, Oscar, don't be such a silly. Besides, Corin's doubled your portfolio, again." Martha turned to Sandy. "She's an investment genius."

"Really?" Sandy looked interested. "I could use good advice. I bought this tour business before I learned getting dependable help would be so difficult."

"Why's that?" Oscar raised his eyebrows.

"Tonight is a full moon and tomorrow is the Autumn Equinox. In Sedona, everyone belongs to a drumming circle. Plus, my drivers call in sick when their planets aren't aligned or their biorhythms are out of sync." Sandy smiled. "Still, I truly love this place and the people. I plan to stay here for the rest of my life." She said the words like an affirmation.

"Sedona's so pretty." Martha looked up at the deep crimson rock formations.

Oscar let out a low whistle. "And look at the size of those houses."

Sandy shook her head, trying to ignore the huge houses that littered sacred canyons.

Two women appeared from the hotel lobby and Oscar yelled, "Hi ho." One was very thin, in black jeans and a long-sleeved black Western shirt. The second woman followed, shorter, solidly built, and wearing a wide-brimmed cowboy hat.

Sandy checked names off her clipboard list. "Corin. And Nora!" She gave the second woman a hug. "Nora! It's really you. You look wonderful. We lost touch after Virginia Beach! What are you doing here?"

Nora stepped back and winked at Sandy. "Don't you just love coincidences. I'm a horse trainer now. My third career. I see you're on a new path, too."

Martha told Corin, "I love all this paranormal stuff."

"If I never see another crystal for the rest of my life, it will be too soon." Corin pursed her lips.

"Stuff it, Corin. We're having a great time." Nora elbowed Corin's ribs, opened the tailgate, and pushed her up into the jeep.

"I don't think I'll see any spirits." Corin settled onto the bench.

"Look at her!" Nora pointed to a pickup truck driven by a woman covered in white feathers.

"That's Angel Woman," Sandy explained. "She's sweet, but very *vatta*. That's Sanskrit for 'very Sedona.' When I see her, I always think of a Boston Common swan boat."

"When I lived in Boston, I didn't have time for that silliness." Corin's voice almost sounded wistful.

"Never mind," Nora told her, "next year we'll go to Boston and ride every swan."

Sandy started the jeep. "Remember there's a chance you may not actually see spirits, but most of my clients have spirits appear in some of their photos. Photos you take tonight will be processed tomorrow." Noting their expensive digital cameras, she added, "Or we'll load your memory cards into my laptop and I'll make prints."

"We'll see." Oscar still sounded skeptical. "You're the owner?" he asked Sandy, as she pulled onto 89A.

"Yes, though I usually only lead Professional Photography Tours."

"You're Sandy Shellborn!" Martha cried. "I saw your work in our hotel lobby. Your photos are as good as I've seen in *Arizona Highways*."

"Some of my work has been published there. Lately, I'm doing more sculpting."

"Are you exhibiting at the Sculpture Walk?"

"One piece is there with my co-op. I couldn't go myself. All my drivers are drumming. Besides, art shows aren't my thing, anymore."

***

Jeff

Jeff leaned back in his director's chair, sipping Ariel's excellent coffee. He was surprised and pleased at the coincidence to find his exhibit space situated next to an old friend.

She refilled his cup from her Thermos. "I love your new image." She examined his white shirt, Dockers, and loafers, and artsy length hair. "The beard is a delightful touch. You look like the picture of a successful artist."

"Hopefully, that's what I am."

"You also look happier and healthier than when I saw you in Florida," she said with a secretive smile.

"Thanks. And thanks for better coffee than I brew in my trailer." Jeff often wondered if she'd been the woman in white in Key West who'd refused to acknowledge him. Ariel, like most psychics, seldom explained her predictions or her behavior.

"You looked like you missed your Starbucks." She smiled easily. "So far, Sedona has more crystal shops than coffee shops."

A white-haired woman covered in feathers rushed up and handed Ariel a three-foot feathered globe. "I'll be right back with the rest."

As the woman hurried away, Jeff saw large, feathered wings attached to the back of her dress.

"Angel Woman," Ariel told him.

"Reminds me of a Boston Common swan boat. After unloading a ton of metal last night, maybe I should switch to feather art." He looked into Ariel's booth. "You certainly work in a variety of media."

"Sedona Visionary Artists is a co-op. A few friends. I do the marketing and the others split show expenses." As he sipped, she surveyed his booth. "I like your kinetic work, but that stone and chrome piece really speaks to me."

"Thanks. In Sedona, do you still read palms or is everyone here psychic?"

She raised her eyebrows. "I work as a psychic to pay my exorbitant Sedona rent and sometimes drive jeep tours."

"Can you still read my mind?"

"Absolutely, let me get my crystal ball, newt toes, and drink a dram of dragon's blood." She paused when Jeff's eyes widened. "Sorry, you looked so serious, I couldn't help putting you on."

Jeff snickered. "So, if I can't get my fortune told, what good is setting up next to a psychic?"

"My great coffee. And during slow spells I tell you about Sedona vortexes." She pointed. "There's Chimney Rock. To the left is Boynton Canyon, a really powerful masculine-feminine vortex. My favorite place—off season."

Jeff laughed off her vortex talk and carried his coffee into her tent. Porcelain masks, fancifully painted and decorated with feathers and crystals, covered one canvas wall.

"The masks are mine," Ariel told him. "I sometimes do workshops where students mold their own faces. I learned from an artist in Nebraska who owns a coffee shop."

"Beautiful." Jeff stood for a long time in front of a mask painted with iridescent rainbow-colored scales, before moving on to a table of wood carvings, surrealistic animals crawling out of twisted tree trunks.

In the center of the booth, pedestals supported large bronze anatomical studies and marble sculptures. Jeff's attention was drawn to a golden bronze woman, realistic, yet surreal. He held his cooling coffee cup to the side of his neck. Distracted by the tingle, more twang than tickle this morning, he asked, "Where can I get a massage? I have this sort of neck crick."

"There are chair massage people near the food tent. I'll watch your booth if you don't think any major gallery owners will sneak in this early?"

"You're an angel. I'd like to see the other artists' work before the show opens. Sedona artists seem a bit more... fanciful."

"We say intuitive," Ariel teased. "Or speculative." Then her face lost the playful banter. She placed her cool fingers at the spot on his neck where he'd been rubbing. She closed her eyes and laid her other hand over his heart. Intense heat flooded his chest. The tingly area throbbed, bubbles burst faster, and a stream of energy passed through him between Ariel's hands.

Eyes closed, Ariel spoke in a deep exotic voice, "You are very close to what you seek. The ocean is in the desert. The love you seek is near. Follow the..."

Jeff squirmed. He liked Ariel, but her psychic stuff had always made him twitch.

"...dolphins," she finished, opened her eyes, and shook her head. "Wow," she said, in her normal voice, "I don't usually channel spontaneously. I saw dolphins. Does that mean anything to you?"

"You channel?"

"Like a cell phone call from the universe."

Ariel's smile was disquieting, but Jeff walked away feeling more curious than afraid. He was comfortable with his life and his art. He wasn't expecting changes.

***

Sandy

Sandy turned right on Dry Creek Road, drove out of town to Boynton Canyon, and pulled off into the small Vista Trail parking lot. As soon as she opened the tailgate, her clients climbed out, milled around, and began snapping pictures.

"Wait. Stand quietly." She collected her gear and herded them together. "Close your eyes and breathe. Smell the pine and the earth. Give spirits a chance to come close."

Oscar sneezed and backed up into a sharp-leafed yucca. "Ouch! Is this when the woo-woo stuff starts?"

Martha yelled, "Oscar, Shush!"

Sandy switched to Plan B. She led her charges along the trail, following markers made from wire barrel containers filled with crushed red rock. "Feel the energy here. Notice the twisted juniper tree trunks. See those two spires, one shorter and thicker, less spire-like than the other. Some people believe the two are vortex energy points, one positive and one negative. Others just call them The Lovers."

"I thought this would be easier," Oscar panted.

"The trail's just one-third of a mile long and not too steep. This spot is lovely at twilight. Move a little to your left and you'll get that lovely pine tree in your shot. *National Geographic* ran this exact photo."

They settled down, aimed their digital cameras, and began clicking.

"Look back to the southwest. See the lights of the Sedona Cultural Park." Sandy showed Corin how to turn off the flash and checked her watch. "Sculpture Walk artists are closing down for today."

Corin said, "My brother owns a famous art gallery in Los Angeles."

Sandy nodded. "There are many great L.A. galleries," and continued, "Boynton Canyon is a balanced vortex, holding both masculine and feminine energy."

"It's like yin and yang," Nora explained to Corin and the Weatherhills. "And that's not just about sex. Exactly like horse training and massage, you need to balance strength with gentleness. Balance in all things."

Sandy nodded. "Follow me up to the knoll to feel for the strongest energy. We'll take photos where a lot of spirits hang out."

Later, driving back Dry Creek Road, Oscar asked, "What's all this vortex nonsense have to do with crystals?"

"Shush." Martha hugged Oscar's arm. "Sorry, he's not very spiritual."

Sandy shook her head to clear the reoccurring light-headed feeling. "Good question, Oscar. My regular tour guide usually gives an introduction at the beginning of the tour. I'm feeling very Sedona today and skipped it. Vortexes are energy whirlpools with electromagnetic charges. Within a five to ten mile radius, Sedona has more vortexes than any place on earth." She pointed. "Look at the side of the road."

They turned to look where a white strip glowed through the red dust.

"That layer is quartz. And red rocks are filled with iron. Ever heard of a crystal set?"

"Sure," said Oscar. "Crystals pick up radio waves. And iron ore has electromagnetic properties. Basic science."

"That's the reason people come to Sedona to talk to aliens," said Nora.

"How'd you know that?" Oscar asked.

Nora smiled. "I know about more than horses."

"A lot more," Corin said proudly.

Sandy grinned at Nora. She remembered how much her librarian friend knew about lots of things, besides horses. And how Nora helped her in Texas and again in Virginia Beach. She couldn't wait to catch up. Nora was someone who'd understand changes in life. "There are three kinds of vortexes. Masculine vortexes are empowering, exciting, and energizing. Feminine vortexes are nurturing, healing, and intuitive. The Boynton Canyon vortex is a cross between the two and sends out both energies. We're on our way to Cathedral Rock, a feminine vortex. I expect we'll have better luck finding spirits there. Remember, no talking after the jeep stops."

"When do we go to a masculine one?" Oscar asked.

"Sorry, not on this tour. But you can easily drive to Airport Vortex. Or tonight, for the full moon, you can join my meditation group. We're going to Bell Rock, a very powerful masculine vortex." Sandy surprised herself by asking these people to join her group, but she was beginning to like Nora's friends and wanted to find out how Nora moved from massages in Virginia Beach to horses in Kansas.

"Oh yes, I want to go," said Martha.

"Meditate? I don't know about that?" said Oscar. "But if that's what you want, sure, why not?"

"Let's buy a timeshare, Oscar. Then we could spend a lot of time here and take all Sandy's tours."

"Anything for you, pumpkin." Oscar's arm slipped around Martha.

Sandy smiled. "Some people think vortex energy heals, alters moods, and inspires artistic people. Many come to Sedona at a crossroads in their lives. Some say Sedona affects relationships. It's believed that if two people are truly meant to be together, they will be pulled close here. I'd guess you two are meant to be together." Watching the loving couple snuggle, Sandy felt that distinctive tingle flow into her heart.

So far Sedona hadn't brought Sandy that kind of love. Her life felt full and content but she'd resigned herself to a possible life without the magic of lasting love. Sometimes she imagined that part of her life was over. While others settled down to build a full life, she'd lived several short episodes. The dream of finding a loving partner who also understood her need for art seemed out of reach. She'd never find love with someone who'd known her forever and remembered the awkward kid with excess eye makeup in too much of a hurry.

***

Jeff

Jeff returned to his booth and complained to Ariel, "The massage therapist wouldn't touch me! I explained the thing about these twinges that come every few years. She said it sounded like a simulation of a cetacean sense organ found in the jaw and bones near the ear and that my sonar must be picking up high frequency vibrational sound pulses." He shook his head. "I just wanted a back rub."

"Interesting." Ariel nodded.

"I was happy calling it beer foam."

She laughed and handed him a business card. "I joked about rich gallery owners, but one did come looking for you. Jerome Oberon, from the Le Oiseau Rouge galleries, including the one everyone calls LaLA. My artist friends would die to meet him."

"Jerome Oberon's my former brother-in-law."

"Said he'd be back." She handed him second card. "This is from his young companion. I'd describe her as exquisite punk."

Jeff looked at the card. "Ginnie Ostergard, *La Oiseau Rouge, L.A.*, Assistant Curator." He grinned. Go Ginza Girl. Be happy.

"And some other friends stopped for you. A big Midwestern farmer and three women."

"That would be Oscar, his wife, my ex-wife, and her girlfriend."

"And you probably think Sedona people are eccentric odd," said a deep voice behind him.

Jeff turned and embraced the tall, older man who'd spoken. "J.J. So glad you could get here."

"Wouldn't miss it. And I love visiting Sedona." He looked at Jeff's display. "I like your new work, especially that big one," he said as he examined the five-foot chrome dolphin that appeared to rise, pulling a granite man up and out of carved wooden waves. "Anything I can do to help?"

"Critique my display. I need your honest opinion."

J.J. stood back and considered. "I like the way you arranged it all." He stepped a few more feet away, angling his body as if he were a customer browsing the aisle. "The kinetic pieces draw the eye in. And create a breeze. But your large sculpture rivets my attention." He pointed to the large piece. "Move it out and to the right. Most of the traffic comes this way."

Jeff placed his shoulder against the massive sculpture's pedestal and maneuvered as J.J. gestured like a traffic cop. "I call him 'Twin,'" Jeff grunted.

"Perfect. Perfect." J.J. moved closer until he stood five feet in front of Jeff's booth. His eyes swept right and left, appraising Jeff's display and the booths on either side, glancing back and forth between Jeff's large piece and the Visionary Artists' booth.

"Looks like you're judging a ping pong match," Jeff joked.

J.J. face remained thoughtful. He walked to Jeff's 'Twin,' closed his eyes and stroked the elegant lines. "This speaks to me," he said softly, then walked into the adjoining space. Ignoring Ariel, he circled the white marble dolphin and bronze woman.

Ariel watched J.J. flick away her 'do not touch' sign and stroke the figure. She gasped when he lifted the heavy piece free from the base and carried it off. "What are you doing?" she began. Then, her face registered his purpose and she whispered, "She's called 'Souls.'"

"They fit together. As if..." J.J. adjusted the woman/dolphin in the arch of Jeff's man/dolphin. "They were made to be one."

Ariel and Jeff stared. The golden bronze woman and white stone dolphin curved against the granite man and chrome dolphin. Jeff's carved wooden waves bound the two art works together.

J.J. beamed at Jeff and Ariel. "I saw what neither of you artists could see. You two have worked together without meeting. I've never seen independently created pieces form one such perfect work." He turned to Ariel. "Bravo!"

"But I'm not the artist." Ariel handed J.J. a brochure.

He read, "Purple Dolphin Jeep Tours—Photograph a Vortex Spirit Tonight?"

"That's the artist's other business. Look on the back."

J.J. flipped the paper over and saw a photo of the dolphin sculpture next to a smiling woman. "Laughing Dolphin Studio, Photography, Mixed Media, Oils, Bronze and Stone Sculpture." He laughed. "It's Sandy! This is the new work she wanted to show me. Jeff, you have to meet my friend, Sandy Shell-born."

"Sandy?" Jeff snatched the brochure from J.J.'s hand. "Sandy is here!"

***

Jeff screeched into the Kokopelli Korners strip mall parking lot, pulled up to the Purple Dolphin Jeep Tours office, and stopped abruptly. Jumping out of his truck, he ran to the purple door. The lights were out, but the door was unlocked. He rushed into the dark shop as a six-foot-tall blonde, face painted with red and black stripes, holding a large drum, came out from behind the counter.

"Sorry. We're closed," she said firmly, blocking him with her body and drum.

"Just tell me where Sandy is," he said breathlessly to the woman who looked really scary in the dim light beneath an 'Expect Coincidences' sign." He held up the crumpled brochure, folded to show Sandy's picture.

"Sir. Breathe. Sandy is out with clients. She'll be in the office tomorrow."

"I've got to find her. Now!" Realizing he sounded manic, he consciously slowed his voice. "I am an old friend. I have been looking for her… for a very, very long time."

The woman backed up from the bearded man. She held her keys at waist level like a gun. "I was just locking up. I'm due at my drumming circle. It's the Full Moon. And the Equinox!" She looked at him as if he should have known. "Please leave. Come back tomorrow and I'll book you a nice tour, maybe Spirit Soul Adventure or Sedona Spiritual Vistas. Both are very calming."

He looked at the woman's nametag. "Chrystal, please help me." He opened his wallet and emptied all his cash onto the counter.

"I don't want your money. You could be a kook?"

"A kook? In this town, how do you tell?" His voice rose. "Am I waiting for a spaceship to pick me up? Am I being massaged with fairy dust? Am I standing on my head in the middle of Rite-Aid? No? Then, I must be a kook?" He continued emptying his wallet. "Take my credit cards, my driver's license, my passport. Can't leave earth without it, right? Help me find Sandy!" Like a drowning man, his life flashed before his eyes. He clearly saw his journey and knew Sandy was the destination. He would not lose her. Not again.

The woman saw the driver's license and screeched, "Jeff Sanders! You're Sandy's Jeff! And my Jeff! It's me! Christopher!" He dropped his drum and embraced Jeff.

***

Sandy

Sandy joined her meditation group in the Bell Rock parking lot. The regulars went on ahead to their usual spot, but she stayed behind with the four Kansas tourists. "Look at your photos while there's still light," she said, giving each one a packet. "Good shots. A few in each have orbs."

Corin flipped to the one she'd taken of the other three standing next to Sandy in the moonlight with Cathedral Rock in the background. Behind each person was a fuzzy white flame-shaped splash.

"Look Oscar, there's something on your shoulder." Martha pointed at the photo.

"Just a white splash." Corin held it up. "But look at Sandy. I can clearly see the shape of a man behind her." She turned to Sandy. "He looks like he's talking to you."

Sandy answered slowly. "Actually, yes. A friend who passed spoke to me."

"What did he say?" Martha wanted to know.

Sandy dropped her voice, hesitant to share this. "He said, 'Be Free to Love.'"

"Do you know what that meant?" asked Corin.

"Yes, I do," Sandy answered quickly. She'd been holding onto the belief that she and Jake had been destined to live and create together. And when Jake was taken from her, that she'd never find that joy again. Changing the subject, she asked, "Did you all enjoy the Sculpture Walk?"

Martha sighed. "It was wonderful."

Oscar added, "She had a chance to see her old artist boyfriend."

"But Oscar is my soulmate." Martha pecked his cheek.

"Positutely," said Oscar. "We saw a full size elk, lots of cute bunny rabbits, and some ugly javelinas. I'd rather take home a steer head with nice horns, than frogs or stuff that doesn't look like anything at all."

"I loved the horses and the Hopi art," said Nora, "and the masks."

"Oh yes, the horses… and the turquoise jewelry." Corin waved both arms jingling with bracelets. "And my ex-, I mean, our friend Jeff does these moving metal pieces, like windmills. I liked those."

Sandy escorted the four to the Bell Rock trailhead and led them on to join the rest of the mediation group. As they walked higher along the path close to the bell formation, she told them, "This is a masculine vortex. Try to feel the power of the energy."

"How can anything that looks like a breast, be masculine?" Oscar mused before Martha shushed him.

When they reached the flat open spot Sandy used for group meditations, she handed Oscar, Martha, Corin, and Nora folding stools. Nora set hers aside and joined the other meditators on blankets on the cooling rock. Sandy started a tiny fire in the circle center and, as Seva taught her, sprinkled tobacco on the flames. As the pungent smell filled the air, she offered a blessing to the four directions. She passed a small deck of cards and each person chose a soul card.

Sandy read hers silently. "To create, to teach, and to love." She had planned to offer other prayers and lead off tonight's meditation with a quote by Deepak Chopra about the power of coincidence. She knew most tourists liked his words because they were often less woo-woo and more scientific. Lightheaded and far from grounded, she asked Angel Woman to lead the meditation tonight. Holding a hand to the intensifying burn on the side of her neck, she stood and walked from the firelight into the shadows.

Commencement

Alone, Sandy kept walking, spiraling higher, closer to the apex of Bell Rock. A coyote howled. She knew she should be more responsible. But tonight her neck bubbled with energy and she couldn't stay still. Shivering, she pulled her denim jacket tight against the night air. The full moon lit her path and caused Bell Rock to glow deep burgundy as if afire.

She heard an airplane flying a sunset tour, yet she felt completely alone, as if time had shifted and she now walked in another dimension. Close to the place she called The Hogan, a natural rock formation that resembled an Old English granary, a silo, she stopped. This spot always called to her, but tonight she moved forward higher. She yearned for another sacred place.

***

Jeff, following Chris's frenzied directions, almost missed the turn into the Bell Rock parking area. His tires squealed and red dust billowed around his truck. Moonlight illuminated the lot as bright as day—day anywhere but in Arizona. The jeep appeared black, not purple, in the moonlight, but the two dolphins in the rear logo were clear. He jumped from his truck, only taking time to put on his faded Boston Red Sox ballcap.

He ran to the trailhead like a mad man, skirting mesquite, jumping cactus, unaware if he even followed a path. Working his way higher, climbing, scrambling, he pulled himself up rounded ledges until he was high enough to look out over the base of Bell Rock to the main path and across 179 to Cathedral Rock outlined against the sky. A balanced energy vortex, that's what the guidebook called it. Here on Bell Rock, he felt far from balanced. His mind spun and his body felt wildly alive. He was running… home. To a beginning.

All was quiet.

Sandy stood in the moonlight looking at the bearded man in the Red Sox cap.

Jeff saw the girl in the denim jacket didn't look surprised to see him. He stopped. This was crazy. They weren't kids anymore. His excitement at finding her here in Sedona deflated. He caught his breath. He had to take a chance. "Once we watched a sunrise together."

She smiled and nodded. "A long time ago." She no longer regretted leaving him. Nor leaving that too-sure-of-herself college girl. "We're not the same."

She looked a little sad.

He didn't know if he could bear it if she walked away. Did he think she'd rush into his arms and pledge undying love?

She walked towards him and took his hand. "We have a lot of catching up to do before dawn."

ABOUT THE AUTHOR

Amber Polo loves to take readers on journeys to places she's lived, visited, and imagined. Escaping her past as librarian and yoga teacher, Amber strives to mix humor and a little fantasy into every genre (so far fantasy, romance, historical, and woman's fiction).

Amber is best known for *The Shapeshifters' Library*, a light urban fantasy series which asks what if librarian dog-shifters faced book-burning werewolves and *The Pharaoh and the Librarian*, blending alternative history with a little fantasy.

Find her at www.amberpolo.com